No wonder Kayla disliked him.

And it was true that his parents hadn't been happy he was dating her. So even if they'd known about Alex and supported her financially, she might have resented taking the money. On the other hand, she might have felt it was owed to her.

"I'm sorry," he murmured.

"I did okay."

"You did better than okay," he told her.

They fell silent again, but it was more comfortable this time. After exactly sixty minutes, DeeDee came running downstairs. "Can we swim now?" she pleaded. "There's a neat pool house where we can change."

"Sure," Kayla told her. "I'll go with you."

Jackson went to his bedroom to put on his swim trunks, then headed outside.

Kayla stood next to the pool in her bathing suit, chatting with Morgan. She looked like a model in one of those "vacation paradise" magazine ads—long legs, hair fiery in the sun and a body that nearly made him howl.

He was in deep trouble.

Dear Reader,

Because my parents were older when I came along, camping was rarely a part of my childhood. The last time we went was before I turned five. I remember the family picking berries and my mom making a batch of jam from them. Having made jam myself, now, I know she was a little insane for doing it over a camp stove.

When my hero in *Kayla's Cowboy* is struggling to find a way of connecting with his rebellious teenage daughter, as well as with the son he's just met, sending everyone camping at Yellowstone seems like a good idea. Besides, Yellowstone is an amazing place, and it felt as if I got a vicarious visit to the park along with them.

But they have to return to reality—and one of Jackson McGregor's realities is his attraction to his son's mother, Kayla Anderson. That's a big problem with their painful history, a mutual struggle to trust and the fact that he's from Schuyler, Montana, while she lives in Seattle, Washington.

I enjoy hearing from readers. Please contact me c/o Harlequin Books, 225 Duncan Mill Road, Don Mills, ON, M3B 3K9, Canada.

Callie Endicott

CALLIE ENDICOTT

—

Kayla's Cowboy

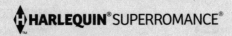

Recycling programs
for this product may
not exist in your area.

ISBN-13: 978-0-373-60946-8

Kayla's Cowboy

Copyright © 2016 by Callie Endicott

Printed in U.S.A.

Callie Endicott often wishes her life would slow down, but so far it doesn't show any sign of cooperating. There aren't enough hours in the day for everything she likes to do, whether it's writing stories for her readers, hiking on a mountain trail, or walking on the beach. Reading is another passion for Callie, along with her cats (Myna and Winston), cooking and travel. Luckily, Myna and Winston are getting along better than they did in the beginning, but Myna remains stubbornly jealous of Callie's guy.

Books by Callie Endicott

HARLEQUIN SUPERROMANCE

That Summer at the Shore
Until She Met Daniel

Other titles by this author available in ebook format.

To Teddy Roosevelt and the other visionaries
who set aside the US National Parks.

CHAPTER ONE

KAYLA ANDERSON STARED at the sign indicating she was still more than a hundred miles from Schuyler, Montana. After driving all night from Seattle, she was exhausted. And scared.

A hitchhiker caught her eye and she leaned forward to get a better look. She sagged with disappointment. It wasn't her son.

Had Alex gotten this far?

Fifteen-year-old kids couldn't rent cars, though they could take a train or bus without raising too many questions.

She shuddered at the idea of her son hitchhiking. Surely he had better sense. Of course, she'd never dreamed he would run away during his two-week visitation with his dad and head for Montana on his own. And how could Curtis have waited all day to let her know Alex was missing? She'd rushed home to see if Alex had come back, only to find a note explaining where he'd gone. Despite that, Curtis still hadn't been concerned, certain Alex was just "exerting his independence."

Her smartphone sounded with a chime indicating she had a voice mail. Could it be Alex? She'd gotten a signal off and on the whole night. Pulling off the road, Kayla checked her messages.

"Kayla, this is your grandfather. Don't worry, Alex is here and he's all right. I imagine you're on your way. Travel safe, and we'll see you soon."

Kayla let out a shaky, relieved breath. She still had dozens of questions, but the most important one was answered. Her son was safe, instead of lying in a ditch or kidnapped, or any of the other terrible things her imagination had conjured. She debated calling her grandparents but decided to wait until they were face-to-face.

Glancing into the rear seat, she saw her nine-year-old daughter was asleep again, the wrappers from her fast-food breakfast scattered on the floor. Curtis had said it was ridiculous to bring DeeDee with her, but he hadn't been that upset to have his time with the kids cut by a few days. As she'd learned during their marriage, Curtis Anderson had a short attention span. Since their divorce he'd slid from one relationship to another. His work history was the same.

Kayla's mouth tightened and she tried to remember that her ex-husband wasn't a terrible father. And he *had* wanted to adopt Alex from the very beginning. He'd just never grown up. He adored romance and falling in love and playing daddy, but relationships were beyond him. He was now on his third marriage since their divorce. Kayla no longer cared, but it was hard on the kids.

Before getting on the road again, she called Curtis to tell him Alex was safe. Two hours later, they passed the Schuyler city-limit sign. Her terror had subsided, but other anxieties had surfaced; the last thing she'd ever wanted was return here.

It wasn't that she'd hated Schuyler. In fact, she'd had high hopes when she and Mom had moved into her grandparents' home. Though it was the first time Kayla had met them, she'd thought the Garrisons were nice and she had started making friends at high school. But less than a year later Mom had been hitting the bottle even harder and they were on the road again. As far as Kayla knew, her mother hadn't spoken to her parents since then.

Kayla pulled up in front of a three-story house that hadn't changed since the day her mother had driven them away from it. As she hurried up the walkway, the front door opened and a familiar figure emerged—like the house, Elizabeth Garrison also appeared unchanged by the years, except that her brown hair was now shot with gray.

"He's all right," Elizabeth assured quickly.

"I know, I got Granddad's message."

"Good. We called the home phone as well but figured you were already on your way."

"Where's Alex?"

"He's gone to the office with your grandfather to clean and organize the supply room." Elizabeth's eyes crinkled with a gentle humor. "We decided it was a suitably mundane thing for a kid to do after running away."

Kayla agreed with a shaky laugh. "What's the number?" she asked, taking out her phone. "I need to hear his voice."

She punched in the numbers and the secretary put her through to her grandfather, who told her how much he loved her before passing the phone to Alex.

"Uh, hello?" her son said cautiously.

"Are you all right?" Kayla demanded.

"I'm fine, Mom, just dusty from some boxes that haven't been moved in, like, *forever.*"

"We'll talk later. We'll talk a lot," she warned.

"I kind of figured."

After hanging up, she couldn't keep the tears from stinging into her eyes.

Elizabeth gave her a quick hug before drawing away to gaze at her intently. "Oh, honey. It's so good to see you."

"I'm sorry it's been so long," Kayla managed to say.

"You're here now, that's what matters."

Kayla still felt bad. She'd had little contact with her grandparents herself over the past sixteen years—just Christmas and birthday cards. That was fine for distant relatives, but the months she'd spent with the Garrisons as a teenager had been the happiest of her childhood. They'd even invited her to stay instead of leaving town with her mother. But

Kayla hadn't been able to bear the thought of Mom being alone. Besides, she couldn't have stayed in Schuyler, not after Jackson had declared that he'd always used a condom, so the baby couldn't possibly be his.

The memory might hurt more if she'd really loved Jackson McGregor, instead of having a short-lived crush. Still, crush or not, she'd ended up pregnant. And while she could never be sorry about having Alex, it hadn't been easy.

Pushing the thought away, Kayla squared her shoulders. "There's something I should tell you—about Alex, I mean."

"It isn't necessary," Elizabeth answered. "Until I saw him in person I hadn't realized how much he looks like the McGregors. A *certain* McGregor, as a matter of fact. As I recall, the two of you were quite an item for a while."

Kayla winced. "Yes. And by the way, Alex doesn't know Curtis isn't his biological father. He adopted Alex right after we were married, and wanted to wait before telling him."

"Don't worry, we won't say anything. Where's DeeDee?" Elizabeth asked. "Is she still in Seattle?"

"She's in the car, asleep."

Elizabeth's eyes lit up and she rushed to look through the Volvo's back window at her great-granddaughter. "She didn't wake up when you turned off the engine?"

"Most kids probably would have." Kayla let out a tired chuckle.

"She looks so sweet lying there, curled up like a kitten."

"Don't get your hopes up. That's my wild child." Kayla's humor faded. "At least she was until Alex pulled this stunt."

"Well, he's fine, and as hard as it's been for you, I can't be completely sorry. It's wonderful to see you."

Her throat choking up, Kayla dashed a hand across her eyes. Lord, she was getting soft. At *sixteen* she hadn't given in to weepiness, not even when hopped up on pregnancy hormones.

"I take it you drove from Seattle, instead of flying and renting a car?" Elizabeth asked.

Kayla nodded. Her grandmother must have noticed the Washington state license plate and the "My kid is an honor student at…" bumper stickers on the Volvo, showing it wasn't a rental.

"I wanted to watch along the roads," Kayla explained.

The Volvo door opened and DeeDee tumbled out, looking rumpled and drowsy. "Mom, I'm hungry."

"That's something I can fix," Elizabeth offered eagerly.

"First things first," Kayla said. "DeeDee, this is your great-grandmother, Elizabeth Garrison."

DeeDee stared at Elizabeth. "I thought you'd

be *ancient*. I mean, great-grandmothers are *old*, aren't they?"

"Not all of them," Elizabeth said with a grin, showing no hint of discomfort.

No, the Garrisons weren't very old to be great-grandparents of a teenager, not with a daughter and granddaughter who'd gotten pregnant as teens themselves.

Kayla followed Elizabeth and DeeDee into the house and a wave of memories swept over her. She'd only lived there for a short time, but she had liked the house and her grandparents and even Schuyler itself, no matter how much she'd felt out of place.

"Where's the bathroom?" DeeDee asked.

Elizabeth took her down the hall, then returned. "Kayla, dear, lie down on the couch and get some rest. DeeDee and I will put a meal together."

"I should help or..." Kayla's protest trailed. Now that she'd spoken to Alex, a different tension was asserting itself—the anticipation of facing the consequences of being in Schuyler again. All the same, she felt limp with exhaustion.

"Let it go for now," urged her grandmother. "At least for today, someone has your back."

Tears stung Kayla's eyes again. Staying strong for her children was a necessary habit, particularly since the divorce, but she felt safe in her grandparents' home and knew her son and daughter were just as safe. So she smiled wearily, kissed her grandmother on the cheek and sank onto the comfortable sofa. It wasn't long before reality drifted away.

The clock was chiming two when she woke. Standing, she went down the bathroom and glanced into the mirror. Yikes, DeeDee would claim she looked worse than the cryptkeeper's wife. Fetching her purse, she found a brush to tame her long auburn hair, though there wasn't anything she could do about the circles under her blue eyes. She blinked. It had never occurred to her before, but she had her grandmother's eyes. The resemblance pleased her.

Kayla washed her face and applied lip gloss, wishing makeup was her thing so she could use it to put on a brave face. Instead, she straightened and headed for the kitchen.

DeeDee looked up from her plate of spaghetti. "Hi, Mom. Grandma said to let you sleep. She told me you call them Grams and Granddad, but that we could say 'Grandma' and 'Grandpa' instead of saying 'Great' all the time."

"Where is she?"

"Bringing in the wash or something."

That was right. Elizabeth loved the smell of clothing hung out to dry in the fresh air.

Kayla served herself spaghetti and salad and began eating, the taste of her grandmother's food carrying her into the past.

"I wanna go explore," DeeDee said as she sucked

a last strand of pasta into her mouth. "Can I walk downtown? Grandma says it's only a couple of blocks."

Kayla thought about it. She tried not to be overprotective. Fortunately her kids were growing up in better circumstances than she'd experienced during most of her own childhood, but there were still dangers, even in a town the size of Schuyler. Since the divorce, it had been even more of a challenge to find a workable balance. Nevertheless, DeeDee was very independent at almost ten, and would rebel if kept on too tight of a parental leash.

"Okay," she told her daughter, "but you know the drill."

DeeDee rolled her eyes. "I got my phone and I won't let anyone close and will scream my head off if anyone tries to lay a finger on me."

"And?" Kayla prompted.

"And I'll be back in two hours and call in the middle to say I'm okay."

"Then, have fun."

"Grandma says there's an ice cream parlor downtown called the Schuyler Soda Saloon." DeeDee had a hopeful look in her eyes.

"You can get three dollars out of my purse to have a cone."

"Thanks, Mom." DeeDee dropped a kiss on her forehead and rushed away.

"It must be hard letting her out of your sight," Elizabeth observed as she came through the screen door and put a basket of dry laundry on the chair next to Kayla.

Kayla picked up a towel and inhaled the scent of the warm Montana day. She glanced at her grandmother. "It's never easy. I want to keep her safe at all costs, and then I try to let go, only to worry that I'm letting her have too much freedom."

"I have a feeling you're a pretty good mom."

"Right. I have a fifteen-year-old son who ran away to Montana."

"I know, but he let you know where he was going. Alex is a good kid. That can't have changed because of one wild act."

Wearily, Kayla ate her last bite of spaghetti and stood up. "I realize that. He's never been rebellious. Art and history are his favorite subjects, and he's strong enough not to be afraid of being labeled a geek. Not that he enjoys the teasing, but he shrugs it off."

"Let's get your luggage in from the car," Elizabeth suggested after they'd cleaned the kitchen. "You're staying for a while, aren't you? Maybe a week or two?" she added hopefully.

"I suppose, if it won't be inconvenient."

"You could move in forever and we'd be thrilled."

"That's awfully nice of you." Kayla had a life and a business in Seattle that she couldn't abandon, but she could stay for a while and let her grandparents get acquainted with DeeDee and Alex. The milk had already been spilled, so there was nothing to do except mop it up. A wry smile crossed her lips. Funny how often her grandmother's old sayings still cropped up in her mind.

"You'll be in your mother's old room. I've already got Alex in the guest room, but I thought DeeDee might enjoy the attic bedroom."

When Kayla carried her suitcase into her mother's childhood room, she saw nothing had changed there, either. Even the posters Mom had tacked up before she and Dad had run off to conquer the world still hung on the walls. Instead of conquering anything, her father had died in an industrial accident a year later, and Mom had started drinking to deal with her pain.

Was love really worth all the anguish? Kayla sometimes wondered about it. Teenagers *could* fall genuinely in love, the way her parents had, but her mother hadn't been able to deal with losing that love. Kayla had believed she loved Jackson, but the feeling had vanished with his harsh rejection and the onset of morning sickness. As for her marriage…? She'd loved Curtis—or at least the man she'd thought he was—only to have him throw it all away.

A hint of melancholy went through Kayla as she unpacked the clothing she'd put together so hastily. She had built a good life, though it wasn't what she'd imagined when she was little.

"You…um, haven't asked about Jackson," Elizabeth ventured as Kayla returned to the living room.

"To be honest, he's low on my list of priorities," she answered. Jackson was the past, and she'd learned to focus on the present. Unfortunately, she'd have to deal with him now. Coming back to Schuyler was going to present a stack of challenges. A number of people had seen Alex, and some of them must have recognized his likeness to Jackson McGregor. Word would probably get around. As a kid she might have done nothing and hoped for the best, but she couldn't do that with two children to think about.

Kayla grinned wryly.

Being a mother changed everything.

Elizabeth patted her hand. "In that case, how about a chocolate soda at the Schuyler Soda Saloon?"

Nostalgia made Kayla smile. Between her grandfather's passion for huge bowls of ice cream and her grandmother's penchant for having it in soda, she'd been well supplied with treats while living in Schuyler.

"It sounds good," she agreed, "but I want to stop at Granddad's office and see Alex first."

"Sure, honey. I figured that's what you'd want."

Walking toward town with her grandmother was another echo from the past.

"In a way, it doesn't seem that long since we last did this," Elizabeth said, clearly thinking the same thing. "In others, it seems a century. So...um, how is your mother?"

Kayla made a face. "Still drinking. She made one stab at rehab and walked out after thirty-six hours. I don't see her that often—it's too hard on the kids. For that matter, I don't even know where she is most of the time."

She could see the pain in her grandmother's eyes and wondered if she shouldn't have mentioned the drinking.

"I'm not sure what we did wrong," Elizabeth murmured.

"You can't assume it was you. People just lose their way sometimes."

"You didn't."

"I got pregnant at sixteen—hardly a sterling example of stability."

Elizabeth shook her head firmly. "That was just a teenage misstep. It's what you did afterward that's important. We just wish you'd let us help."

"That money you gave me when we left Schuyler was a *big* help."

"I'm not just talking about money."

"I know." Kayla thought back through the years. "But Granddad was the mayor. I didn't want what I'd done to embarrass either of you. Even now, there's going to be gossip."

"The hell with that," Elizabeth shocked her by saying. She stopped and asked gently, "Is that why you stayed away?"

"Partly. I was the one who'd screwed up and felt I should deal with it. But it's also because I didn't want to see Jackson after some things he'd said. I guess life just…settled into a habit. Besides, it would have meant Alex finding out about his biological father, and Curtis didn't want that."

"I understand, but Alex spoke to a number of people while trying to find our house. I've already gotten calls about how much he resembles the McGregors," Elizabeth said.

"I know, and word will get around to Jackson, as well. I'll talk to Alex about it tonight."

At her grandfather's law office, Kayla didn't scold her son, just gave him a fierce hug. "Be thinking about what you're going to say later," she said when he looked at her cautiously.

"Uh-huh."

"I'm glad you're helping Granddad," she added.

Alex hastily went back to the stockroom where he'd been dusting and sorting office supplies.

Granddad was meeting with a client, so they continued walking downtown, her grandmother introducing her to everyone they saw. Schuyler still had the charm of a Western town with a blacksmith and farrier, saddle shop and spots for locals to hitch their horses if needed. It was just everyday life and tourists loved it.

As they stepped into the Schuyler Soda Saloon, the eerie workings of fate seemed to stir around them. Across the room she saw Jackson, or someone who looked an awful lot like him.

It had been sixteen years, and her old boyfriend's

face had become fuzzy in her memory. Now she was startled, realizing how much Alex took after Jackson. Yet as Jackson strode forward, some of the resemblance seemed to fade. Alex was a sweet, awkward, open-faced teenager, whereas Jackson radiated the pent-up energy of a stalking mountain lion.

Jackson cast a glance at her, kept walking, then stopped and turned around.

"Kayla Garrison?"

Kayla tensed, hoping gossip about Alex hadn't gotten around quite *this* quickly. "Actually, it's Kayla Anderson now. It's been a long time."

"Yeah, high school," Jackson said. He stirred restlessly and his gaze swept the ice cream parlor.

"Is there a problem?" Elizabeth asked politely.

"No, nothing. Good to see you, Mrs. Garrison. Welcome back, Kayla." Jackson tipped his cowboy hat to them and hurried out the door.

They ordered chocolate sodas and found a small corner table.

"I wonder what Jackson was doing here. He was never crazy about sweets," Kayla murmured.

"Who knows? This is one of the local hot spots to get the latest gossip, though I admit he doesn't seem to be one for idle chitchat. It could be something to do with his daughter—I hear she's turned into a real handful."

Kayla clenched her fingers, unable to decide how she felt about seeing her old boyfriend; she was too tired and frazzled. But meeting Jackson had emphasized the need to speak with Alex about his biological father as soon as possible. It wouldn't be the easiest discussion. Maybe she shouldn't have agreed to keep the adoption a secret, but it was what Curtis had wanted.

"I think we should change our order to takeout," Elizabeth announced suddenly. She went to the old-fashioned marble counter and spoke to the cashier, returning a few minutes later with two large plastic cups.

Grateful, Kayla took hers and they headed for the door. They strolled around town, sipping their ice cream sodas and trying to catch up on the past sixteen years. Yet in the back of her mind, Kayla kept wondering if Jackson remembered his reaction when she'd told him she was pregnant...that *he'd* used condoms, so obviously the other boys were right about her sleep-around reputation.

Kayla straightened her back. Her son was safe and she'd already weathered some of the worst stuff life could throw at her. She would handle Jackson, one way or the other.

"I HATE YOU," Morgan yelled, her blond hair bouncing. "Go ahead, hate me back."

Jackson McGregor glared at his daughter, though he still chose his words carefully. Unfortunately, he'd had plenty of practice lately. "I don't hate you," he said. "But right now I'm struggling to like you as much as I usually do."

"You think you're so clever. Why can't I go to the lake for the weekend?"

"At your age? A girl? With a bunch of the wildest kids in school, with no adults? Do you think I've lost my mind?"

Morgan stomped her foot. "If I was a guy you'd let me go, and that's not fair. It's a…a double standard. The other kids will think I'm a nun. Can't you *try* to remember what it was like in high school?"

"I remember all too well, and I'll be damned if I make it easy for you to repeat my mistakes."

"Yeah, I know all about your mistakes."

"Then, you should realize that I know what I'm talking about," he told her.

"Yeah, you had fun, but you don't want me to have any at all."

Jackson counted to ten as his daughter disappeared around the corner of the barn. Morgan had always been strong willed, but lately she'd gone completely ornery and seemed determined to drive him crazy. It was a miracle if a day passed without a shouting match. As for being grounded, she did her best to make it appear as if she was disobeying him. Just that afternoon she'd hidden in the hayloft of one of the barns, letting him think she'd sneaked into town. He'd wasted hours looking for her. Lately he'd been in Schuyler far too often, tracking her down for one reason or another.

Just a few months ago she'd hacked her hair into a hideous spiky cut. As if that wasn't bad enough, she'd begun adding a dramatic fluorescent streak down one side, using a selection of temporary dyes. Every morning it had been a different color. Though her hair had grown out, it put him on edge, wondering what she'd do next. Hell, much as he loved her, raising a boy might have been easier.

Jackson trotted up the patio steps and into the house, tempted to call his mother and ask for advice. But it wasn't fair to load his problems onto her. His parents had raised their own family and two of his cousins, as well. They'd done their duty.

He glanced at Flora, the woman he'd hired to keep house. "Any pearls of wisdom to share?" he asked.

Flora shrugged. "Afraid not." She was sitting at the kitchen table, snapping string beans. She worked hard and was a great cook but hadn't connected with Morgan as much as he'd hoped. Not that it was a housekeeper's job to provide motherly guidance.

"What are you doing here?" he asked. "I thought you were spending the night in town."

"My sister canceled on me. She got a hot date at the last minute."

The brevity of the comment made him wonder if Stella was going out again with his great-uncle, who was definitely enjoying his retirement. The image of Stella Charlton on a hot date with Uncle

Mitch was almost too much for Jackson's stressed-out brain. Stella was a gum-snapping, determined strawberry blonde, whose ample curves were often poured into the kind of tight clothes normally seen on a twenty-year-old.

He drew a deep breath, trying to dispel the mental picture of Uncle Mitch and Stella together.

"Er…Morgan wants to go camping at Flathead Lake with friends from school, a totally teen party of girls *and* guys."

"She should know better than to ask."

Yeah, she should. But lately it seemed as if his daughter was determined to cross every line, test every boundary and break every rule she could find. And she was so blasted angry while she did it. Who'd have guessed that she used to be a sweet kid who loved to spend time with her daddy while he worked on the ranch?

Jackson rubbed the tense muscles on the back of his neck. What was he doing wrong? And now Morgan was throwing out comments about *his* teenage exploits…?

Hell. He'd tried to live down those years, but it was inevitable that she'd heard some of the stories. No doubt Morgan considered him a complete hypocrite and was angry that he was making her toe the line. But hypocrite or not, he didn't intend to let his daughter head down the same road that he'd traveled. Not if he could prevent it.

Hmm. What if he tried to make her wear those

dresses he'd bought her? Would traditional feminine clothes encourage her to behave more appropriately? But dresses weren't practical on a ranch, and Morgan would just accuse him once again of having double standards.

"I'll be out for a while," he said.

"Going to ride fences?" Flora guessed.

"Yeah."

As a rule, Jackson rode fences whenever he needed to think or to regain his cool. And with Morgan constantly acting out, he'd spent a lot of time in the saddle checking fence lines.

The next few hours allowed him to relax and clear his mind, only to get uptight again when Morgan refused to come out of her room for dinner.

After eating alone, he went into the ranch office, built on the side of the house so it wouldn't intrude on the backyard or pool area. Paperwork wasn't his favorite activity, but he dived into his breeding records with grim determination, only to have the office phone ring soon after he started.

Jackson reached to pick it up, then saw the caller ID on the display... K. Anderson.

He dropped his hand back to the desk.

Seeing Kayla that afternoon had brought a rush of mixed feelings. Pleasure at first—once he'd been fascinated by the outsider who was so different from the other girls in Schuyler. But the memory of their last discussion in high school had intruded on the pleasure. No guy enjoyed being treated as a chump, and Kayla's claim that he'd gotten her pregnant had been ridiculous; he'd used protection and half his classmates had boasted about sleeping with her.

After a minute Jackson dialed in and listened to Kayla's voice mail message.

"Jackson, this is Kayla Anderson. It's urgent we speak as soon as possible. I'm staying with my grandparents, but please call my cell phone." She gave the number and got off quickly.

He sat back and frowned.

What could Kayla want? Surely not the same old thing. She couldn't hope to raise the issue again after so long. Or maybe she could. What was it about women and the way they thought?

Twenty minutes later a knock on the door provided a welcome distraction. Jackson got up to answer and found his younger brother there. Behind Josh the July sun glowed low on the horizon. It was a time of day Jackson especially loved on the ranch, but lately he'd been too distracted by dealing with Morgan to appreciate it.

"Hey, Josh. You want a beer?" Jackson went to his small office refrigerator and extracted a couple of bottles.

"Thanks." Josh popped the lid and settled onto a chair with a groan.

"Something wrong?"

"Same as always. I came up from Texas since Grandpa was making noises as if he was finally ready to give up the ranch. Then I get here and it's business as usual, so I'm heading back in a couple of weeks. I'd leave earlier, but you know Mom. I thought she'd have kittens when I said I wasn't staying."

Jackson nodded sympathetically. The family plan had been for him to get Great-Uncle Mitch's ranch, and Josh their maternal grandfather's place. The second part of the plan kept getting delayed.

"Never mind," Josh said. "I just need to unwind."

"Yeah." Jackson thought for a moment, then opened his mouth. "You want to know something weird?" he asked. "I saw Kayla Garrison in town today, except she's Kayla Anderson now. Remember her?"

"Who could forget Kayla? I saw her, too, on my way to the post office. She's even hotter than in high school. Say, are you still interested in her?"

Jackson almost let out an emphatic no before recalling that Josh didn't know the history between him and his old girlfriend.

"Can't say that I am," he said slowly.

"Then, would it bother you if I asked her out? That is, if I run into her."

Jackson gulped a mouthful of beer rather than reply too quickly. He didn't know what kind of woman Kayla had become, any more than he knew what she wanted to talk about with him. She might have even called to apologize for claiming he'd gotten her pregnant—unlikely, but not impossible.

He finally shrugged. "It makes no difference to me. Just employ the usual caution when it comes to women."

"Amen to that, brother."

CHAPTER TWO

ALEX SQUIRMED AS he listened to the faint murmur of his mother and her grandparents talking downstairs after dinner.

The discussion he'd dreaded all day was coming. Okay, so he'd been dreading it since the moment he'd decided to ditch Dad and head for Montana.

He just hadn't been able to stand the way Dad got so excited about spending time with Brant, his new stepson, but didn't seem to notice when his other two kids were around. Dad used to claim he didn't care about sports, but now he was doing all that outdoor stuff with Brant and wasn't interested in the things he and Alex had once done together. And it sounded as though the two of them had really gotten buddy-buddy on that camping trip they'd taken right after school got out.

Maybe it wouldn't be so bad if Brant wasn't such an obnoxious little creep.

Nah, Alex decided. Finding out his dad had adopted him when he was little would have been rough no matter what, though Brant being an obnoxious creep hadn't helped.

Worst of all, Alex realized he should have figured it out a long time ago. He and Dad weren't at all alike. Maybe, deep down, he *had* known and hadn't wanted to admit it.

His sister slid into the room. "I gotta say," DeeDee said, "I never thought you'd have the gazoomba to run away from home."

Alex pulled himself up and faced the squirt. Why did she have to make up such strange words? You'd never know she was practically a genius. *Maybe.* Personally, he thought she'd just fooled the teachers and school counselor.

"I didn't run away from home," he informed her haughtily. "Guys who run away from home don't leave letters to tell their mothers what they're doing. Besides, I also emailed Sandy about it." Sandy had been his best friend for as long as he could remember.

"That's a technicality. Boy, was Mom *pissed.*"

"You're too young to talk like that. Besides, Mom doesn't get pissed, or at least I don't think so."

"Shows how much you know. She was pissed at Dad, too, at first because he thought you'd gone off for the day without telling anyone and hadn't done anything about it, and then because he didn't call her right off."

"So she wasn't mad at me?"

"Of course she was. Mom gets mad when she's scared."

"Really?"

DeeDee snickered. "You can build a computer, but you're too much of an idiot to figure Mom out."

"I wasn't too much of an idiot to get here on my own, was I?" he countered.

"Probably just dumb luck."

There was a knock on the door and Alex called, "Come in."

It was Mom, and he couldn't tell if she was angry or not. "DeeDee," she said, "please go watch the baseball game with your grandpa."

His sister grinned. "I'd rather stay and watch Alex get shredded."

"Out."

"Jeez, I never get to have any fun."

"DeeDee," Mom warned.

"Okay, okay." His sister winked at him as she slid through the door.

"Close it," Mom ordered.

"But closing it means I'll have to work even harder to hear what you're saying."

"I don't think so, young lady." It was Grandpa, who'd come down the hallway and put his arm around DeeDee's shoulders. "We're going down to the family room to see how the Cubs are doing."

"Okay." DeeDee stuck her head back into the room again. "By the way, Alex, I am glad you didn't get splattered on the road or kidnapped and taken by pirates to Shanghai or something. Surprised, but glad."

"Get out of here, squirt."

DeeDee simply grinned, and Alex was almost sorry when she was gone since their mother's attention would have been split between them.

"Okay, I'm really sorry," he rushed to say. "I guess it was a stupid thing to do, but I—"

"You *guess* it was stupid?" Mom interrupted, sounding incredulous. "I thought we'd brought you up with more sense than to do something so dangerous." Her face was so tired and pale that Alex felt awful.

"You did, but…uh, Dad spends all his time with Brant and doesn't notice us anymore, even when we're there." He'd meant to ask her about Dad adopting him, but the words got stuck in his throat.

Her lips pressed together, then relaxed. "What was the real reason? You've seen your dad in other relationships, and how he gets…er…swept up in them." It was true—his father was an ass a lot of the time. Even when he was just dating some woman with a kid, he did the daddy thing with them and seemed to forget him and DeeDee.

Alex stuck his chin up. "Isn't that good enough?"

Mom sat on the edge of the bed and rubbed the back of her neck. "Nothing's good enough to justify a fifteen-year-old running off on his own. And why Schuyler? You could have come home if it bothered you that much."

She was always so logical, it was hard to argue with her.

"I didn't run away. I just took a…an unauthorized vacation."

"You're fifteen. An unauthorized vacation for a fifteen-year-old *is* running away."

"Grandpa says he's always admired the logical way you argue," he said, hoping to avoid more questions. "He says you'd make a Vulcan proud. Imagine an old guy like that knowing about *Star Trek*."

"Don't try to slide around this, Alex. You scared me half to death. I almost…" Her voice choked up and he could swear she was ready to cry.

Crud. If he'd felt rotten before, now he was neck deep in pond scum. But it was mostly her fault, because she hadn't told him the truth.

She straightened. "Alex, I want to know right now. Why did you run away?"

"I… Okay. That is, I thought…"

Now he wasn't completely sure why he'd done it. He'd just been so angry the way Dad acted around Brant and how they'd kept the adoption a secret. Heck, he knew they'd gotten married three years after he was born, but that wasn't unusual. Half his friends could tell the same story.

"I wanted to get back at Dad somehow, and you, too, I guess," he blurted out.

"Why me?"

"Because you never told me that Dad isn't my real father," he said in a rush.

His mom's face turned pale. "That was wrong,"

she admitted slowly. "Your father wanted it that way, so I agreed. Later I knew it was a mistake, but Dad still thought it was best to wait. And it doesn't change anything to say he isn't your birth dad. He's your real father. Adopting you was his idea. He really wanted to do it."

She stopped talking and waited, but Alex didn't know what to say.

"How did you find out?" she finally asked.

"From Brant. Dad told him when they went on that stupid 'bonding' camping trip."

"Bonding?" Mom's mouth tightened.

"That's what Dad called it when he said I couldn't go. I guess he was trying to be buddy-buddy with the obnoxious little creep. Brant couldn't wait to spill everything."

"Oh. Well, now that you know, you must have some questions."

Mostly Alex had thought about how to run away without getting killed. Face it, he was a wimp. When he'd run away, he'd gone to his great-grandparents' house; how lame could you get?

"Do you want to know anything about your biological father?" his mom prompted. "You have to hear about him now anyway. He lives in Schuyler."

"Here?" Alex gulped.

"Yes, and since there's a strong resemblance, folks in town may have already realized you're his son."

Alex nervously rubbed his nose. People had

looked at him funny and said he seemed familiar, but he'd thought it was because of his great-grandparents.

"Uh, what's my birth dad like?"

His mother shook her head. "It's hard to say. I briefly ran into him today, but that's the first time I've seen Jackson since before you were born. I'll talk with him as soon as possible, and should know more after that. In the meantime, I also need to explain everything to your sister."

"DeeDee doesn't have to know," Alex protested.

"She does unless we leave Montana immediately, which isn't going to happen. And it might even follow us back to Seattle. This is like breaking an egg—we can't put the pieces back together again in the same way. So start thinking about whether you want to meet your birth father. I've left a message at his house so we can get together and talk. I can try to arrange for you to meet him, but to some extent, the timing is up to you."

That made him feel a little better.

Mom stood up. "I'm going to see DeeDee right now. I don't want her to hear what's happening from anyone else."

"Uh, okay," Alex said reluctantly, then realized there *was* something he wanted to ask. "Wait. Why didn't my birth dad ever come to see me?"

His mother looked uncomfortable. "It's complicated. We'll talk more tomorrow."

Alex settled back on the bed, convinced she wasn't telling him everything.

THE NEXT MORNING, Kayla turned in at the road with the Crazy Horse Ranch sign arching over it. She'd been tempted to come over the evening before, but dealing with Jackson when she was so tired hadn't seemed wise. Instead, she'd called a second time, leaving another message on voice mail when no one had picked up.

Maybe Jackson would be more reasonable than the last time they'd really spoken. After all, there was a vast difference between a grown man and a boy confronted with his girlfriend's unwanted pregnancy. On the other hand, Jackson hadn't returned either of her calls, despite her saying it was urgent, so maybe he was as pigheaded as ever.

Rather than wait, she'd decided to drive out to the ranch before someone mentioned Alex's resemblance to Jackson or his family. She didn't care if it embarrassed Jackson, but it would be rotten for his daughter to learn something of that sort from anyone but her father. And the McGregors had been nice people. They hadn't approved of her, but that didn't mean she wanted them to be blindsided by gossip.

Parking in front of the house, Kayla climbed from the car and straightened her shoulders. The two-story structure was surprising—too new and modern to fit the open, rolling land. But the two vehicles parked to one side—a huge black SUV and a pickup truck—fit with every stereotype she'd ever had of Montana ranchers.

The doorbell seemed loud and tension crawled up her spine as light footsteps approached…definitely not those of a man of Jackson's size.

The door opened, revealing a woman with iron-gray hair and a stiff expression. Probably a house-keeper. Grams had mentioned that Jackson was divorced from Marcy Lipton.

"Yes?"

"I'd like to speak with Jackson McGregor," Kayla said.

The woman assessed her up and down. "Name?" If she *was* the housekeeper, she hadn't been chosen for her personality.

"Kayla Anderson."

"I'll let him know you're here."

The door swung partly shut, but from the little Kayla could see of the house's interior, it was more of what she'd expect to see on a ranch—big com-fortable leather furniture and a pair of women's rid-ing boots near the fireplace. A lady friend's boots, or did they belong to Jackson's daughter? Impa-tiently she pushed the thought away.

Heavier footsteps sounded, then the door opened again and Jackson's tall, powerful frame filled the space.

"Hello, Kayla. What do you want?" His expres-sion was less friendly than it had been the day before.

"I have something to discuss with you."

"We have nothing to talk about, last night or today."

She pressed her lips together, a remnant of her old anger at him surfacing, but she pushed it away. They weren't kids any longer; it was the present that mattered.

"You're wrong. Is your daughter here?"

His eyebrows lifted in surprise. "She's in her bedroom."

"Then, we should speak someplace more private. How about Riverside Park at ten?" she asked.

Kayla still hoped to protect the youngster from accidental discoveries...such as the way Alex had learned that Curtis had adopted him. How could her ex-husband have been so careless? He'd told his new stepson about the adoption. Had he expected Brant would keep it to himself?

Of all the rotten things that could have happened, Alex learning the truth from his stepbrother was one of the lousiest. Kayla had met Brant a few times and her son was right, the kid *was* obnoxious.

Jackson's eyes narrowed. "If you're so sure we have something to discuss, why didn't you let me know you were coming to Schuyler? I don't appreciate being ambushed."

She kept her temper with an effort. Honestly, did he think the entire world revolved around him? His old-fashioned attitudes hadn't bothered her in high school, but they didn't go down well now.

"Forty-eight hours ago I didn't *know* I was coming to Montana, and this isn't something that can wait. Now, do you really want to have this discussion within earshot of your daughter?" she asked in a voice that wasn't quite a whisper.

Jackson's eyes darkened. "Fine. Ten at the county park. I'll see you there."

"Make sure of it," she said calmly. "I'm not going away just because you don't want to deal with this."

Head held high, Kayla walked to her car, climbed in and drove away, only relaxing her posture after the house was out of sight.

Fifteen minutes later she parked in the lot near the group picnic site, a sense of unreality coming over her. How could she be back in Schuyler? Two days ago she'd spent the afternoon with her manager debating whether to hire a new insurance billing specialist. To unwind, she'd stopped at a friend's house to visit, only to have Melinda talk about fixing Kayla up with her recently divorced brother. Kayla had paid less attention to her friend's matchmaking than usual; she'd been missing the kids and thinking about their pleas to go camping at Yellowstone that summer.

Then her cell phone had rung. It had been Curtis, telling her that he hadn't seen Alex that day, but he was sure everything was fine.

"It's after 7:00 p.m.," she'd screamed, panic overwhelming her. "You don't know where he's been since he went to bed *last* night?"

"We just… I mean, Brant and I left early to go kayaking. We invited Alex to go with us, but he wanted to sleep in. I'm sure it's just normal teenage independence, going off and doing his own thing. About time, if you ask me."

"I *didn't* ask you," she'd snapped. "Where was DeeDee all day?"

"At a friend's place."

Bitterly, Kayla had wanted to point out that the kids were there to have time with their father, not to spend the day alone or with their friends. But she had stayed silent, her first priority being Alex. She'd rushed home. Frantically searching his room for a clue, she had finally spotted a note peeking out from under his computer keyboard, possibly in hopes it wouldn't be found for a while.

Her son's claim he'd gone to Montana had seemed so incredible that she'd wasted precious time contacting his best friend to confirm it. Sandy had reluctantly admitted to getting an email from Alex, explaining he was on his way to Schuyler, but that his phone was nearly dead, so he'd be out of contact until he could recharge it. After calling police stations, sheriff's offices and hospitals from Seattle to Schuyler, Kayla had collected a sleepy DeeDee from Curtis's house and headed for Montana herself.

Part of her wanted to strangle her ex-husband, but it was also her fault. She'd known they should tell Alex the truth about the adoption from the beginning, but she'd been in love and it was what Curtis had wanted as his wedding gift. And yet when she'd called him the night before to explain why Alex had run away, Curtis had said, "Oh, well, I guess it's best he knows."

Forcing herself into the present, Kayla watched the clock on the dashboard tick off the minutes. At ten the black pickup truck she'd seen next to Jackson's house pulled up and she got out of the Volvo.

"I only came because I don't want my daughter overhearing any nonsense," Jackson growled as he marched around the hood of his Chevy. He was the classic image of a rancher—lean, skin tanned, wearing jeans, a worn shirt, boots and a cowboy hat pushed back on his head.

"It isn't nonsense," Kayla said evenly. "And remember *I'm* the one who tried to be considerate by suggesting we meet elsewhere."

"Considerate would be leaving me alone."

"No, considerate would have been listening sixteen years ago instead of dismissing me and saying I slept around."

Jackson made a visible effort to calm down. "Kayla, I realize things must have been difficult for you and I'm sorry about that, but you can't expect me to take responsibility for someone else's child."

She gave him a narrow look. "Didn't it *ever* occur to you that I might have been telling the truth?"

He sighed. "I've thought about it, but I was very careful about birth control and half the guys in school were boasting about being with you. I didn't believe them until you claimed I'd gotten you pregnant."

"Condoms can fail."

"I always checked after we were done and they were intact."

Kayla remembered him checking and how she'd interpreted it as thoughtfulness. "There must have been something you missed."

"A million-to-one chance against a girl that every guy in the school knew had a birthmark on her hip."

"It would have been easy for someone to find out about a birthmark without having had sex with me," Kayla retorted. She'd always figured it was Marcy who'd shared that information after Jackson had stopped dating her and asked Kayla out. Marcy's locker had been close to hers in gym class, so it would have been easy to spot something normally covered by clothes.

"Regardless, you're going to drop this, now and forever," Jackson ordered.

Kayla raised her eyebrows. Would he have been so peremptory toward another man?

"Perhaps I could have been more tactful when you announced you were pregnant," he continued, "but that was a long time ago. I have my daughter to consider, and girls are very sensitive to this sort of thing."

"Girls are sensitive to…?" Kayla repeated in disbelief. "That's pretty damn patronizing. Teenagers are sensitive to *everything* and gender doesn't make much difference. You're obviously even more chauvinistic than you used to be."

Jackson made a dismissive gesture. "I don't care what you call it. I didn't sleep all night, trying to think of ways to protect Morgan from any wild rumors you might start."

There were lines of exhaustion under his eyes and dark beard stubble on his jaw, so he *might* have stayed up all night. Jackson was more gorgeous and sexy than ever, but otherwise, she wasn't impressed with what she'd seen of him as an adult.

"I'm going to try this again," Kayla said carefully. "No one is asking you take responsibility for Alex. I'm well able to take care of him myself. I wouldn't have called you in the first place, except my son is here in Schuyler. We can get genetic tests and I could go through the court to force it, but I doubt a judge will consider it necessary. The resemblance between the two of you is unmistakable. Because of it, people are already talking, and I don't think it's fair for your daughter to learn about it on Facebook or get a tweet that she has a brother."

Her words seemed to pull Jackson up short. In the silence Kayla took out her smartphone and brought up Alex's latest school photo.

She held it out. "Let me introduce you to your son."

As he stared at the screen, the stunned expression on Jackson's face spoke volumes.

JACKSON FELT THE way he had when a bronco had tossed him at the Schuyler Rodeo Days and he'd landed on a fence railing. By comparison, having two broken ribs and twenty-three stitches was a picnic. Deep down he wanted to believe the picture was a fake and didn't prove a thing. But the kid *looked* like him. No question about it.

Pain went through Jackson's gut. He might have been a rebellious teen, but the McGregors took care of family, no matter what. It was part of their code. The idea that he had a son he hadn't known or supported was a hard pill to swallow.

"Well?" Kayla prompted.

"I suppose he's overdue for a father," Jackson choked out.

She crossed her arms over her stomach. "You're assuming I stayed a single mom? Maybe on welfare or delivering pizzas?"

"Of course not. You have a different last name, so I figured you'd got married."

"Divorced now, but I got married when Alex was three. Curtis is an accountant in Seattle. He legally adopted Alex the year we were married."

Adopted? Jackson was floored. "How could the court allow it without my permission?"

"They didn't need permission—you weren't on the birth certificate," Kayla retorted.

"Didn't you think Alex had the right to have his father listed?"

"Oh, gee, let me think. I was barely seventeen

and the father of my baby had denied any possible responsibility, calling me a slut and—"

"I never called you a slut," Jackson said hastily.

"It boils down to the same thing. I didn't want your name anywhere near my son. Frankly, I'm not crazy about having you near him *now*. I was hoping you'd changed, but the only change I've seen has been negative."

Jackson pulled a slow breath into his chest, reminding himself that Kayla was the injured party and he had only himself to blame for missing so much of his son's life.

"Look, I'm sorry for not believing you, but you *did* have a reputation," he reminded her, still wanting to believe he hadn't screwed up that badly.

Too late, his conscience mocked him.

"My so-called reputation was almost certainly invented by your on-again, off-again girlfriend," Kayla informed him crisply. "If any boys claimed something else, it was bravado talking. Marcy was spiteful and wanted you back. And she got what she wanted—you dumped me without a word and got engaged to her. I understand you married her right after graduation."

Kayla's expression reminded Jackson of the chin-up, ready-to-take-a-hit attitude she had exuded as a belligerent kid. Back then she'd fascinated him, the street-savvy newcomer, so different from the girls who'd grown up around Schuyler. She'd also been one of the prettiest girls he'd ever seen. And

Josh was right—Kayla was still hot. Her long legs were topped by a tight rear end covered in formfitting jeans, while her snug T-shirt revealed the kind of curves that made a man's blood simmer. The mother of a teenager shouldn't look so provocative.

As for Marcy being spiteful enough to spread malicious lies? It was possible. Hell, it was more than possible. She'd turned out to be less than admirable, more interested in his generous trust fund than in him. In fact, he suspected Marcy had gotten pregnant deliberately, hoping he would marry her. Maybe if she'd realized her mother had inherited a fortune that would come to her one day, she wouldn't have been so eager to get married.

"We can discuss what happened later, but right now I want to see my son," Jackson said.

"That's up to Alex."

"Kids don't always know what's best."

"I agree," Kayla told him, "only it isn't that easy. He…uh, ran away to Schuyler. That's the only reason I'm here. I never planned to return."

"Is he okay?" Jackson demanded. "How far did he get on his own?"

"We live in Seattle. He showed up at my grandparents' house rather quickly and says nothing bad happened on the road, but it scared the hell out of me."

"It scares me, and I didn't even know about it beforehand. But don't you think Alex running away to Schuyler had something to do with wanting to see his birth dad?"

An odd mix of emotions crossed Kayla's face. "No. Alex had no idea where his biological father lived before last night. Actually, the whole thing started a few days ago when he found out that Curtis had adopted him. We were waiting to tell him about it."

Jackson opened his mouth to make a snide remark about Kayla's parenting decisions, then stopped. He wasn't in a position to pass judgment. "Well, now that Alex knows, doesn't he want to meet me?"

"I'm not sure."

"You didn't ask?"

Kayla gave him a hostile look. "Of course I asked, but in case you don't know it already, teenagers don't always give direct answers."

Yeah, Jackson knew it. If Morgan responded to a question at all, it was usually a yell or a sarcastic comment. It was disturbing to hear that his "new" son might be acting the same way.

He glanced around the park. It was a popular make-out spot for kids and he'd seen his share of action under the trees at the far end. As a matter of fact, he and Kayla had spent a couple of evenings there, enjoying each other in the front seat of his old truck. But he didn't fool himself that nostalgia had made her pick the place for their talk;

she'd simply hoped that no one would be around to overhear them.

"What do you think Alex will decide about seeing me?" Jackson asked finally.

"I'm not sure. I brought it up with him last night, but this morning all he would talk about is getting back to Seattle for a sci-fi convention, an upcoming Mariners game with the Yankees and whether we could go camping at Yellowstone this year."

Jackson tiredly rubbed the back of his neck. Science fiction conventions and Mariners baseball games? It was a reminder that his son had grown up in a different world than a Montana ranch. Alex was a city kid, and the enormity of what Jackson had missed struck him again. What would they have in common?

"Safeco Field? So Alex plays baseball," he murmured.

"Because he goes to major league games?" Kayla shook her head. "Sorry to disappoint the tough rancher, but he's never played sports that much. Both Alex and DeeDee are Mariners fans."

"DeeDee?" Jackson asked, alarmed that Alex might have a twin sister. He loved Morgan more than anything, but dealing with her was going to shorten his life by twenty years.

"DeeDee is my daughter with Curtis. She's nearly ten and *does* play sports."

"I see." He stopped and tried to clear his brain. "There's something I don't understand—why didn't your family insist on a paternity test when Alex was born and ask for a financial settlement?"

"Because my mother didn't know you were the father, and my grandparents only learned about it yesterday. I didn't even tell Mom that I was pregnant until we were a long way from Schuyler—I was afraid she'd remember we had dated and empty a shotgun into your crotch. She can be hotheaded after a few drinks."

The imagery was painfully vivid.

"Uh, well, thanks. I think."

Kayla smiled grimly. "It wasn't to protect *you*—I just didn't want Mom going to prison for castrating an underage cowboy."

Jackson winced inwardly. "About Alex. I can't believe he won't want to meet his own father. I mean, don't you think he wants a strong male role model?"

Kayla's eyes opened wide. "A strong male role model? What, because Curtis is an accountant? I suppose you don't think that's manly enough."

"I'm just trying to think what Alex wants."

"What he wants is to process everything after his world getting upside down. As for myself, I'd prefer knowing more about you before allowing you any time with him."

"What does that mean?"

Kayla made an impatient sound. "It means I want to protect my son. Good heavens, Jackson, I haven't seen you in sixteen years. I barely knew you back then, and I definitely don't know what kind of man you are now. From what I've seen so far, you've got a macho thing going that raises questions about whether you'd be a healthy influence on a sensitive kid."

"I'm not macho, I'm his father."

"Only through biology. It takes more than DNA to truly make you a parent."

A headache began throbbing in Jackson's temples. "I agree, but I want to rectify that as soon as possible. As for knowing more about me, surely your grandparents have told you the pertinent details."

"Some of them, but I want to hear what you have to say."

Jackson rolled his shoulders and a trickle of perspiration traveled down his back. In the past half hour his own world had been turned upside down, and a sane man… No, scratch that, he hadn't felt completely sane since Morgan had started acting out. And with another teenager entering his life, he might be headed for a straitjacket.

"All right," he said. "I don't know what you think is important, but obviously I'm a rancher. We raise both cattle and horses and have a respected breeding program. My great-uncle Mitch deeded the Crazy Horse to me a while back, though I've been working there since I graduated high school. I'm well able to provide support payments."

"I don't want or need money from you."

"Kayla—"

"Drop it," Kayla interrupted sharply. "I remember you used to talk about ranching, though your folks wanted you to attend college first. What else?"

"Marcy and I got divorced eight years ago, which I'm sure you've also heard, and I doubt I'll ever jump into marital waters again…too many sharks."

"I understand." Kayla's voice was neutral, but since they were both divorced, he wondered if she felt the same way about marriage. "I know you have custody of your daughter and that her name is Morgan. How old is she?"

"Er…fifteen last November."

Kayla's eyes widened. "Good lord, Jackson, that means Marcy was already pregnant when we started dating, yet this morning you were *still* sure you couldn't be Alex's father?"

"That's because I didn't use protection with Marcy the last time we were together," he replied stiffly. "She claimed it was safe since it was right after her period. I decided to be more careful when I starting dating other girls."

"Peachy."

A long time ago Jackson had made an uneasy peace with the fact that he had been a normal teenage boy with raging hormones. Well, perhaps more normal than some. But how many teenage boys got *two* girls pregnant in less than two months? While it probably wasn't a record, it also wasn't something to be proud about.

"I don't know what else to say about myself," he said. "I'm not a criminal. I work hard, pay my bills and respect my parents. What now?"

"For one, we both need to sit down with our kids." Kayla's right eyebrow lifted. "You *were* planning to tell Morgan about her brother, weren't you?"

"Of course."

Tension went through Jackson at the possibility Morgan could have found out already. If folks in town had seen Alex and realized he was Kayla's son, they might easily have put two and two together already. Schuyler loved to gossip, and while he'd taken away Morgan's smartphone and cut off her internet access, her friends had switched to calling the house phone.

"Okay, I'll go home to tell Morgan while you go talk to Alex," he suggested.

"Don't worry, I'll be having a number of discussions with my son. Good luck explaining yourself to your daughter. I'll let you know when, *and if*, Alex wants to meet."

Jackson watched Kayla's trim form slip behind the wheel of her car and drive out of the park. Then he climbed into his Chevy and drove toward the Crazy Horse, his gut knotting tighter than before.

How was he going to tell Morgan that she had a heretofore-unknown brother, just a few weeks younger than her? It was hardly the sort of thing a man wanted to admit to his daughter, especially one who'd done little more than snarl at him for months.

MORGAN WOKE UP, groaning at the sharp knock on her bedroom door. She'd stayed up until 4:00 a.m. playing video games. It was summer—she didn't have to do anything except her chores. And thanks to her dad, she couldn't do a lot of what she *wanted*, though she couldn't figure out why he cared enough to punish her.

Why was he being such a hard-ass? Hell, the sooner she was out of this house, the better.

The knocking continued.

"What?" she shouted.

"Morgan, we need to talk."

"I was asleep."

"It's well after ten and I'm not going to wait. Drag yourself into the living room. I don't like you staying up to all hours, then sleeping the entire day."

"I was playing a video game."

"Why couldn't you do that in the morning?"

"Because I don't want to."

He muttered something behind the door. "I want you out here for a talk."

"If I do, can I go to the lake with my friends? You only grounded me until Friday."

"This isn't a negotiation, Morgan. I have something serious to discuss."

Jeez. Her dad thought everything was important, everything that mattered to him, at least. He didn't give a crap about the things that mattered to her.

"Morgan?" he prompted sternly.

"Gimme a minute, I have to get dressed." That way she could escape to the barns as soon as he was through with his lecture. And she knew it'd be a lecture, because it was always a blah-blah lecture about something.

Yawning, she pulled on her clothes and boots. The one thing her dad hadn't taken away was her riding privileges; she could still go out on the Black when she wanted. That was, she could go if she didn't ride too far and if she took the satellite phone and if she made sure someone knew where she was going. From what she'd heard, he'd never needed to do *any* of that when he was her age.

Three years ago she'd thought she was old enough to ride alone and he had said "no way." He'd even admitted it would have been different if she was a boy. She wasn't supposed to know, but Grandpa and Grandma had told him they thought he was wrong, so he'd finally backed down, except for the rules she had to follow.

Tying a bandanna around her neck, she cast a quick glance at the mirror. It was depressing. Okay, she wasn't Katherine Heigl or anything, but she didn't want to *try* to be pretty, did she? Dad probably wanted her to, though. He'd bought her a load of dresses for Christmas. Sometimes she thought that if he couldn't have a son, he wanted a girlie-girl type daughter who wore dresses and got As in home sciences.

Throwing the door open, she stomped downstairs

to the living room, hoping Flora was around. Her dad's lectures didn't last as long when the housekeeper could hear them, but she was probably in town doing the shopping.

Morgan dropped into an easy chair and muttered, "So what is it?"

"Don't sulk."

"I'm not." She stuck her chin out. "Did you find some other way I'm screwing up your life and my life and everyone else's life?"

"I never said you were screwing up anyone's life and you know it."

Okay, he hadn't, but she knew what was behind the things he *did* say. She was tired of being the burr under everyone's saddle. Maybe it was possible to get emancipated, the way she'd seen kids do on TV. The thought made her sick to her stomach, but it was something she should check out.

Her dad didn't say anything else right away and Morgan wondered why. Was he saving up breath for yelling? Maybe, but he didn't seem as angry as usual.

"There's something I need to tell you," he finally started again.

"So tell me," she said flippantly.

"Er…you obviously know I did a few things in high school that weren't the smartest moves I could have made." He said it as if he'd memorized the words.

"Yeah," she answered slowly. "I've heard stuff. I

know you were supposed to go to college, but you and Mom got married because she was pregnant with me, so everything had to change."

He seemed a little surprised. "I suppose I should have discussed that with you."

She shrugged. "Doesn't matter."

"Well, it turns out there's more to the story."

Dread hit Morgan's stomach. She really didn't want to discuss *all* the details. Her dad stared out the window as if he'd rather be anywhere but there. So what else was new?

"What about it?" she asked, unable to stand the suspense.

He turned around. "Your mother and I broke up briefly in high school and I dated other girls. One girl in particular. She'd only lived in Schuyler a few months, but her parents grew up here, and her grandparents still live in town. You know the Garrisons, don't you? Kayla's mother is their daughter."

Sure, Morgan knew Mayor Garrison. He ate ice cream at the parlor almost every afternoon, right when school let out. She also knew he had a son who was a lawyer in town, and another kid who'd left Schuyler a long time ago. But Morgan didn't know much else except he was nice and didn't seem to mind if a bunch of kids came in at the same time he was there.

"So?" she pushed, now curious.

"So Kayla left and I haven't heard anything about her since then. But now she's visiting with her children. The oldest one's name is Alex. This morning… Well, I learned that Alex is my son, and of course, that means he's your brother."

CHAPTER THREE

JACKSON STUDIED HIS daughter's face as shock spread across it, along with other emotions that were harder to identify.

He'd hated revealing how badly he had messed up as a teenager. It had been a relief when he'd gotten back to the house and found her still asleep. The delay had given him time to think about how to tell her and rehearse it in his mind. The problem was, there wasn't any way to make the situation sound better.

As for her guessing that he'd married her mother because she was pregnant…? Well, *of course* she had figured it out—all she'd had to do was compare her birth date with the day he and Marcy got married.

He ought to have already discussed it with Morgan, but he hadn't wanted to take the chance of her guessing how much he had dreaded marrying Marcy. After all, while he'd dated Marcy on and off, he had never considered a future with her. But with a baby on the way, getting married had seemed the right thing to do.

"How do you know he's your kid?" Morgan said after a long silence, an edge in her voice.

"I met with his mother this morning and saw his picture. He's a McGregor."

"Why didn't she tell you before?"

He cleared his throat. "She *did* tell me, but I didn't believe her. Anyway, her son looks enough like me that people may guess the relationship and talk. I didn't want you hearing about it that way."

"Why are they here now?"

"Alex wanted to meet his great-grandparents. He'd just learned he was adopted by Kayla's husband and was upset they never told him."

"I'd be pissed, too."

"Don't use that sort of language," he said on autopilot.

"Yeah, I know, it isn't 'ladylike.'"

She rolled her eyes and Jackson took a deep breath. What was wrong with a girl using nice language?

"What's he like?" Morgan asked.

"We haven't met yet, but I know he's a baseball and science fiction fan."

"Probably a geek. What's *she* like?"

It was a question Jackson hadn't anticipated. "Oh, Kayla has dark auburn hair and blue eyes. I don't know. Smart, I guess."

"Cripes, Dad. If that's all my boyfriend could say about me, I'd give him the old heave-ho."

"This isn't about Kayla and…you have a boy-friend? Who is he?" he demanded.

"No one steady at the moment."

"But you *used* to have a steady boyfriend?" Jackson asked, his heart rate accelerating. A child grow-ing up on a ranch was familiar with the facts of life, but he wasn't ready for Morgan to experience those facts firsthand. "You're only fifteen—that's too young to go steady."

Morgan gave him an inscrutable look that didn't admit or deny anything. "How old was Kayla when you knocked her up?"

Damn. Okay, he was an even bigger hypocrite than he liked to think about, but he was determined to keep his daughter from having to grow up too quickly.

"I don't remember for sure," Jackson replied. "And it's none of your business, so don't ask if you meet her, or Alex, either."

"*Am* I going to meet him?" she said, angry defi-ance creeping back into her attitude.

"That's partly up to Alex, but it's fine with me and I don't think his mother will object. Is that what you want?"

His daughter's nose wrinkled, but he still couldn't tell what she was thinking.

"I guess," she said after a while.

"Is there anything you want to discuss?" he asked, wishing she'd give him a hint about her feel-ings. It would have been easier if he'd found out about Alex before she turned so ornery. Or perhaps when she was older and they'd figured things out.

Morgan hunched her shoulder. "What do you mean?"

"I mean…how do you feel about all of this?"

"What do I care if you have another kid? Maybe he won't cause you as much trouble as me."

Jackson leaned forward. "Morgan, we might be going through a rough patch, but it doesn't—"

"Save it," she interrupted and jumped to her feet. "I'm going for a ride."

"Take the satellite phone," he reminded her.

He counted to ten as Morgan disappeared, their faithful German shepherd at her heels. The discussion hadn't gone as well as he'd hoped, but slightly better than expected. His mom would say…

Ah, *hell.*

His parents also needed to be told about Alex, and it was news that should come from him. Jackson was reasonably certain they hadn't heard yet or they'd have contacted him; nowadays his folks were pretty direct.

Suddenly he smiled with grim humor. His mother had *not* been thrilled when he and Marcy needed to get married so young, especially since going to college had seemed unrealistic with a family on the way. Still, when Morgan was born, Mom had loved her granddaughter wholeheartedly, saying a baby was always a blessing. And lately she'd begun complaining that her *other* grown children hadn't settled down and given her more grandkids.

Punching his parents' number on the phone, Jackson waited for an answer.

"Hi," greeted Sarah McGregor's voice.

"Hey, Mom, it's Jackson. Do you remember the old saying, 'be careful what you wish for'? Well, get Dad on the extension and grab a chair. I've got the perfect example."

KAYLA LET HERSELF into the house and found her grandmother in the kitchen.

"Sorry for taking so long," she apologized. "I stopped at Granddad's office and we talked about the situation with Jackson and Alex."

"It's no trouble, dear," Elizabeth said. "The kids are napping in the hammocks."

"They'll stay out there all day if we let them— I rousted them out of bed early for your terrific breakfast and they're not morning people."

"As I recall, neither were you."

Kayla's smile grew more strained. Her mother's lifestyle had made sleep a challenge when she was growing up. It was ironic that with their more or less normal home and childhood, her kids hated going to bed. Of course, it was different when you *wanted* to stay up—Alex and DeeDee had never been forced to stay awake all night because of loud parties or feeling uncomfortable about who might be in the apartment.

Shaking the thought away, Kayla peeked into the pots on the stove. "It looks as if you're making potato salad."

"And fried chicken, yeast rolls and coleslaw. Also chocolate cake and sour cream lemon pie for dessert," added Elizabeth. "Pete has been out of town for a few days, but he's coming over tonight to see you and meet the kids. The weather is so pleasant, I thought it would be nice to have a picnic on the patio."

Kayla had almost forgotten Uncle Peter. She'd only met her mother's much younger brother a couple of times. He'd left for college shortly before Kayla's stay in Schuyler.

"I should have asked before...how is Pete?" she asked.

"Doing well. He moved back last year to work in the practice and people are starting to, um, *appreciate* him as their lawyer."

From the tone of her grandmother's voice, Kayla suspected Schuyler was struggling to accept a young Garrison in place of the elder one, but "That's nice" was her only comment. She didn't have enough experience with small towns to know what was normal.

Elizabeth opened the refrigerator and studied the contents. "I had the grocer send over three chickens," she said over her shoulder. "But maybe I should get another one."

"Heavens, that's more than enough. DeeDee

doesn't have a teenager's voracious appetite yet, and while Alex may eat a little chicken, he'll mostly fill up on the bread and salads."

"I know. He's trying to be a vegetarian."

"This month, at least," Kayla said wryly. "Anyway, you mustn't wear yourself out cooking for us."

"A picnic is nothing. I made ten gallons of chili and all the corn bread for the church's booth at the rodeo."

Kayla grabbed a carrot stick from a plate on the table and crunched it down. "Okay, so what can I do to help?"

"You don't need to—"

"Yes, I do," Kayla interrupted firmly. "And I want the kids to do chores while they're here. They need to learn self-discipline." Her grandparents were terrific people, but they were too indulgent.

"I'm sure you're right," her grandmother agreed slowly, a flicker of melancholy in her eyes.

Abruptly Kayla wished she hadn't said anything—Granddad had spoken of how they blamed themselves for how their daughter had lived her life. Maybe they *had* made mistakes, but people needed to take responsibility for their decisions… such as having sex at sixteen. Kayla didn't blame anyone else for her teen pregnancy. She might not have been as experienced as Jackson, but she'd known there could be consequences.

An hour later she was peeling eggs for the potato

salad when Granddad arrived with sandwiches and milk shakes from the Roundup Café.

"Lunch," he called.

The kids appeared at the back door, blinking sleepily.

"Don't worry, I got a grilled cheese for you," Granddad said to Alex. "They don't serve much vegetarian food in Schuyler, but the toasted cheese isn't bad."

Kayla restrained a smile while her son tried not to look envious as everyone else unwrapped their hamburgers. The Roundup Café made a mean burger, stacked high with juicy, fire-grilled patties, sliced onions, pickles, lettuce and tomatoes. If possible, they were even better than she remembered.

DeeDee smacked her lips when she was finished. "Yum. Too bad you're a vegan, Alex."

"Shows how much you know. I'm not a vegan. Vegans don't eat cheese." Alex popped a French fry into his mouth and chewed grumpily.

His sister shrugged. "Mom, can I go out and explore Schuyler some more?"

"Not yet," Kayla said. "I'm going to talk with your brother right now, and after that we need to have another discussion."

"Ah, Mom. Why can't you talk to both of us together?"

"Shove it, squirt," Alex warned, getting to his feet. "You don't have to be in on everything."

DeeDee stuck out her tongue.

"Careful," Elizabeth warned. "A fly might land there."

"Or it might get stuck that way," Granddad added, "and you'll have to go through life with your tongue hanging out like a sheepdog."

"Oh, puleeze," DeeDee groused.

Elizabeth's eyes twinkled at her husband. "I'm afraid we're behind the times, Hank. Our jokes are dated."

"And proud of it."

DeeDee giggled.

Even after such a short time with her grandparents, Kayla could see how comfortably the kids were settling in. It was something they'd never experienced, the sense of extended family. Curtis had been a foster child and Kayla's mother was in and out of their lives—mostly out—depending upon her sobriety.

Back in Alex's room he sat on the bed, while Kayla took the chair.

"I saw your birth father this morning," she told him. "And I thought you might have some questions. I'll tell you whatever I know."

"No more secrets?"

"No more secrets," she promised. "If I don't have an answer for you, I'll try to get one."

"Okay. Last night you said it was complicated, you know, about why my birth dad never visited me in Seattle. Didn't he know about me?"

Kayla swallowed. Depending on how she told her son, Alex might never want to meet Jackson. But as tempting as it was to keep him out of their lives, it wouldn't be fair to her son.

"I told Jackson I was pregnant," she explained carefully, "only he didn't think it was possible because he'd used condoms. We were kids, and kids don't always handle that sort of situation well. That's one of the reasons I don't want you to jump into an intimate relationship too young. Accidental pregnancy, STDs, they're all out there, and protection isn't a hundred percent, no matter what you use."

"Jeez, Mom, you sound like a broken record."

"I don't care. I don't regret having you, but that doesn't mean I want you to become a father before you're ready."

Her son's face scrunched up, reminding her of when he was small. He'd always been such a serious child, as if contemplating the weight of the world.

"Maybe this Jackson guy wasn't ready to be a dad, either," he said slowly. "And that's why he didn't believe it."

Kayla blinked. "You could be right, but that's water under the bridge."

Alex stared at his shoes for a minute. "What's he like?"

"If you mean what kind of man is he, I don't know yet. But I can tell you some facts. He's a rancher, which is what he wanted to be when he was in high school. His spread is called the Crazy Horse and he raises both cattle and horses. The McGregors go way back in this area. So does his mom's family, the Nelsons. They were kind of rivals, I guess, until Parker and Sarah got married."

"After I found out about the adoption I figured my birth dad would be an artist or something."

Her son focused on his shoes again and Kayla's heart ached for him. Montana was a world away from Seattle, and he was probably hoping his biological father would be more like him. "You should also know that Jackson was rather reckless as a teenager," she said. "He was quite sexually active by the time he was seventeen."

"Duh. I wouldn't be here if he wasn't."

"Yes, but it turns out that one of Jackson's other high school girlfriends also got pregnant. He has a daughter named Morgan about a month older than you."

Alex stared. "Jeez, Mom! That's messy."

Kayla couldn't help laughing at the apt description. "It *is* messy," she agreed. "But we have to deal with it. The other girlfriend, Marcy, lived on the ranch next door to his parents'. They broke up and he went out with other girls, including me. Not long before your grandmother Carolyn and I left Schuyler, Jackson went back to Marcy and they got married right after graduation."

"You mean his other girlfriend was already pregnant when he was dating you, and they got married when he found out?"

"I'm not sure why they decided to get married. I didn't ask."

"I bet they won't like me suddenly showing up. I don't think *Dad's* new family likes having DeeDee and me around, either."

Kayla learned forward, wishing she could protect her children from every hurt and disappointment. "If your dad's new family doesn't enjoy having you around, that's their loss," she said carefully. "As for Jackson's family, I don't know how they'll react. He's divorced now, but the rest of his relatives may want to meet you."

Jumping up, Alex went to the window and gazed outside.

"How about it?" Kayla asked after a minute. "Do you want to meet your birth father?"

"I'll think about it," he muttered. "Not yet anyhow. I feel sort of…mixed-up."

"Okay. I'll let him know you aren't ready. We'll be in Montana for at least another week, so you have some time. If you can't make up your mind before we leave, you can meet him later."

"Thanks, Mom. Can you find out more stuff about him?"

"I'm planning to. Are you especially curious about anything in particular?"

Alex shrugged. "I dunno. Just stuff."

Sighing, Kayla climbed to the attic bedroom and gave her daughter a version of the story suitable for a nine-year-old. However, it was apparent that DeeDee wasn't shocked, and Kayla had a feeling they were overdue for a frank discussion about sex. Loneliness settled over her at the thought; it was one more thing she'd have to do alone because Curtis was a perpetual Peter Pan.

Kayla went downstairs and found her grandmother knitting on the living room couch. Elizabeth glanced at her sympathetically. "How did it go?"

Kayla groaned and dropped into a chair. "Alex isn't ready to meet Jackson. He wants me to learn more about him, but when I asked what he's curious about, he just said 'stuff.' 'Stuff' is a little vague."

"He's a teenager."

"Too true." Kayla yawned. "Do you have any sense of what kind of man Jackson grew up to be?"

"I don't know much. He isn't wild any longer. From what I've heard, he works hard and his ranch has a good reputation. The gossip at the beauty parlor is that he dates regularly but is resistant to getting married again, which seems to annoy several of our single women."

Kayla didn't know how accurate beauty-parlor gossip might be, but Jackson had already confirmed his aversion to marriage. What had he said... Too many sharks? Considering he'd been married to

Marcy Lipton for eight years, she wasn't surprised he was soured on women.

"It turns out that Morgan is only a month older than Alex," she murmured.

Her grandmother had an apologetic glint in her eyes. "If we'd known Jackson was so good at getting girls into bed, we would have tried to stop you from seeing each other. At the very least we should have cautioned you about birth control."

Kayla shook her head. "It wasn't your place to step in. Jackson used condoms. I don't why they failed, but I wasn't ignorant. I was educated about the facts of life before Mom brought me here. She didn't shelter me growing up."

Elizabeth's shoulders slumped. "I never knew what to do with her. She was always restless. We tried to find her and your father after they ran away, but it was as if they'd vanished from the face of the earth."

"It is what it is," Kayla said firmly. "And things might have been different if Dad hadn't died. She can't let go of his memory, which is probably why her other relationships haven't worked. Anyway, don't beat yourself up about it."

Elizabeth nodded. "Okay. No more agonizing over past mistakes. We concentrate on being a family from now on."

"That sounds good to me." Kayla chuckled. "Alex calls the situation messy and he's right, so we need each other to deal with it."

JACKSON SADDLED HIS STALLION, his ranch foreman watching with raised eyebrows.

"Going to ride fences again?" Greg asked as Jackson checked the tools in Thunder's saddlebag. The black-and-white Appaloosa sidestepped lightly, eager to get moving. "You've got ranch hands to take care of that."

"Drop it. I'm not in the mood."

"Whatever you say, boss."

Jackson rode north, trying to let go of his tension. The way he saw it, time riding fence lines wasn't wasted. Besides, he'd never enjoyed being indoors all the time, which was why giving up college hadn't bothered him as much as it had bothered his parents. Since then he'd realized how much he had missed, but at least he'd supplemented his education with online and extension courses.

While he hadn't told Morgan she was expected to attend college, he'd raised her with the assumption she would do so. Lately her grades had been poor enough that no decent school would take her, but she still had time to get her act together…if she tried. With the new bombshell in her life, it was hard to say what would happen.

It was ironic to learn he had a second child. Marcy had refused to consider having another. She'd been too busy reading fashion magazines and nagging him about wanting to move to the city.

Jackson reined in Thunder and gazed at the horizon, unable to imagine living anywhere else.

It was a beautiful time of year on the ranch. Everything was lush and green, the brilliant blue sky arching overhead, broken only by puffs of scattered white clouds. If he turned a certain direction, he didn't even see fences, just miles of rolling grassland and trees, the way it must have looked when his ancestors had settled here.

Morgan loved the ranch, too, or at least she'd loved it when she was smaller. It was difficult to tell how she felt now. Who would have guessed that her mother, who'd grown up on the ranch adjacent to his parents' spread, would hate Montana so much? Then, not long before Marcy had taken off for New York, he'd discovered she was sneaking around with other guys.

Thunder snorted, tossing his head, and Jackson realized his hands had gone tight on the reins.

"Sorry, boy." He patted the stallion on the neck and urged him back into a walk.

In all honesty, he shouldn't have let Marcy's cheating bother him so much, but the one place they'd gotten along was in bed, so why had she gone looking for it somewhere else?

At least she hadn't fought him for custody of Morgan, which meant his marriage had ended with more of a whimper, than a bang. Of course, by then he'd basically seen the worst Marcy could dish out. The cheating had been the final knife thrust to end a long, miserable period that had seemed more of a prison sentence than anything else.

"I can sure pick 'em, can't I, Thunder?" he murmured, thinking about the woman he'd dated for a while after his divorce.

Patti had been a paralegal for his divorce attorney. Very sympathetic. Supportive. *Nice.* At least that was what he'd thought. It turned out she'd seen the documents on his net worth and had decided it was her chance to catch a rich husband. She lived in a nearby town and he'd surprised her one evening with a pizza...and caught her longtime boyfriend hopping out a side window.

Perhaps he ought to be grateful he'd learned his lesson about women. Since then he'd vowed to keep life uncomplicated, yet now he had a huge complication. And the complication wasn't just Alex, it was also Kayla.

She'd claimed that she didn't need any money, but whether or not that was true, what about a college fund? Or sharing parental responsibility? The fact that another man had adopted Alex didn't mean a damn thing. The guy might be all right, but it was Kayla, *not* her ex-husband, who'd driven to Schuyler looking for her runaway son.

If their positions had been reversed, Jackson knew nothing could have kept him from searching for Alex, as well.

Jackson spotted a slack wire on a fence and reined in Thunder again. He swung down from the saddle and took out his tools, thinking about the frosty expression in his former girlfriend's eyes.

He was quite certain she'd prefer to keep him away from Alex, so to have a relationship with his son he'd have to figure out how to get along with Kayla.

Still, it wouldn't hurt to call the Garrison household and make sure she hadn't made a beeline for Seattle. For that matter, he had only Kayla's word that she'd told Alex the identity of his birth father. If there was one thing he'd learned from Marcy and Patti, it was how many ways a woman could shade the truth.

CHAPTER FOUR

SOONER OR LATER Alex figured his mom would tell her grandparents to stop spoiling him and DeeDee. They kept doing all sorts of nice things. Like today. The Garrisons had cable, but they didn't get the Mariners games, so Grandma had called the cable company and ordered a sports package.

That was okay. Alex didn't mind being spoiled.

Now he and DeeDee were watching the Mariners in the family room. His mother had gone for a drive with Grandpa and his great-grandmother was in the kitchen. She was such a terrific cook it made him wonder if he wanted to stay a vegetarian, even the kind of vegetarian who sometimes cheated with chicken or fish. He missed hamburgers and pepperoni pizza awful bad.

"I like it here," DeeDee said, lounging back on the cushions with the bowl of popcorn Grandma had made for them.

"Me, too, but just for a visit." Baseball on TV was okay, but it wasn't the same as going to Safeco Field. Besides, Sandy was in Seattle. Not that he was worried Mom would move them to Schuyler. She could only leave her business for a while, and he knew how much she cared about her work. He sure didn't want to leave Seattle for good.

Another inning passed and the Mariners weren't doing much better than in the first three. Then they pulled off two singles, a double and a home run in the sixth.

"I knew that pitcher was losing his arm," DeeDee said smugly as the opposing team's starting pitcher left the mound. "Hit the road, Jack," she called at the TV screen.

"Mariner batting didn't hurt," Alex countered, getting up during the break. "I'm gonna make more popcorn."

In the kitchen he popped a batch and stood at the window for a few minutes, munching from the bowl. Montana backyards sure were different from anywhere in Seattle.

The phone rang. It had been ringing a lot because Grandma and Grandpa's friends kept calling to ask about him and DeeDee. Alex yawned, not much interested until his ears caught, "Hello, Jackson." He crept to the connecting door between the kitchen and Grandma's sewing room. It wasn't nice to listen in, but he wanted to hear what she was saying to his birth father.

The half of the conversation he could hear, broken by silences, was weird.

"No…Kayla is still here…Well, *of course* she's told him." There was a longer silence. "I'm not interested in what's fair to you, Jackson. It wasn't fair to take a sixteen-year-old girl out for a date and return her home pregnant, even if Kayla says she takes responsibility, as well. You were older and I expected better."

Wow. Alex was proud of his grandmother. She was plenty tough when she needed to be.

"You'll just have to be patient," Grandma said after another minute. "I can't promise, but where do you want to meet?"

Alex heard a car door slam in the driveway and hurried back to the hot-air popper. He was dumping another batch of kernels into it when his great-grandfather walked through the back door.

"Great idea," Grandpa said. "Make some for me."

"Uh, sure."

"That's a very serious expression you're wearing, young man. Is something on your mind?"

Alex made a face. He wasn't good at playing it cool. "Yeah, maybe...I don't know."

Grandpa grinned. "That kind of answer would drive a courtroom judge crazy."

Alex started the popper. It was noisy and he was glad to have an excuse not to say anything. He didn't *know* what to think. Mom had said it was his choice to see Jackson, so why was the guy calling the house?

After giving Grandpa a bowl of popcorn and topping off his own, Alex went back to the family room. DeeDee was on the floor next to the bookshelf, studying the contents.

She rolled over and grinned at him. "Guess what I found?"

"Not interested."

"Bet you will be—it's the yearbook from when Mom was in high school here."

It was a pain to admit, but DeeDee was right. Grabbing the book she was waving in the air, he sat on the couch and thumbed through the pages.

He stopped at the junior class photos and looked at the picture of his mother. She didn't look that different from now. In the senior class section he rolled the pages until he came to Jackson McGregor.

DeeDee must have guessed whose picture he was staring at. "What does your birth dad look like?"

"Kind of like me."

"Nah," she denied. "Can't be two faces that ugly in the world."

"You've been waiting to use that line, haven't you?"

"Natchramento."

Alex closed the book and tried to concentrate on the ball game. The Mariners had pulled even further ahead, so he ought to be cheering, but something was bugging him. What if his birth dad tried to make trouble? Was that why he'd called?

Maybe this Jackson guy wanted him to move in…or to get custody. He could be trying to make Mom do something else she didn't want to do. Grandma hadn't sounded happy on the phone.

Alex didn't want to live anywhere else, even if he

was still mad that Mom hadn't told him about the adoption and...well, everything. Maybe he should just tell her he'd decided not to see his birth father and ask how soon they could go back to Seattle.

THAT EVENING KAYLA steamed into Ryan's Roadhouse, where her grandmother had said Jackson wanted to meet for another discussion. He was seated at the bar, talking on his cell phone as she came closer.

"Hell, no, Morgan...Well, you aren't a boy, you're a girl and...Okay, so the rules *are* different and you...Morgan?" He held out the phone and stared at it. *"Hell,"* he growled. Glancing up, his eyes narrowed when he saw Kayla standing a few feet away.

"Thanks for coming," he muttered. "I've reserved a table in the back."

Stiffly Kayla followed him, ignoring the not-so-subtle glances of the other restaurant patrons. She slid into the seat and scowled as Jackson sat across from her.

"I told you I'd be in contact if Alex wanted to meet you. Why did you call the house today?" she demanded.

"What's the big deal?"

"Oh, nothing, except now it might take another fifteen years for Alex to decide he wants to meet you."

Jackson's jaw dropped; he seemed genuinely surprised. "It was a private conversation. How did Alex even know I called?"

"If you'd take your head out of your ass for a minute, you'd remember that teenagers sometimes eavesdrop."

"A good mother should teach her son not to listen to other people's conversations," Jackson shot back. "Of course, he's probably just following your example."

"Excuse me?"

"You listened to *my* call at the bar."

"That wasn't eavesdropping," Kayla said tartly. "Everybody in the room heard you explain there are different rules for girls than for boys. It's obvious where *you* stand on equal rights for women."

He glared.

"But I must say," Kayla added in a sugary tone, "with such high standards of parenting, your daughter must be an absolute paragon."

Despite the restaurant's low light, Kayla could see the antagonism in Jackson's face. He had to know she'd heard stories about Morgan's outrageous behavior.

"Leave Morgan out of this," he said curtly.

"Hey, you're the one who brought up the issue of parenting skills. As for Alex, meeting you is his choice. But if you do, my concern will be finding the right words to vaccinate him against your influence."

"What is that supposed to mean?"

"Think about it. You got two girls pregnant within a few months, so who knows how many *other* children you might have fathered? As I recall, you dated quite a few girls after breaking up with Marcy. Maybe we should plan a reunion and find out." Perhaps she wasn't being fair, but at the moment she didn't care.

"There aren't any others," Jackson shot back.

"Oh? I bet a few days ago you would have sworn Morgan was an only child."

She had him there, as the dull red on his neck could testify. To think she'd once felt lucky because he'd asked her out. Jackson McGregor might have been the biggest heartthrob of the high school, but that didn't excuse her teenage self from being an idiot. After all, she'd seen her mother in action for years and should have known better.

As for the adult Jackson?

Kayla didn't particularly like him. He was more attractive than ever but still seemed to be the same stubborn jackass who'd gotten her pregnant and left her high and dry. It wasn't that she'd expected a romantic marriage proposal, but to be accused of sleeping with half the boys in school?

"All right," he said through gritted teeth. "But I didn't have sex with most of the other girls."

"*Most* of them?" Kayla let out a mock groan. "Damn, that means Marcy and I were among the few who were foolish enough to fall for your line."

A muscle twitched along the edge of Jackson's jaw.

"What's the matter?" she taunted. "You can dish it out, but not take it?"

"Look, can we just talk about my son? To be frank, I called your grandparents because I thought you might take Alex away without telling him about me."

Kayla narrowed her eyes. A hot temper was one of her weak points, and right now she wasn't motivated to keep it in check. "I *told* you that I'd explained everything to Alex. You thought I was lying?"

"Not exactly, but I couldn't be sure you were telling the truth, either. Marcy proved how many ways a lie can be told. Since then, I've encountered more than my share of women who do the same thing and—"

He cut off his words, possibly because he'd realized how sexist he sounded. Obviously it wasn't people in general he distrusted, it was the opposite sex.

"Let me guess," she said. "I'm a woman, so my integrity is automatically in question."

"I didn't say that."

"You didn't have to. Growing up with a misogynist must be delightful for your daughter."

Jackson glared. "I don't hate women."

"No, as long as they stay in their place, follow special rules and have a man vouch for them." She folded her hands and assumed a meek expression.

"Please, Mr. McGregor, I'll have my grandfather testify that I told my son the truth."

"Oh, God," Jackson muttered.

"I've missed Schuyler," Kayla continued, ignoring him, "but now I realize how lucky I am to be raising my children in the twenty-first century. I'd recommend restraining your macho attitudes if Alex ever agrees to see you. His best friend is a girl and he firmly believes she'll be president someday—of the United States, not the ladies' guild."

"Fine, I'll vote for her. In the meantime, what upset Alex about a simple conversation?"

Kayla fought a new surge of temper. The memory of her son's worried eyes was hard to forget. As soon as she'd returned to the house he'd asked if they could go back to Seattle immediately. The reason? Because he didn't want to meet the guy who'd "ticked off Grandma on the phone." And that was all he would say.

So she'd asked Grams about the call. Elizabeth had muttered something about Jackson wanting to be sure Kayla hadn't run off with Alex to Washington and how he'd talked about his rights as a dad, so she'd put him in his place.

It had been a revelation. Apparently Elizabeth Garrison shared her granddaughter's quick temper, at least when it came to defending her family.

Just then a food server came by with menus and a flirtatious smile for Jackson.

"Just decaf coffee," Kayla said.

"Plain cherry pie and coffee," Jackson ordered. "Thanks."

Neither of them said anything until their cups were filled and the pie delivered. As the server walked away, Jackson shoved his plate to one side and leaned forward. "Kayla, what's going on with Alex?"

She gazed at him for a long minute. Her grandmother and son had probably overreacted, but Jackson had only phoned in the first place because he'd assumed the worst of her.

"Alex asked if we could go to Seattle today or tomorrow," she explained reluctantly. "I talked him into staying, but it wasn't easy."

A LEAD WEIGHT settled in Jackson's stomach. It was a damned poor introduction to his son, provided Kayla was accurately relaying Alex's reaction.

"Why is he worried about meeting me?"

Kayla sighed and pushed her rich auburn hair away from her face. The motion drew attention to the delicate curve of her cheek and brilliant blue of her eyes and he wondered if it was a deliberately provocative gesture, intended to distract him.

"I'm not sure," she said. "I know he's disconcerted because you aren't what he'd imagined his birth father would be like."

"What sort of man did he think I'd be?"

She shrugged and Jackson averted his gaze from the movement of her breasts against the emerald-green T-shirt she wore.

"Somewhere between Seattle and Schuyler Alex got the notion that his biological father was an artist or something similar. It's quite an adjustment to go from envisioning you as an artist to discovering you're a big tough cowboy his grandmother has to fight off."

"That isn't what happened," Jackson growled, unable to think why Elizabeth Garrison had implied such a thing. Well, she *had* gotten irate, so maybe it was understandable.

"I'm just saying how it sounded to a kid hearing one side of the conversation. Alex has an active imagination, and there's no telling what else he might be thinking."

Massaging the tense muscles at the back his neck, Jackson decided to try a new approach. "I apologize, but try to understand where I'm coming from. Less than twenty-four hours ago I found out I have a son. Then I had to explain it to my daughter and—"

"Frankly, any sympathy I might have had vanished when I had to deal with a freaked-out teenager," Kayla interrupted.

He had no one but himself to blame. It had been stupid to imply to Elizabeth Garrison that Kayla might have failed to explain the situation to Alex.

As for rushing her son back to Seattle? Kayla could have done that before talking to him in the first place.

"Okay," he said. "What can I do to make Alex more comfortable?"

"I'll try to find out, for his sake, *not* yours. At least he's still asking questions, such as what sort of person you are, what you like and dislike, if you get mad easily. That sort of thing."

"I don't…uh, usually don't get mad easily," Jackson said. It was mostly true; it had taken months of Morgan's resentful rebellion to turn him into a crazy person with a hair-trigger fuse.

"I'm sure that's debatable," Kayla observed wryly. "But tell me about your hobbies, or something that Alex can relate to."

"I raise horses."

She hiked an eyebrow. "Not helpful. Alex has a cat and grew up in the city, so horses aren't something he normally encounters. Sandy—that's his best friend—went on a ranch vacation last year and fell in love with riding, but Alex hasn't shown any interest. Anything else?"

Jackson tried to think. How did he connect with a kid who attended science fiction conventions? Maybe the biggest thing he shared with Alex was being nonplussed that they had so *little* in common.

"I enjoy baseball," he said finally.

"That's good. What team?"

"I'm partial to the Cubs. Oh, and I'm not crazy about the designated-hitter rule in the American League."

"Alex will look forward to trying to convert you."

"When do I get a *chance* to be converted?" Jackson asked.

She made an exasperated sound. "A shred of patience would be helpful. I need to give Alex more than baseball to make him comfortable. Have you seen any of the *Star Trek* movies?"

"Uh, yeah. Sure. *Star Trek*. Great film."

Kayla gave him a stern look. "Don't say something just because you think that's what we want to hear. Alex can spot a phony even better than I can."

"Fine, I didn't pay that much attention when Morgan watched the last *Star Trek* flick," Jackson admitted. "But I'll put it on again if it will help."

Rolling her eyes, Kayla nodded. "What about art? Any likes or dislikes?"

"Some. M. C. Escher is interesting. But have you raised Alex to only get along with people who are exactly the same as him, or am I the only one who has to fit into a box?"

"No, but it's one thing to make a friend who doesn't enjoy the same things, another to meet a complete stranger who's actually your birth father. He doesn't know what you expect or think and he's nervous."

A second food server approached their table. "Are you sure you don't want dinner, Jackson? The chili is real good today. I'll get Walt to slice a few of those fresh jalapeño peppers you like."

Jackson smiled tightly; normally he appreciated the attentive service at Ryan's, but not tonight. "Thanks, Cora, we're fine."

Kayla cocked her head as Cora retreated to the front of the restaurant. "She seems familiar. Was she in high school when we were there?"

"She was. And *no*, I haven't dated her."

"That wasn't what I was asking, but at least I can leave Cora off the family reunion invitation list."

Finishing his coffee, Jackson reminded himself that he only had himself to thank for the current mess in his life.

MORGAN CLICKED THE Internet Explorer icon and watched it come up on the computer screen. Flora had enabled her access at exactly nine o'clock, the hour ending the no-internet part of being grounded.

Her dad had gone out, saying he had an appointment at Ryan's Roadhouse. It had to be a date. He never brought anyone home that he'd hooked up with, and he never spent the entire night away, but she knew the score. She'd called to ask about going the lake again, just to annoy him, then hung up when he started repeating that crap about different rules. It wasn't as if she'd expected a different answer.

Morgan logged on to Facebook to see if her new

half brother had an account. She searched for an Alex Anderson in Seattle, Washington, and scrolled through the list until she saw a face that was eerily familiar.

Morgan gulped.

Cripes, he looked an awful lot like her dad. She clicked on his profile and saw the stuff he'd entered about his interests. Her dad had said he was a science fiction and baseball fan, but Alex had also listed art and computers.

For a second she kept the curser away from the friend request button. It would be a bummer if Alex didn't want to be her friend, and she was already sick inside from not being wanted, but…*no*. She wasn't going to be a stinking coward.

Morgan lifted her chin and punched the request button. Then she went on to chat with her buddies, though the really cool ones had already left for the lake and didn't seem to be logging on. After a while she saw a post from Alex pop up on the screen.

Hmm. He'd confirmed her request. Now she wondered if he'd recognized her name or merely *always* accepted friend requests. Did Alex know who she was? Curious what he thought about being in Schuyler and finding out about his birth dad, she clicked on his page and read through his recent posts.

Nothing. He'd written about being in Montana and meeting his great-grandparents, saying they weren't that ancient and were really awesome. But not one word about his birth father, or a new sister.

Then a message popped up—it was from Alex. She noticed he didn't write in shorthand texting language, so she didn't, either.

Hi. Are you who I think you are? Alex wrote.

Yeah, unless you think I'm Xena the Warrior Princess.

Are you a Xena fan? he asked.

Morgan hesitated for a moment before entering, Used to be.

Do you like Star Trek?

Yeah, except maybe the Enterprise series. Morgan had never gotten into *Enterprise*, though she liked Scott Bakula, who'd played the captain.

Into Darkness is the best movie ever. Thought I'd die laughing when Spock talked about attitude, Alex wrote back.

Yeah. Which Khan do you think is best?

That's like comparing apples to dogs.

I guess.

It was an odd conversation and not as fast as talking on the phone, but it gave her more time to think. She hadn't told anyone at school that she was a *Trek* fan—the cool kids weren't into it.

They went back and forth awhile longer about *Star Trek*, then Alex said he needed to watch a Mariners baseball game with his little sister and great-grandparents.

Since her dad always ordered the cable sports package, Morgan was able to find the Mariners game on her TV. She wasn't sure what to think about becoming Facebook friends with Alex, but she thought it might be okay, even if he was a geek from Seattle and she was a cowgirl.

Later that night when her dad came home, she came out of her room. "When are we going to meet Alex?" she asked.

"I'm still not sure, Morgan. I'll let you know."

FOR HOURS AFTER she'd gone to bed, Kayla lay awake, trying to sort out her feelings.

She'd come home from Ryan's Roadhouse to find everyone cheering on the Mariners. But once the game was over, she had reassured her son that Jackson knew the choice to meet was Alex's decision, not his.

Now it was past midnight and she couldn't sleep. Granted, she was a chronic insomniac, but usually it wasn't this bad. Punching her pillow, Kayla rolled over, closed her eyes and tried not to picture anything, but Jackson's face kept intruding. Once he'd been the cutest guy she'd ever met, and now he was even better looking, his archaic views notwithstanding.

She squirmed, not wanting to find *any* man handsome. Some of her friends kept saying she didn't have to make a career out of being a divorcée. That wasn't what she was doing, or at least she hoped not. They couldn't understand, and the blind dates they set her up on were lame, to use her kids' language for it. Maybe she just had bad luck with men, or maybe she couldn't stop making lousy choices about them.

Perhaps when she was a sassy old lady, she'd retire to sunny Florida and chase the guys around, but right now she'd been too busy with the children and running her company to have time for romance. Besides, dreams had never worked out very well for her. She was better off planning for a sound financial future than getting her heart broken again.

Still, sometimes it was hard to stifle her romantic side. It was scary, because Kayla had always thought her mother would be better off if she could stop remembering how desperately she missed her first love.

The next morning Kayla went out for her regular run, despite the short hours of sleep. It was cool and she ran for miles, letting everything else slip from her mind. The way the sky arched overhead seemed especially beautiful—Big Sky Country was certainly living up to its reputation.

By the end of her run, some of the stress had

eased from her muscles, only to spring back in when she checked her smartphone and found a message from Jackson. He wanted to meet for lunch to discuss an idea. Lord, the guy was full of ideas, most of them *bad*. But she shrugged and dialed his number.

"Hello," a female voice answered.

"Hi," Kayla said. "Is Jackson McGregor there?"

"Yo, Dad!" the voice yelled. "It's some woman for you."

In the distance there was a low "Please don't shout when you're on the phone," before Jackson came on and said hello.

"It's Kayla."

"How about lunch?" he asked, and she guessed he was trying to make his tone sound casual.

"I suppose so."

"I'd offer to pick you up, but thought Alex might be uncomfortable if I come by the house."

Now he learned discretion?

Aware that DeeDee had come into the room, Kayla restrained the tart response that popped into her mind.

"You're probably right," she said. "Name the place."

"How about Simpson's Deli? We could get sandwiches and go to the county park. It's quieter than the one downtown."

And more private, Kayla added silently. Unlike the anonymity of city life, everybody in Schuyler seemed to know everybody else's business. She didn't want inquisitive ears to overhear them any more than Jackson did.

"Sounds fine," she told him. "I'll be there at half past noon."

"Great."

At exactly twelve thirty, Kayla arrived at the deli. Jackson was already there, waiting outside the door.

"Hi, Kayla. We don't need to go in, my housekeeper packed a meal."

Whatever speeded things up sounded terrific. Insisting on driving her own car, Kayla followed Jackson to the pleasant park at the edge of town. They found a picnic table in the shade and he handed her a foil-wrapped plate holding a selection of sliced meats and salad.

"This looks good," she said, "but I don't want to pretend it's a social occasion. What's your idea?"

"Well, I usually take Morgan on a vacation this time of year, and since you mentioned Alex wants to see Yellowstone National Park, I thought I could take her there with Alex. It would be neutral territory and we'd have an opportunity to get acquainted."

Kayla dropped her fork and stared. "What makes you think I'd let you take my son to another state?"

"Right, that won't work," Jackson said hastily, his expression almost comical as he regrouped. "Perhaps we could all go together—you and DeeDee, and maybe your grandparents. Alex would feel he's got plenty of support."

She frowned. The last thing she wanted to do was spend time with Jackson, but there were aspects of the idea that might work. DeeDee and Alex enjoyed camping and they'd been bugging her about wanting to visit Yellowstone and see the Old Faithful Geyser. It would mean more time away from Seattle, but it was feasible; a friend was checking the house and feeding the cat, and her business manager was top-notch. Roger could easily keep things going in her absence. Besides, she had both a smartphone and computer, so she was available if needed.

The big question was whether Alex would be interested. But at least Jackson was asking instead of trying to give orders. Considering his temperament, she'd expected a list of demands that would tempt her to kick him where it would hurt the most.

JACKSON WATCHED KAYLA'S FACE, hopeful she was considering his hastily revised proposal. In the early a.m. hours he'd once more come to the conclusion that insanity must be an inevitable outcome for parents of teenagers.

In his case, being a jackass hadn't helped. He should have thought everything through before contacting the Garrisons. Instead, he'd made matters worse. *Again.* Of course, the situation was only worse if Kayla was being up front about Alex's reaction. No matter what she said, he didn't have any particular reason to trust her word for anything.

Shortly after 4:00 a.m., the possibility of taking Alex and Morgan to Yellowstone had occurred to him. Getting Morgan out of her routine for a while might be helpful, and a fifteen-year-old boy would surely enjoy a camping trip. He should have realized Kayla wouldn't let Alex go alone.

Come to think of it, what had made him think *Alex* would be okay with the idea?

"So?" Jackson prompted. "What do you think?"

Kayla ate a bite of the chicken. "I'll talk with him. He wants to see Yellowstone, so he might be tempted."

Suddenly Jackson had an appetite, and he dug into his potato salad. He wasn't accustomed to waiting—usually there wasn't time on a ranch to sit around and weigh the options, so he just did whatever had to be done. Planning a trip to Yellowstone might not be action, but it was a step in the right direction.

CHAPTER FIVE

ALEX STARED IN amazement at the fish he'd just landed.

Grandpa chuckled. "What's the matter, son?"

"Nothing." Alex carefully removed the special catch-and-release hook so he could toss the fish back into the water, glad Uncle Pete and Grandpa didn't want to eat what they caught that day. "I just didn't know what fishing was like."

"I told you," DeeDee said, rolling her eyes. "You put a worm on a hook and try to see if there's a fish too dumb to know there's no such thing as a free lunch."

Uncle Peter laughed. "I never heard it described quite that way, kiddo."

He'd taken the afternoon off to go fishing with them. He was a lot of fun, joking around and teasing about everything from Grandpa's waders to DeeDee's hat, the one she'd gotten at Disneyland the previous year.

If it wasn't for the birth father mess, Alex knew he'd be enjoying Montana a whole lot more. Grandma and Grandpa were terrific and so was Uncle Peter. Well, he was really *Great*-Uncle Peter, except that he was pretty young and had said to just call him Pete.

The night before had been kind of weird. Morgan McGregor had sent Alex a friend request on Facebook. He'd stared at it awhile, unsure of what to do. But curiosity had got the best of him, and he accepted then went straight to her page.

The selfie on Morgan's profile wasn't much help. She'd spiked her blond hair and had a streak of pink up the right side. He didn't think they looked alike.

Not that sisters and brothers always had the same nose or anything. Except for her hair, DeeDee looked like Mom, and, well, *he* looked an awful lot like his birth father. So it wasn't strange that Morgan was so different. Besides, officially she was his half sister, the same as DeeDee. Not that halves mattered. Mom was big on people sticking together; she said that halves and quarters and that stuff was fine for math, but family was family, no matter what. He just hadn't known she might be talking about *their* family.

He baited the fishhook again and cast it into the lake the way Grandpa had shown him. Suddenly DeeDee yelped and started turning her reel.

"I've got one," she gasped, then pouted as a boot came dragging onto the shore.

"You sure do," Pete said, "but it'll be tough to cook."

"I bet it's from a murder victim," DeeDee announced. "The mob probably dragged an informer here and tossed him into the drink with chains around his waist. 'Take that, squealer, goner fer good.'"

"Right," Pete agreed. "What do you think his name was?"

"Luigi."

"Poor Luigi," Grandpa said sadly. "We didn't know him well, but we'll miss him."

DeeDee grinned, baited her hook and threw it back into the water. So far she'd pulled in a branch, some weeds and now Luigi's boot.

Briefly Alex wondered what his mom was talking about with Jackson McGregor. That *had* to be what she'd gone off to do, since she didn't have any friends in Schuyler.

When he got back to the house he'd write about Uncle Peter on Facebook, and also more about Grandma and Grandpa and Montana.

After getting the friend request from Morgan, he'd decided it was best he hadn't posted something on there about the McGregors. His friends probably thought updates about his great-grandparents were boring, but they weren't hitting Space Needle heights with *their* summer reports, either. Most of the guys didn't share much on Facebook anyhow. Sandy said it was because they were scared it would make them sound dorky. They'd think the stuff about his birth father was interesting, but when he'd started to write something, it had felt as if he was undressing in public.

Sandy knew. She'd been his best friend forever, so he'd emailed to tell her what was happening. He would have phoned, except she was still mad at him for going to Montana and had called him an idiot in her last text. But no matter how angry Sandy was, she wouldn't blab.

Alex suddenly wondered if Jackson McGregor had a Facebook page. He'd have to check—not because he wanted to be friends with the guy, but to find more out about him.

WHEN THEY FINISHED, Jackson watched Kayla walk toward her car. She was wearing black jeans that hugged her curves and a deep blue shirt that set off her auburn hair. Her hips swayed gently, making him swallow. If he'd seen an unattached woman with her looks and figure at Ryan's Roadhouse, he'd have done his best to introduce himself.

Hell.

Jackson crumpled a sheet of foil into a ball and tossed it in the picnic basket. Kayla was opinionated, sharp-tongued and possessed a temper that was quick on the draw, but for a brief liaison, he wouldn't have minded those qualities. And *brief* was the only kind of relationship he'd consider. Dating a woman once in a while was fine, as long as he could go home afterward.

He wanted to keep life simple—raise Morgan and develop the best damned cattle-breeding program possible, figuring he'd be one of those guys who dies in the saddle and gets buried on the spot he falls. Except now their lives were getting turned upside down again.

He got up and stretched as Kayla drove away. Hell, she was beautiful. But he was dealing with her as the hostile mother of his son, so he couldn't let her physical appeal cloud his thinking.

Remembering he hadn't spoken with Morgan about the Yellowstone plan, Jackson strode to his truck and started for home.

Back at the ranch he found his daughter in the barn, grooming her horse. The stallion had been a gift for her eleventh birthday and she'd named him the Black. He watched unnoticed for a few minutes, her blond braid swinging with each swipe of the body brush. Morgan's hands were small, so she compensated with a firm grip and shorter swipes. Her face wasn't angry, more sad and puzzled at the moment, though that changed as soon as he said her name.

"Morgan."

She looked up and her chin rose instantly. "Yeah?"

"I want to discuss something we might be doing in the next week or two. Alex is uncomfortable about meeting me, so I thought a camping trip might break the ice. It would be us, Alex, his mom and sister, and maybe Mr. and Mrs. Garrison. If Alex agrees, we'd go to Yellowstone. How does that sound?"

She shrugged. "Whatever."

Weariness went through Jackson. How was he supposed to get through to her? He'd been a rebellious, reckless teenager himself, but somehow, this was different.

"Morgan, anger isn't getting us anywhere. We need to talk. You suddenly have a brother. How do you feel about that?"

Tossing the body brush aside, she patted her horse's neck. "It's no big deal."

No big deal, as if it hadn't turned *his* world inside out. But he couldn't expect his fifteen-year-old daughter to appreciate what it was like to be in his shoes. He didn't even *want* her to understand. It wasn't just because of Alex, it was seeing Kayla again. Though she reminded him of his youthful mistakes, she also reminded him of how it felt to be young and wild with desire.

"Actually, it *is* a big deal," he said with more patience than he felt. "It changes our family structure, for one thing."

Morgan's eyes widened. "You mean he's gonna live with us?"

"I doubt Alex is interested in that," Jackson returned quickly. "He's got a good home and we're still strangers. Nonetheless, he's a member of the family and that changes things."

"Yeah, well, maybe you'll get what you want from him."

"What do you mean by that?"

She put a saddle pad on the Black's back. "Nothing. I'm going for a ride."

Jackson lifted the saddle for her and tightened the girth, trying to act as if everything was normal. "Have a good time. We can talk more this evening," he said as she tucked the satellite phone into her saddlebag and mounted.

"Whatever."

She rode out of the barn and Jackson headed to the storage room at the back, thinking it was a good thing kids started out as babies. If they were born as teenagers, no family would ever have more than one, and the human race would dwindle to nothing.

His shoulders slumped. However aggravating Morgan tried to be, he loved his little girl with all his heart. Something was going on with her, and it hurt that he couldn't get at the problem.

Then a stray thought crossed his mind. If the trip to Yellowstone came together, Morgan would inevitably spend time in Kayla Anderson's company. Kayla might be able to pick up on something and give him a few pointers. After all, Morgan was essentially growing up without a mother and might relate to another woman.

Yet almost as soon as the idea formed, Jackson dismissed it. Kayla had shown concern for Morgan when she'd tried to keep the news about Alex from leaking out accidentally, but that didn't mean she wanted to bother with someone else's rebellious kid. She had her own children to worry about.

Jackson unlocked the cabinets and started removing camping equipment. The sleeping bags had been cleaned after the last time they were used and stored in tight plastic, so they should be fine. There was a good propane cookstove and full set of camp cookware, along with ice chests and sturdy lockers for food.

Assuming the Garrisons went on the trip, they'd probably need three tents, one for the older couple, one for Kayla and the girls, and a third for him and Alex. In view of their age, he should buy camp cots for the Garrisons.

It was easier to focus on organizing the prospective trip than to dwell on parenting an angry teenager, while trying to convince another one to even *meet* him. He still wanted to believe Kayla was simply stonewalling when it came to Alex, but that excuse was wearing thin.

KAYLA TRIED TO decide if considering Jackson's suggestion had been wise, but there was no way to be sure. When she got back to the house, her grandmother was sitting at the kitchen table with a glass of iced tea, so she poured one for herself and joined her.

"What did he want this time?" Elizabeth asked.

"He suggested a camping trip to Yellowstone, thinking it would be a good place to get to know Alex."

Grams looked disappointed. "We were hoping for more time to visit."

"You and Granddad are invited, too."

"Oh." Elizabeth's eyes cleared. "That would be fun, and we enjoy camping. I'll talk to your grandfather, but I'm sure he'll want to go."

"Good, and I'll see if Alex is interested."

Her grandmother leaned forward. "How do you feel about seeing Jackson so much?"

Kayla thought about the question as she sipped her iced tea. "It's awkward after all these years, but I can handle it. And compared to some things, this isn't so difficult."

Elizabeth squeezed her hand. "If the trip works out, shouldn't we plan ahead for DeeDee's birthday?"

"Yes. It could land in the middle of the trip."

"Then, let's go shopping."

The shopping went well, except that Kayla had to restrain Grams from being too extravagant. For her own gift, Kayla found the telescope she knew DeeDee had been wanting. She also bought clothing for herself and the kids to supplement the small supply they'd brought to Montana.

"Don't they insist on choosing their own?" Elizabeth asked.

"For school things they do, but this is leisure gear

and pretty standard," Kayla told her. "I can return anything they don't like when we come down to get shoes for hiking."

After they finished, Kayla helped her grand-mother fix dinner. The others were back by five, and she took her son aside for a talk; his expression grew guarded as soon as he sat down.

"What does he want now?" Alex demanded.

"It's very simple. Jackson suggested a camping trip to Yellowstone, all of us together, including Grams and Granddad. That way you can get to know him and Morgan, but still have the rest of us around as backup. What do you think?"

"I don't know."

His face was still reserved and she tried to project enthusiasm. "Hey, it could be a lot of fun, and you've been bugging me to see Yellowstone."

"Yeah."

"Don't be a sap," DeeDee advised from outside the family room door. "This is our chance to go!"

"DeeDee, what have I told you about respecting private conversations?" Kayla scolded, reminded of Jackson's snide comment about teaching kids not to eavesdrop.

"It was an accident," DeeDee protested. "I was going to wash my hands for dinner and the door was open."

"It's okay," Alex said. "She'd be coming, too."

DeeDee marched inside and dropped into a chair. "Cool. How long would we stay?"

"We haven't decided," Kayla explained. "I needed to check with Alex before we made plans."

"Don't I get a say?" DeeDee asked.

"Not this time, and don't act offended. Your brother has to decide for himself."

"Okay, okay. How would we get there?"

"The five of us would probably go in Grams and Granddad's RV."

Alex relaxed at the reassurance. It was understandable. The forced intimacy of a long drive together could be overwhelming.

"If I...if we didn't like being there with him, could we leave?" he queried.

"That's a possibility. But remember, you don't bail out at the first bump in the road. I'd want you to try to make it work."

Kayla hoped she was saying the right things. Now that everything was out in the open, she believed it was best for Alex to get to know Jackson. There probably would be uncomfortable moments, but she didn't want her kids to be easy quitters. She was still worried about Jackson being a bad influence, but it might also be an opportunity to point out inappropriate male attitudes.

Alex bent over and retied his shoelaces, hiding his face. "Would we have to spend *all* our time together?"

"What do you mean?"

"Um, could me and DeeDee do things on our

own, or with you and Grandma and Grandpa? Or does it have to *always* be with them?"

Kayla wasn't sure what Jackson had in mind, but she'd never force Alex into nonstop contact with someone he was reluctant to see in the first place.

"No. You don't have to spend every minute with the McGregors," she promised. "But Jackson will want to do *some* things with you, and of course we'd all eat together."

With so many questions, Kayla would definitely have to meet with Jackson again to work out the details.

"Just think about it," Kayla suggested, not wanting him to feel rushed into a decision. "Let me know in the morning if you have more questions and I'll talk with Jackson to figure it all out."

"Thanks, Mom."

Kayla sighed as she left the room. Alex usually wasn't this uncertain, but he'd also never dealt with something so momentous. Besides, his sense of security had been shaken by finding out he was adopted. Being adopted wasn't a bad thing—it meant someone had *chosen* him—but having it dropped on him like a ton of bricks was hard.

A ghost of old frustration shivered down her spine. It wasn't fair to lay all the blame on her ex-husband; she'd messed up, too. But when they'd gotten married it had been easy to believe that everything would work out just fine. How could she have guessed Curtis was a perpetual adolescent when it came to romance, with a short attention span for everything else, as well? Sometimes it seemed she'd spent half her time trying to shield her children from knowing exactly how flaky their father really was.

Shaking off the memories, she went to borrow a notebook from Granddad to jot down Alex's questions and concerns about the Yellowstone trip. She wanted to be sure everything would be addressed. Then she called Jackson and made arrangements to meet the following afternoon.

JACKSON GLANCED INTO Morgan's room before leaving for his appointment with Kayla. She was busy on Facebook.

"I'm heading out," he told her.

She hit the minimize button to hide what she'd been doing before swiveling around.

"Yeah?"

Concerned, Jackson took a step into the room. "Morgan, you're careful on the internet, aren't you? You wouldn't go meet with someone you don't know, or give strangers personal information?"

She rolled her eyes. "You've only told me that, like, a *gazillion* times. And the school gave us a booklet about it, too."

"Okay. Don't forget to stay cautious."

"Whatever."

Jackson clenched his jaw. "I'll see you later."

"Yeah, later."

KAYLA WALKED INTO the Schuyler Coffee Shack and was surprised to see Cora from Ryan's working behind the counter.

"Two jobs?" she asked.

"Yup, I'm saving for a trip to Tahiti."

"That's nice." Kayla ordered a decaf iced latte and dropped a dollar in the tip jar. "The patio is open, right? I'm meeting someone."

"Sure." Cora grinned as she made the latte. "Let me guess…you're meeting Jackson. Schuyler is going to buzz tonight—he *never* sees the same gal two days in a row."

"We're simply working out some family matters," Kayla answered drily.

"Yeah, I heard the two of you committed parenthood back in high school."

"That's one way of putting it."

Cora chuckled and Kayla realized there was no point in being offended. The McGregors were a prominent family in Schuyler, and her grandfather had served five terms as mayor before retiring. It was inevitable that the gossips were having a field day.

"Good luck," Cora said, handing a tall cup across the counter. "Jackson is a hot dish that lots of local gals would love to sample. Of course, since his divorce, he's kind of developed a he-man attitude, but I bet he's a real take-charge guy in the bedroom."

"Really?" Jackson's voice said behind Kayla.

"Yep, call my number anytime you want," Cora informed him, unabashed. "I don't mind sampling the caveman for a night or two. Black coffee, right?"

"Uh, right." Jackson took the cup Cora handed him. He and Kayla walked outside to a table in the deserted patio.

"Gossiping?" he asked as they sat down.

"Cora was gossiping. I was waiting for my latte. But maybe you should take her up on the offer. She seems nice and very astute."

He frowned. "No, thanks. So when do we leave for Yellowstone?"

Kayla's eyes widened. Straight to business. That seemed different. "Assuming everything is a done deal might work for a car salesman, but Alex is very careful. He has a few more questions. And possibly more to come." She took out a notebook and pen.

Tamping down his impatience wasn't easy, but Jackson kept his expression neutral, wary of any reports Kayla was bringing back to Alex.

"I'm anxious to move things forward," he said. "And not just for my sake—my parents and the rest of the family are eager to meet him, as well. What does he want to know?"

"I've already dealt with some of his concerns, such as how we'd get there. My grandparents have an RV and I explained we'd ride with them, while you and Morgan drive separately."

"An RV?" he questioned. "But it's a camping trip."

Though Kayla smiled blandly, there was steel in her eyes. "My grandparents may not look old, but they're in their seventies. Having a comfortable bed isn't too much to ask. Plus, there's a small kitchen in the RV."

"I've got a terrific cookstove."

"Fine, bring it. Maybe we'll use that instead, but when Grams bakes a cake, she'll do it in the RV."

A cake?

Jackson's vision of a hardy outdoor excursion began to erode; he'd hoped it would be easier getting to know Alex with fewer modern distractions.

"Uh, why would she make a cake? We can buy sweets."

"We certainly can, but I guarantee Grams will do some baking, too. It's DeeDee's birthday next week and Grams wants her to have a cake she's made herself."

"Oh."

The whole thing was exasperating, but only a louse would argue against a child's birthday cake. He'd do well to remember Kayla had two kids to consider, along with her grandparents. "You're right," he conceded. "An RV is a good idea for your grandparents, and DeeDee *should* have a home-made cake."

Kayla put a hand over her mouth as she yawned. "Sorry, I was up early on a call to Seattle."

With a boyfriend?

The speculation annoyed Jackson. Kayla seemed to be a decent mother, so her dating habits weren't his concern. Most divorcées in her situation would be searching for a new relationship, and with her looks, she probably had them lined up at the door.

Still, the prospect of a new stepfather might be hard on a teenage boy. Jackson considered how he'd feel in Alex's place and decided he *should* know what sort of men were in his son's life.

"Are you seeing anyone seriously?" he asked.

Kayla's eyebrows lifted. "That's none of your business."

"Anything that affects Alex is my business."

She snorted. "As if you have a clue about your biological son's life."

"That isn't my fault. And don't call Alex my 'biological son' as if you'd gone to a fertility clinic."

"Do we have to cover this again? Biology and relationship are two different things. So far, you only have DNA in common. As for it not being your 'fault,' don't rewrite history," she said coolly. "I told you I was pregnant and you rejected both of us. What was I supposed to do, come back to Schuyler every year and find out whether you'd grown up enough to face your responsibilities? I don't think so."

The justice in her retort was indisputable. Even

the argument that Kayla could have returned at least *once* put him on shaky ground, yet a part of Jackson remained angry. He *had* treated her poorly, but he'd also lost fifteen years with Alex, making it unlikely they'd ever share the kind of relationship a father and son should share.

"As for me dating," Kayla continued, "you probably think a woman always wants a man, except that isn't true. Though it's *really* none of your business, I've gone out a few times since my divorce, but only because I was pushed by friends. I'm not sure I want to fall in love again. And certainly not until Alex and DeeDee are grown."

"Your divorce must have been rough."

"It wasn't happy. How did it feel when you and Marcy split?" she asked.

"Mostly relief." *And loathing*, he added silently.

"Then, you can't understand what it's like when someone you love says he doesn't want to be married any longer."

Though he saw pain in her eyes, a curious envy went through Jackson—at least Kayla and her ex-husband had *started* by loving each other. He'd never expected the kind of grand passion that poets extolled, but it would have been nice if he and Marcy had felt more for each other.

"Anyway," Kayla said, "I'm here to get Alex's questions answered, not to discuss my personal life." She glanced at her notebook. "Among other things, Alex wants to be assured that if he's really unhappy, you won't go ballistic if we pack up and leave your little tea party."

Jackson set his jaw at the deliberate goad. "Of course not," he answered in even tones.

"The same goes for trying to spend every minute together. He knows the point of the trip is to get acquainted with you and Morgan, but he doesn't want to commit to anything too intense."

"Doesn't he even *care* about meeting me?"

Faint sympathy filled Kayla's face. "It's hard to say. Alex won't explain what's bothering him the most. All I get from him is little stuff."

"All right," Jackson said wearily. "I won't mind if he wants to spend time doing other things. But you need to start encouraging him in my direction, or this will never work."

The sympathy instantly vanished from her expression. "You seem to assume I've been pushing the two of you apart. While it's a temptation, I happen to think it's best for Alex to face this, instead of backing off."

"Fine," Jackson muttered.

"Why do you seem to assume I'm working against you?"

Jackson's jaw set. "Sorry, that's what Marcy does."

"Well, I'm not Marcy." Kayla put her cup aside. "If you were so relieved when your marriage ended, how did you become one of those bitter divorced men they talk about in advice columns?"

"I'm not bitter, and now you're butting into *my* private business."

"What's sauce for the goose is sauce for the gander, as my grandmother would say. I've told you, I don't want Alex picking up your attitudes. It's hard enough teaching kids to be wary in a dangerous world and still have a basic faith in people. He doesn't need to learn distrust vicariously."

His head pounding, Jackson tried to think rationally. There was a kernel of truth in what Kayla was saying, but it wasn't *just* Marcy who'd made him so cautious about the opposite sex. The seemingly nice woman he'd dated after his divorce had just been using him. And then there were others over the years, including a buddy's wife who had hit on him shortly before Marcy left for New York. And the wife of another friend who'd actually suggested talking her husband into a threesome. Two years later she'd quietly cleaned out their joint bank accounts and disappeared.

But he didn't plan on telling Alex about such things.

"I'll watch what I say around him," he said finally. "What's his next question?"

Kayla regarded him for a long minute before looking back at her notebook. At least two pages were covered with writing and Jackson resigned himself to the inevitable.

They were going to be there awhile.

CHAPTER SIX

KAYLA WAS PRIVATELY amused when Jackson walked her to the car. Even in high school he'd held doors and pulled out chairs for girls, all the while with condoms in his wallet and a seductive glint in his eyes.

"Nice ride," he said, looking at her silver SUV. "Rental?"

"It's mine."

"I would have pegged you for something more unconventional. Did your ex-husband pick it out?"

"Nope. I bought it last November. I like Volvos because of their safety record. When you work on insurance billings, you hear about too many accidents."

"Didn't you do insurance billing at Dr. Wilson's office for your after-school job?"

"That's right." She grinned unexpectedly. "At the time I was bored out of my skull, but I'm grateful. He paid well and it gave me the skills to get my business started."

Jackson seemed surprised by something, but she didn't have time to find out what it might be. It was late and she wanted to get back to help Grams with dinner.

"Oh, wait," he said as she opened the Volvo door. "Can you send me some pictures of Alex?"

"Sure." Kayla groped in her purse and pulled out her phone. "Here, type in your email address." When he'd entered it, she sent him three of her favorite photos. "I have our family albums on my laptop, so I'll pick out a selection of Alex when he was younger, too."

"That's great. Let him know we can work everything out."

Kayla didn't crack a smile until after she'd climbed into the Volvo and was driving away. At least for the moment, Jackson had improved his tactics. It was a smart move, since his bullheaded approach had failed.

Yet the meeting with Jackson had underscored another worrisome concern for her—what sort of expectations did he have for a son? His dismay over her grandparents bringing a recreational vehicle had raised an instant image: rugged frontiersman who conquers the wild with nothing more than a knife and flint—flint optional.

Alex, on the other hand, wasn't outdoorsy.

He enjoyed camping, but in limited doses with amenities to make it comfortable. For Alex, baseball was a spectator sport with snacks. He was quiet, reflective, interested in art and science and computers, and wanted to learn everything. It was possible he'd have turned out differently growing up on a Montana ranch, but maybe not.

Schuyler's shady, tree-lined streets should have been soothing, yet Kayla was still troubled when she arrived at her grandparents' home. Uncle Pete and Granddad were in the backyard, scrubbing the barbecue grill. She waved before stepping into the kitchen and giving Grams a determined smile.

"Did you talk Alex into eating chicken again?" she asked casually.

"He's wavering," Elizabeth said. "He tells me it's cheating, and real vegetarians don't cheat. What made him stop eating meat?"

Kayla took salad makings from the fridge, grateful Grams hadn't immediately asked about Jackson McGregor.

"Nothing dramatic. Two months ago, his church youth group visited a farm," she explained. "They fed the calves, hunted for eggs and watched a baby lamb being born. He came home and announced he was now a vegetarian...and that the miracle of birth was *really* gross."

Elizabeth chuckled. "How about DeeDee?"

"She wanted steak for dinner."

"That's our girl—a tough cookie when she wants to be."

They worked in companionable silence while Kayla thought about the contrast between her kids. DeeDee loved animals, but she'd visited the same farm as her brother and had returned unfazed about the realities of animal husbandry.

So how would Alex react to another trauma? Hell, he'd *run away* after learning Curtis had adopted him. It would be awful if Alex got to know Jackson, only to think his birth father was disappointed in who he'd turned out to be.

Honestly, if Jackson hurt her son, she'd have his head.

"Take it easy, darling," Grams said, breaking into her thoughts. "You're slicing carrots, not pounding rocks."

"Oh." Kayla looked down at the cutting board and sighed. She swept the mangled carrots into the salad bowl. "I should speak with Alex. I'll be back in a while."

"No need. The only thing left is putting the meat and veggies on the grill, and they haven't started the barbecue yet."

To give him more privacy, Kayla took Alex for a walk and told him the details that she'd covered with Jackson. Predictably, he responded with further inquiries.

"I'll ask any questions you really need answered," she assured. "But don't let them become a delaying tactic. A camping trip is a big commitment, so maybe having a quick meeting with Jackson here in Schuyler would help make you more comfortable with the idea."

Alex kicked a pebble into the street. "I don't know."

"Promise me you'll think about it. The longer you put off seeing him for the first time, the harder it's going to be."

"Okay."

They returned to the house, where he promptly headed for the family room computer.

Since she wasn't needed in the kitchen, Kayla went out to the hammocks. As a teen in Schuyler she'd spent hours in the backyard, reading or thinking. Even on hot days the shade was deep and comfortable.

She closed her eyes and inhaled the scent of warm canvas and grass. There was no simple solution for her worries about Alex. All she could do was watch and listen. And remain vigilant with regard to Jackson.

Kayla put a toe down on the grass and sent the hammock swaying.

In many ways Jackson McGregor had cleaned up his act since high school. By all accounts he worked hard, was honest and ran his ranch well. Plainly he didn't live like a monk, but he remained a determined bachelor who avoided women with marriage on their agenda.

But she obviously wasn't the only one to find his attitudes about women to be dated. Cora had called him a caveman, though it hadn't bothered her enough to stop flirting with him, so finding casual partners probably wasn't a problem for Jackson. And it couldn't *only* be because he was so ruggedly handsome—part of the attraction had to be his dark, angry reserve and the feminine urge to be a reformer.

Damn.

This wasn't helping. Determinedly closing her eyes, Kayla tried to focus on the sway of the hammock and clear her mind of everything else.

MORGAN STUDIED THE instant message Alex had sent her on Facebook. His mom and her dad had talked about the camping trip and he was thinking he might go. She messaged back. Could be fun. Do you like camping?

Yeah. We take a trip every summer to a different national park. Last year we went to Crater Lake.

Geography wasn't her best subject. Never heard of it.

It's a lake in the middle of a mountain where a volcano was. So much rock blew out from underneath that the top fell back inside. Oops, gotta go, Mom's calling.

Morgan rested her chin on her hand and thought about it. That was how she sometimes felt, as if everything had blown up and she was going to fall back into the strange empty place inside.

Everything was messed up and she didn't know how to fix it.

THE NEXT DAY Jackson rode north on Thunder to check on an injured cow his cowhands had found and doctored. He trusted his men, but lately he'd spent less time than usual working the ranch, and he needed to feel as if he was accomplishing something. It certainly didn't seem as if he was getting anywhere with Morgan *or* Kayla.

Well, that wasn't entirely true. Earlier that morning Kayla had reluctantly shared her electronic family albums on the portable hard drive he'd given her.

When he returned to the house, Flora called him into the kitchen. "Any chance you could hang out at the pool for a while?" she asked. "Morgan wants to swim, but I'm going into town and can't sit with her. Now she's sulking."

One of the rules Jackson had made was that Morgan couldn't be in the swimming pool without an adult present. He had threatened, entirely seriously, that he'd bulldoze it full of dirt and plant petunias if she ever swam unattended.

Though he was impatient to look at the photos Kayla had given him, Jackson went upstairs to Morgan's room. The door was ajar and she looked up as he knocked.

"How about a swim, kiddo?" he asked. "I'd like some time in the pool."

Her face brightened. "Okay."

"Let's put on our suits and meet out there."

She was waiting when he reached poolside and jumped in, turning on her back and floating happily. Morgan had always been an excellent swimmer.

Diving into the cool, clear water, Jackson gave himself up to enjoying it, as well. Some folks in Schuyler regarded the large pool as an extravagance, but his trust fund kept him comfortable, and he saw no reason not to enjoy the benefits from it—especially since he'd encountered his share of drawbacks to having money. And in the water, Morgan lost her angry resentment, even shooting a beach ball back and forth with him. In his book, the pool was worth the cost, if only for a single untroubled afternoon with his daughter.

Two hours later they dried off and went in to eat the supper Flora had left baking in the oven.

After their dishes had been rinsed and stacked in the sink, Jackson thought about asking if Morgan wanted to look at the Andersons' photos with him, but he didn't want to change the comfortable atmosphere that lingered.

"I know we've seen them, but would you like to watch the last two *Star Trek* movies with me again?" he suggested instead.

"Really? I didn't think you were interested."

"I should give them another shot. It's early. We can make popcorn and have a movie night."

Morgan bit her lip. "I just have to, uh, go message somebody to say I won't be online for a while."

"Go ahead. I'll get the popcorn and sodas."

This time through, Jackson realized the films were quite good, though he didn't enjoy watching the sexier scenes with his teenage daughter. Still, they were mild compared to lots of movies and TV, so he tried to ignore his discomfort.

"I like the sequel even better than the first," Morgan said as the credits rolled on the second film.

"It's pretty good, all right."

"We should bring all the *Star Trek* movies to Yellowstone. I bet the Garrisons have a TV and Bluray player in their RV."

"Sure," he said, wincing internally. So much for a back-to-basics camping trip. "Alex likes science fiction, so he'd probably enjoy it, too."

Morgan's eyes suddenly flicked back to the resentment he'd seen so often. "Oh. *That's* why you want to watch *Star Trek*. Because *Alex* likes sci-fi."

Jackson wanted to kick himself. "If that was all, I could have watched them alone. I wanted to share the movies with *you*."

"Yeah, whatever."

Without another word she marched up to her room and he shook his head in discouragement. How could she go from one mood to another so quickly? Had he been that way at the same age, or was it an aspect of female adolescence?

Obviously Morgan wouldn't want to look through the Anderson family albums with him now, so he went into his office and plugged the portable hard drive into his computer.

Everything was neatly organized, the albums being represented by folders. Each file name included the date taken, and he started with the earliest. It was a teenage Kayla in the picture, and an odd sensation went through him as he looked at the nervous girl sitting in a hospital bed, holding a baby wrapped in a blue blanket.

Curious, he looked at several more photos in the folder and didn't see any of Kayla's mother. He'd never met Carolyn Garrison and only recalled bits of gossip that had circulated when they lived in Schuyler, mostly about her being seen drunk. Not long afterward, Kayla and her mom had left town. Jackson had been relieved since it meant Kayla wouldn't be around to keep making false accusations. He was already headed to the altar with Marcy, feeling as if he was being dragged into a sinkhole. Ironically, of the two girls, he would have preferred marrying Kayla, except when she'd told him about the baby, he'd decided the rumors about her reputation must be true.

He reopened the shot of Kayla and her newborn son in the hospital. As he gazed at it, guilt crawled through him. There she was, not much older than

Morgan, facing single motherhood. If some boy got his daughter pregnant, he'd want to wring the kid's neck. He would do anything to undo the day Kayla had come to him, saying she was pregnant. He couldn't have married two girls, but he could have supported her and been a part of Alex's life from the beginning. Instead, he hadn't even considered the possibility Kayla was telling the truth.

Clicking away from the photo in the hospital, Jackson saw numerous shots of Alex as a plump, healthy baby. The pictures were mostly of Alex as he grew, rarely including Kayla.

But in the second album, around the time Alex turned two, a young man started showing up. Soon after Alex turned three, there was a photo of a radiant Kayla in a long white gown, standing next to the same man in front of a church altar.

So this was Curtis Anderson, the guy who'd let his family down. Knowing the end of the story made Jackson ill at ease to see the happy photos that followed, though it was interesting to see that Kayla hadn't deleted the ones of her ex-husband. The pictures advanced chronologically until Curtis Anderson was no longer present. For a while the faces weren't as cheerful, but slowly everyone appeared happier.

Jackson had done his best to forget Kayla, yet he still remembered her talking about finding a soul mate, as if that one person could fill the hungry, empty places inside her. He had news for Kayla—

everybody screwed up, and soul mates were few and far between, if they even existed.

Jackson emailed some of the photos to his parents. They were anxious to meet their grandson but were trying to be patient until he'd gotten to know Alex himself.

He'd started to get up from the computer when a message came in from Kayla, explaining Alex had agreed to a quick meeting, but she wanted to talk first.

Letting out an impatient breath, he wrote back, suggesting their usual time at the Coffee Shack.

KAYLA WAS DELAYED a few minutes the next day and Cora waved her through to the patio. "Jackson already got you an iced latte," she said.

While the afternoon heat was softened by the overhanging trees, it was still warm as Kayla slid into a chair across from Jackson. He handed her a cup and she took a long swallow.

"I don't know how you drink hot coffee in this weather," she murmured, eyeing his steaming cup.

"It's a cowboy thing."

She cocked her head. "You seem tense."

He groaned. "Morgan threw another fit this morning because I told her she couldn't go any farther than Halloran's Meadow by herself. She's a girl, for God's sake. I'm only trying to protect her. Honestly, teenage girls are the moodiest creatures on earth."

"Moodiness isn't limited to the feminine gender," Kayla said mildly. She couldn't turn every stupid-ass comment Jackson made into an argument. "I'm raising a teenage boy, and he has his own share of moody moments."

Jackson gave her a suspicious look. "Whatever. I want to thank you for sharing the pictures."

"You're welcome." Giving him a copy of their electronic family albums hadn't been easy—it was like opening both her joys and heartbreaks for a stranger to view.

"I noticed there aren't many photos of your mother."

Kayla shrugged. "Mom isn't around much. She drinks heavily and gets involved with the wrong people. I had to give up taking care of her when I started taking care of a baby."

Jackson's eyes widened. "You didn't have any help?"

"I stayed with Mom until Alex was two months old, though I never risked leaving him alone with her. After that we moved someplace else. Not great, but better. Growing up I learned all the ways you could survive. Before Alex was born I found one of those guys who make fake IDs so I could get a better-paying job—a lot of employers won't hire pregnant, underage girls. I started my business when I turned eighteen."

"I'd figured your mother was there for you."

"I had me, and that was enough. We were okay."

She wasn't about to admit how scary that first year had been, underage and alone with a baby. Fortunately she'd saved the generous farewell gift from her grandparents, plus every penny from her after-school job in Schuyler. Elizabeth Garrison had delicately hinted it would be wise to keep her money secret. Carolyn hadn't meant to be a bad mother, but she was an alcoholic, and when the craving hit, her other instincts failed. If she'd known her daughter had some money, it would have eventually gone toward a bar tab.

Kayla hadn't needed Grams's advice to keep her savings hidden. She'd memorized the bank account number and destroyed the paperwork; Carolyn had never known it existed.

Jackson was staring at the passing traffic as if he didn't know how to respond. "It still must have been rough," he said, finally. "Alex is my son. *I should have helped.*"

Kayla saw genuine remorse in Jackson's face... and heard a note of anguish in his voice. The ranching world he came from was filled with tradition and rigid codes of behavior. He hadn't wanted to believe he was the father of her baby, so he'd broken that code. Now he was paying the price.

"You can help now by letting Alex be himself," she suggested carefully. Jackson McGregor might be chauvinistic, impatient and demanding, but he was also the kind of man who could make an adolescent boy feel inadequate, especially if he thought the man in question looked down on him.

"What do you mean?"

"Just that Alex *isn't* a cowboy. I suspect that's part of why he's so reluctant to meet you. He may worry you won't approve of him, or that you might expect him to be different than he is."

Jackson jerked with surprise. "He thinks I won't like him if he isn't a jock or something?"

"I don't know, but I have to wonder. And even if he isn't worried about it now, he might be later. Just be excited about who Alex is, not who you think he *should* be."

"Surely you know I'd never intentionally hurt my own kid, Kayla." Jackson sounded faintly offended.

She sighed. "It's the unintentional damage I'm concerned about. You obviously have very... *traditional* ideas about male and female roles."

His mouth snapped shut and she gave him credit for not going ballistic.

"Anyway," she continued, "I'll bring Alex to the park in the morning. I'm hoping it will help him make up his mind about going on the camping trip."

She drove back to the house and sat down with her son. "Okay, we're all set for tomorrow."

Alex chewed the inside of his lip and looked ready to run for the Montana state border.

"This is not the time for second thoughts," she said gently.

"Jeez, Mom, I know, but the thing about tomorrow…and Yellowstone…" His voice trailed into silence.

"Yes?" Kayla prompted. She knew he was mixed-up about a lot of things, but if he didn't talk to her, she couldn't help.

"I'm afraid I messed up our family," he said in a rush. "What if that guy tries to make me stay in Montana?"

"Alex, I don't think that's what Jackson wants, and even if he does, he couldn't make you stay. No judge would let it happen."

"Really?"

"Honest," Kayla assured him. "But would it be terrible to come back for visits? We'd see Grams and Granddad, and if you and Jackson hit it off, you can spend some time with him and your sister Morgan. That doesn't sound bad, does it?"

"No, I like Montana. I just don't want to stay here forever."

Kayla couldn't resist ruffling his hair the way she'd done when he was three. "Do me a favor. Next time you're worried about something, *ask* before twisting yourself into a knot."

He grinned. "Okay."

She went to her bedroom, shaking her head. Jackson thought moodiness belonged to teenage *girls*?

At least she'd learned what some of Alex's foot-dragging was about, though she could kick herself for not figuring it out earlier. If she'd believed Jackson might try to seek custody, she'd have been bothered, too…and lining up lawyers from Schuyler to Seattle.

But custody wasn't a serious concern. Aside from Alex running away to Montana, he'd never been in any trouble. He got excellent grades in school, was well-adjusted and his home life in Seattle was stable. Even if Jackson decided to seek custody, no Seattle judge would give him the time of day. And her grandparents were so respected, he wouldn't get far in Schuyler, either.

Yet Kayla frowned. Her motherly instincts remained uneasy. Alex's "unauthorized vacation" had been a drastic step, and she still thought there was more to it than he'd confessed.

THE NEXT MORNING Kayla pulled in at the park and turned toward Alex, sitting next to her in the front seat. He looked sick to his stomach.

"Ready?" she asked.

"Do I have to?"

"You said you would, and Jackson came into town just for this."

Alex nodded, but he still scrunched down and tried to spy over the edge of the dashboard so he could see his birth father without being spotted.

Jackson stood near a picnic table and was staring intently at the car as if he had X-ray vision, making Kayla wish she could tell him to dial it down a few notches. Projecting the energy of a stalking mountain lion was *not* the way to make Alex more comfortable.

"How long do we have to stay?" Alex muttered.

"Give it thirty minutes, okay?"

They got out and Alex dragged his feet as they walked toward the picnic table. He visibly gulped when they got close. "Uh, hello."

"Hi, Alex. I'm really glad to meet you."

"Yeah. Sure."

"Do you want to sit down?" Jackson gestured toward the table.

"Uh, no, I'm okay."

As Alex shifted his weight from one foot to another, Kayla had a feeling that it was going to be a really *long* half hour.

MORGAN GIGGLED WHEN she read Alex's latest message about how the previous year he'd injected blue dye into the shampoo of some jock jerk at his school and red dye into this other jerk's shampoo. But the joke had fallen flat because everybody thought they'd done it deliberately to show the school colors. The jerks had taken all the credit and then used the shampoo for every game after that.

They never even tried to figure out who did it, Alex wrote. Not that they could have. I was careful.

Did you want them to know? she asked.

Are you kidding? I'd rather not get pounded. You're only the second person I've told. Sandy knows, but my other friends might blab.

It was awesome that Alex's best friend was a girl. Morgan had friends, but she didn't have a *best* best friend, so it made her feel good that she and Alex were sharing a secret. She hadn't told her dad they'd been messaging each other. So that was another secret. Well, she didn't know for sure that it was a secret—Alex might have told his mother— but Morgan had a feeling he hadn't.

It was weird getting to know her brother this way. The night before they'd messaged back and forth for over two hours.

She typed, Have you decided to go on the trip to Yellowstone?

Yeah, I told Mom I would. I guess your dad already has reservations at a campground. Mom is like a superwoman planner. Your dad must be, too.

Not usually, except for stuff to do with his cows, Morgan wrote back, shrugging off the "your dad" thing. She was really glad Alex had decided to go. He and Dad had met at the park, but since he wasn't writing anything about it, she felt funny asking what had happened.

Maybe, if she got to know Alex well enough,

she'd ask what he thought about the whole teen-pregnancy thing. Especially whether he thought his mother was sorry she'd had him, the way her own mother was sorry.

CHAPTER SEVEN

THREE DAYS LATER Alex dragged his eyes open when his grandfather knocked on the bedroom door and told him it was time to rise and shine.

He blearily checked the clock. Five a.m. Crap, they were going on vacation—why did they have to get up so early? Grandma had told him it was part of the fun and she wished they were leaving when it was still dark—it was what she called an indelible experience. He didn't know what that meant and didn't care.

After another fifteen minutes, a sharp rap woke him up again and his mom stuck her head inside the room. "Second warning, kiddo. Breakfast is almost ready."

Rats. He sat up and started taking off his shirt before remembering he'd slept in his clothes so he could stay in bed longer. So he yawned and stuck his feet into his sneakers. He'd been up late messaging with Morgan on his phone long after Mom had sent him to bed.

Morgan was turning out to be okay. They'd gone back and forth about practically everything... except Jackson McGregor.

It was hard to wrap his head around the idea that the guy was his birth dad. As soon as Alex had seen Jackson at the park he'd thought, *Holy crap, he really* is *my father.* But it still didn't seem real.

Alex finished tying his shoes and trudged down to the living room, where DeeDee was groggily brushing her hair. Mom was bright and energetic, double-checking their luggage and joking with Grandpa.

"Jeez, Mom," DeeDee mumbled. "You went for a run, didn't you?"

"A short one."

Alex groaned along with his sister. Running made Mom all perky in the morning.

After a few minutes a big shiny black SUV pulled up in front of the house and Jackson McGregor got out, looking as if he'd been up for hours.

Alex rubbed his face. Cripes, the guy was a cowboy. That was the same as finding out his father was a Klingon.

Everyone headed toward the front yard. Mom stopped and looked back at him. "How about it, Alex?"

"In a second."

"Okay."

Why had he said he'd go? Spending time with Morgan would be okay, but he wasn't sure about anything else. While his birth father might not be able to get custody or force him to stay in Montana, everything would be different from now on.

Alex swallowed hard and wished he was on another planet, even the Klingon home world.

NERVOUS ENERGY RAN down Kayla's spine as she walked toward Jackson's Chevy Suburban. Jackson stepped onto the sidewalk and a teenage girl with a sulky expression followed him.

Morgan was pretty, with wavy blond hair and green eyes. Kayla had expected her to resemble her mother, but there were only a few similarities. Marcy had fancied herself a dark-haired Marilyn Monroe, complete with pouty mouth and dramatic poses. Unlike Marilyn, however, nothing about Marcy had suggested a hidden vulnerability.

"Morgan," Jackson said, "this is Kayla Anderson. She's Alex's mother."

Morgan stared with open curiosity, something Kayla understood. Maybe she was comparing her half brother's mother to her own.

"Hi, Morgan," Kayla said with a friendly smile. "It's nice to meet you."

"Uh, hello."

"This is my daughter, DeeDee," she introduced as DeeDee came up beside her.

"Your shirt is so dope," DeeDee said, looking at Morgan's black T-shirt with a white tiger lunging across the front.

"Thanks."

Despite her taut nerves, Kayla noted Jackson's jeans and the muscles rippling under his blue shirt.

With his cowboy hat and boots and powerful physique, he was the epitome of a confident outdoorsman, which made him the opposite of Alex, who was suffering through a skinny, gangly period of self-conscious adolescence.

Jackson was obviously trying to act casual, though she noted his gaze shifting around, looking no doubt for "his" son. Lord, hopefully she wouldn't have to coax Alex out of the house. If he'd changed his mind and didn't want to go… well, she'd have to remind him that he'd agreed and needed to follow through.

Fortunately the front screen door opened before she had to do anything, and her son came down the steps. Jackson urged Morgan up the walkway. It was painfully awkward as they all came together.

Alex swallowed. "It's…uh…nice to see you again, Mr. McGregor."

The muscles tightened visibly beneath Jackson's shirt. "Same here, but you don't need to call me Mr. McGregor."

"Okay," Alex said, "I'll call you Jackson."

Aside from breathing faster, Jackson seemed to be keeping it together. Kayla suspected that Alex was testing him, though she didn't know if he was doing it consciously. But what else had Jackson expected? Alex already had somebody he called Dad.

"That's a good place to start," Jackson returned pleasantly.

"Hey, Alex," Morgan stepped forward to say.

Alex's face changed as he grinned. "Hiya, Morgan. What are you doing up in the middle of the night?"

Morgan's eyes rolled and the teenagers exchanged a laugh. "I slept in my clothes."

"Me, too."

Jackson watched them with a puzzled expression, and Kayla wondered if they were thinking the same thing. Morgan and Alex acted almost as if they already knew each other, though she was sure they hadn't met. Alex had avoided going around Schuyler by himself alone for fear of accidentally running into Jackson.

"Breakfast is ready," Elizabeth announced. She was a great believer in the power of eating together. Along with oatmeal and a pitcher of cream, she'd prepared huge platters of country potatoes, deluxe scrambled eggs and sliced ham.

Jackson had been obviously impatient when he learned Kayla's grandmother planned to serve a meal before they left, and his reaction had worried Kayla. Apparently when Parker McGregor had taken his sons and nephew camping or fishing, they'd left before it was light and eaten what they had packed. But if Jackson was trying to replicate the experiences that had bonded his own family, the trip to Yellowstone would be an abysmal failure.

"It looks delicious, but you didn't need to fix anything this elaborate," Jackson said.

Elizabeth waved her hand. "I thought we should

start with a meal. If you and Morgan don't like your eggs with mushrooms and such, I have plain scrambled in the pan."

"I love the extra stuff," Morgan asserted.

Jackson's eyebrows rose slightly and Kayla wondered what it might be about, especially when Morgan ate a good serving of the mushrooms and other chopped vegetables in the eggs.

All three kids were eating and chatting at one end of the table and while Jackson sent quick looks in their direction, he didn't intrude. Kayla almost felt bad for him. His one meeting with Alex had been horribly uncomfortable, and now they were in a room with five other people and no chance of private conversation. For a man accustomed to being in control of his universe, he must be churning with impatience.

At least the kids seemed at ease with each other, and they ate piles of food, making Elizabeth glow.

"That was terrific, Grams," Kayla told her as they quickly did the dishes in the kitchen.

"It's wonderful having children to feed again."

"So why hasn't Uncle Peter gotten married and given you more grandkids?"

"He was engaged years ago, but his fiancée died. He's never found anyone else."

"I'm sorry to hear that," Kayla said, glad she hadn't teased her uncle about his single status. She collected her purse and made a quick check to be sure she and the kids hadn't left something behind that they'd need, while Elizabeth did the same. Then they locked the door and came out to where Hank had pulled the RV around to the front of the house.

"Hey, Mom," DeeDee exclaimed, "Morgan wants to ride with us. Is that okay?"

"It's up to her father."

Disappointment flashed across Jackson's face, but he quickly rallied. "It's fine if she wears a seat belt."

"We have three places in the back of the RV with belts," Hank told him, sending a worried look at Kayla.

But Kayla had already read the handwriting on the wall—with only three seat belts in the back and her grandparents in the front, she'd have to ride in the SUV.

"Looks as if you're stuck with me," she told Jackson cheerfully, not wanting the kids to guess she'd rather be anywhere else.

Alex chewed his lip and seemed torn; he probably hadn't realized the outcome of their invitation to Morgan.

Kayla winked at him to smooth over the moment. "Give the grandparents a break, you guys, and keep the noise down." Then with a silent groan, she climbed into the Suburban's front passenger seat.

THOUGH JACKSON HAD known Alex expected to ride in his great-grandparents' RV, a part of him had hoped for more. Nevertheless, he smiled in Morgan and Alex's direction and asked the Garrisons to take the lead.

Grimly he followed the RV out of town and onto the small highway.

"Do you honestly think trying to get acquainted with a teenager at fifty-five miles an hour would be that effective?" Kayla asked after a while, her voice sardonic.

"Of course not. But the morning didn't start well—Morgan and I had a royal battle when I told her that our German shepherd couldn't come with us."

"Why? I've seen pets in the national parks."

"So have I, but I didn't look up the rules for Yellowstone until late last night. Dogs have to be leashed at all times. Even worse, Cory couldn't come on the trails and he'd be miserable being left in camp or in the Suburban. So right now Morgan is probably telling Alex that I'm cruel and inhumane for leaving her dog behind. It isn't as if I tied Cory in the backyard with nothing but a sack of food and bowl of scummy water," he said indignantly. "My foreman is taking care of him."

"Maybe you could have a park ranger explain the rules when we get there."

Jackson grimaced. "I doubt she'll pay any attention. I just hope by not objecting to the riding arrangements, it will help Alex be more comfortable with me."

"It would also help if you stop doing an impression of a pressure cooker getting ready to blow," Kayla advised.

"I don't do that."

"Really? I've been hoping my seat has an emergency ejection system installed."

He released a harsh breath, knowing she had a point. His frustration wasn't just about Alex. It went back to the prior summer when Morgan had suddenly become angry and defiant for no apparent reason. His mother said teenagers went through phases, but he couldn't help thinking it was more than a phase.

Under the circumstances, maybe it *was* best the kids had gone in the other vehicle.

Jackson tried to relax and concentrate on the road. Hank Garrison appeared to be a good driver, and it was less tedious than expected to follow the RV. If they kept up a good pace, they should reach Yellowstone by early afternoon.

An hour out, Kayla pulled a bottle of water from the tote bag at her feet.

"Want some?" she asked.

"Sure, thanks."

Silence returned. But now that he'd unwound a little, he started noticing other things…such as how long and smooth Kayla's legs were beneath her black shorts. Her lightly tanned skin sloped over sleek muscles and then tapered into extremely nice ankles, and her aqua T-shirt hugged curves that were exactly right.

Hell. He did *not* need to keep noticing Kayla's physical attractions, but the reminder didn't stop him from observing the soft, dark auburn hair brushing the curve of her cheek and falling over her collar bone. He liked long hair. When so many girls at high school had sported short pixie cuts, Kayla had stood out with her flowing auburn locks.

Jackson clamped a tight reign over his body. He wasn't a randy high school boy any longer; an experienced man of his age ought to have discipline over himself.

"I thought it was interesting how easily Alex and Morgan got along," he commented finally. "If I didn't know better, I'd think they were already friends."

"Sometimes teens have fewer inhibitions—it depends on their mood."

"True, but is there any way they might have spent time with each other?"

"Not in Schuyler. Alex hasn't wanted to go anywhere alone in case he ran into…"

Her voice trailed and Jackson sourly finished the sentence in his head…*in case he ran into you.*

"They could have connected through one of the social networks," Kayla said. "Does Morgan do Facebook?"

"Constantly. I have a page for the ranch and post

periodic updates, but she's on it all the time. I'm always warning her to be careful."

Kayla chuckled ruefully. "That sounds familiar. I do so many safety lectures, I should just tattoo them on my forehead to save time."

"I suppose DeeDee would be insulted if she thought you were directing them all at her."

"You're making assumptions again. Boys are at risk, same as girls."

"I know," Jackson said, realizing he probably had assumed boys were safer than girls. "I've just never needed to think about it. Now I'll have to start looking at the other side of the coin."

"There's no need to rush. I've got it covered."

"I'm not implying your care is lacking, but I need to take responsibility."

"No, you don't," Kayla said stubbornly.

"I'm his father. I've already talked to my accountant about setting up a fund for his education and sending regular support checks."

"Not needed." She enunciated the words precisely, with an underlying edge in her tone. "We're doing fine. And as for college funds, both Alex and DeeDee have one, though we've never planned to pay for everything. I happen to think kids take their education more seriously when they have to work for it."

Everything she'd said was reasonable...and annoying. The "we" was obviously a reference to her ex-husband, and it was reminder that Alex thought of Curtis Anderson as Dad, not Jackson McGregor.

"What's the matter?" Kayla asked. "I can tell you're uptight about something. *Again*."

"Don't be ridiculous."

"Good grief, Jackson. If you don't want me to know when you're unhappy, you'll have to start relaxing your jaw. I could crack walnuts on it right now."

Jackson frowned. Was he that easy to read, or was she more observant than most people?

"Fine, something is bothering me," he admitted. "But I don't want to discuss it."

Kayla already knew how he felt about missing most of Alex's childhood, and mentioning it again would just earn another tart remark about it being his own fault. For any hope of a relationship with Alex, he *had* to build a working partnership with Alex's mother. Like it or not, they'd be dealing with each other for the rest of their lives—graduations, a wedding, grandchildren, they'd share them all.

Grandchildren?

He suddenly felt old, and he was only thirty-four.

Hopefully Alex wouldn't follow in his footsteps when it came to early fatherhood, but they'd have to know each other better before discussing the facts of life. So far Jackson had mostly listened to his son interacting with other people. Still, he should be glad he'd been able to do that much. For a moment after arriving that morning, he'd wondered whether Alex would refuse to come out of the house.

"What would you have done if Alex had changed his mind about going today?" he asked curiously.

"We would have talked, but ultimately I would have said he needed to follow through on his word."

"I thought you were leaving all the power in his hands."

"Power?" she questioned. "That's an odd way of putting it. He's a boy, not a wild young steer to be thrown and branded."

"You know what I meant."

"I know you don't approve of letting him choose about meeting you, but he's fifteen, not eight. How would you have reacted as a teenager, being told you *had* to meet your birth father for the first time, regardless of how you felt about it?"

Jackson thought back to when he was Alex's age. From fifteen on, he'd pushed for more and more independence, been wildly interested in girls and ready to wrestle the world to its knees.

"I guess I would have met the guy without thinking much about it. Honestly, I wasn't that introspective," he admitted. "I know Alex isn't like me, but I want to be the best father possible."

"What kind of father do you imagine he needs?" There was an edge in her voice.

"Someone to rely on, back him up when things get tough."

"His mother also does that."

"I didn't say you don't. But I can do what a father usually does—if he needs to talk about girls, for example. I should have a discussion with him about sex. I can also do things like teach him to drive and ride a horse."

Kayla cocked her head. "Is riding a horse one of your definitions of manliness?"

"Dammit, Kayla, why do you have to pick everything apart?"

"It's my job as Alex's mother. Though, come to think about it, it's also my job working on insurance billings. We examine everything to help ensure an insurance company doesn't inappropriately reject the claim."

"Tell me about your business," Jackson urged, hoping to divert her from yet another debate about his male attitudes.

Her sideways glance told him she wasn't fooled. "We're called Smooth Billings. I have twenty-seven employees and contracts with dozens of medical and dental offices. More and more, small providers are outsourcing insurance billing and other services to companies like mine, rather than hiring someone to take care of it in-house."

Jackson blinked. Smooth Billings had even more employees than the Crazy Horse.

"Do you enjoy it?" he asked.

"I enjoy knowing we make a difference. Now I primarily do training and manage our contracts—most of the day-to-day insurance work is handled by the staff. My manager is top-notch, but I do regular spot checks to be sure we're on track. It's hard on patients if their billing hits a snag."

"Does that occur often?"

"It does if the doctor puts down the wrong word or writes an incorrect code. I insist our employees really think about what they're seeing, especially buzzwords that insurance companies may use as loopholes. And if there's a problem, I expect my staff to follow up aggressively."

The enthusiasm in Kayla's voice impressed Jackson. She seemed to believe in her work, and it was easy to see how it *could* make a difference. It was tough enough being ill, but fighting forms and balky insurance companies would make things worse. It was nice; she seemed to see her business as a form of service rather than simply paperwork.

Kayla stretched, and Jackson determinedly fixed his gaze on the RV ahead of them. He knew she wasn't being deliberately provocative, but his body was harder to convince. Hell, it was just the dry period he was going through—normally he had a reasonably adequate sex life, but the longer Morgan's rebellion had gone on, the harder it had become to go out for an evening.

The RV's turn signal went on and he followed into a roadside picnic area, hoping it meant Alex had decided to ride in the Suburban. Being alone with Kayla raised his blood pressure in more ways than one.

CHAPTER EIGHT

MORGAN DIDN'T LOOK at her dad when he came to the driver's window of the RV.

"We thought it would be a good idea to stretch our legs," Mr. Garrison told him.

"Yes, of course."

Morgan leaned over and whispered to Alex and DeeDee, "My father doesn't like stopping. He thinks we should leave by 4:00 a.m. and gnaw on beef jerky when we get hungry."

DeeDee giggled, but Alex shrugged. "My dad used to tell us everyone should walk around every couple of hours when they're traveling—something about blood and circulation and stuff. For a while he was going to be a doctor, but then he…um, did something else. He gets bored easy."

Morgan thought it was strange having Alex talk about his dad that way. DeeDee had already said some odd things, too. It was as if they loved him but didn't like him very much, all at the same time.

Alex's little sister had made Morgan uncomfortable, staring at her with rabid curiosity.

"You don't look like your dad," she finally said.

Yeah, as if I don't already know that.

Wishing she could stop thinking about it, Morgan unbuckled her seat belt and followed the others from the RV. DeeDee immediately took off running. Alex had said she was a runner, same as their mom, only she didn't want to get up early in the morning to do it.

When she looked at Alex's mother, Morgan decided there were worse things than being a runner. Cripes, even though she was a mom, the guys at school would think Kayla was really hot. So maybe running was a good idea.

"Come on," she said to Alex, "let's go, too."

He went, though he didn't seem thrilled about it.

After fifteen minutes Morgan was breathless, but it felt good in a way. Mrs. Anderson had been nice, keeping pace with her and the others.

"Do you want to ride in the Chevy for a while?" her dad asked once they'd stopped and were drinking water.

"Nah," she said, "I like the RV."

"Do you kids want to play a game?" Mr. Garrison asked when they got in again. "We have a nice selection in the compartment over the table."

DeeDee nodded eagerly. "How about Monopoly?"

Morgan thought Monopoly was lame, but Alex seemed willing to play, so they got the box out and unfolded the board.

"I always enjoyed Monotony," Mrs. Garrison told them.

"It's Monopoly," DeeDee reminded her. "Not Monotony."

Mrs. Garrison looked back, her eyes twinkling. "Really?"

Monopoly might be lame, but it was okay playing with DeeDee and Alex. They made crazy deals and called the properties names like Farpoint and DS9 and the Klingon Home World—that one had the cheapest rents because the neighbors were so loud. With the Garrisons throwing in jokes from the front seat, it was pretty fun.

THE DRIVE SEEMED painfully long to Kayla, though it was broken by various sightseeing stops her grandparents wanted to make. The biggest delay was their idea to drop down and go through the east entrance of the park in order to tour the cowboy museum in Cody, Wyoming.

It had to be making Jackson crazy with impatience. He was goal oriented: meet Alex. Get to Yellowstone. Set up camp. Do manly stuff. Become a father-and-son team.

But Kayla had news for him—it would be the little things that built a relationship with Alex, such as goofing off at a rest stop and spraying water at each other, or speculating whether ghosts ever haunted a museum instead of somebody's creepy old house.

Luckily, her grandmother had taken a stint in the Chevy Suburban, giving Kayla a break. And in the RV it had been heartening to see the kids getting along, comfortable enough with each other's company that all three fell asleep.

Back in the SUV it was silent part of the time, but the quiet would slowly become more uncomfortable than conversation and one of them would start talking. It worked best when they got onto books or movies and stayed away from personal subjects. To Kayla's surprise, they had more in common that she'd expected.

They pulled into their campsite in late afternoon and quickly hit a snag.

"I brought two large tents," Jackson explained. "One for guys, the other for the ladies."

Alex took a step backward. "I don't want to sleep in a tent," he announced. "Mom, can I just throw my sleeping bag on the ground and watch the stars the way we did at Crater Lake and Yosemite?"

"Me, too," DeeDee exclaimed.

"Same here," Morgan added. "It's almost time for the Pleiades meteor showers. Hey, Alex, are those the same thing as the Perseids?"

The two debated the subject as disappointment crossed Jackson's face. Kayla barely kept from grinning. If he'd asked, she could have told him that Alex wouldn't agree to a guys' tent. But he'd only said he was bringing enough for everyone, and it hadn't occurred to her that enough meant *two* with a gender division.

"Morgan got a D in science this year," Jackson

muttered. "How in *hell* did she come up with Pleiades and Perseids?"

"It's one of life's great mysteries. So I'll take one tent, and you'll take the other," she said. "They can use them for changing clothes and storing gear."

Jackson gave her a dark look.

"We'll put down tarps and pitch the tents on either side to shield you from any wind," he announced, interrupting Morgan and Alex's debate. It had shifted from meteor showers to whether or not they'd spot wolves in the park. "But if there's rain, you'll need to come inside."

As they set up the tents, Kayla insisted hers face the kids' sleeping area, saying, "That way they won't trip over lines or poles."

It was mostly an excuse…she planned to leave the front open at night to keep an eye on her son and daughter. Jackson's half smile suggested he knew what she had in mind, but she didn't care if he thought she was being too protective. And she noticed he faced his own tent the same way.

Jackson had agreed to leave the food arrangements to Elizabeth, and soon after everything was squared away, she announced supper was ready. On the campsite picnic table was an enormous pan of roast beef hash, with a large bowl of salad and corn bread on the side.

Grams handed a dish to Alex as they sat down. "Here you go."

"Allergies?" Jackson asked, looking at the

contents—potatoes with mushrooms and cheese instead of beef.

"I'm a vegetarian," Alex replied.

"Vegetarian?" Jackson choked and Kayla kicked him under the table as a warning.

Alex stuck up his chin. "Yeah. Got a problem with that?"

Kayla nearly choked herself—on a laugh. She suspected her son had enjoyed telling his cowboy birth father that he didn't eat meat. The possibility pleased her; a little defiance could help Alex deal with the situation.

"No, it's fine…great," Jackson said hastily.

Morgan gave the pan of roast beef hash a speculative look and Kayla got the feeling she was considering a sudden conversion to vegetarianism to bait her father. Finally she spooned a large serving of the traditional hash onto her plate.

"You don't know what you're missing," she told Alex.

DeeDee nodded. "He's a sap. No meat on his pizza. That's just *wrong*. I live for pepperoni."

"I like veggie pizza just fine," Alex argued.

"Me, too," Morgan said, "but it's better with pepperoni."

"Or bacon." DeeDee smacked her lips.

"What about Hawaiian?" Morgan asked. "Plain pineapple isn't the same."

Suddenly Kayla's gaze met Jackson's and she realized he'd gone from being disconcerted to amused at the girls' attempts to convert Alex. They both chuckled.

"What's so funny?" Alex asked suspiciously.

"Nothing much," Kayla said. "Let's enjoy our hash. It's beef for us, and mushroom cheesy for you."

"The vegetarian version also sounds delicious," Jackson said. "You're a fine cook, Mrs. Garrison."

"Please, call me Elizabeth."

"And I'm Hank," Kayla's grandfather urged. "Morgan, that goes for you, too. None of that Mr. and Mrs. nonsense. We're all family now."

Kayla blinked back tears. Growing up, her mother had claimed her parents would be humiliated by their daughter's teen pregnancy. "I couldn't go home," she'd often declared. "They would have slammed the door in my face." But once Kayla had met the Garrisons, she'd realized it was Carolyn's embarrassment about her drinking and succession of men that had kept her away, not concern over her parents.

After dinner Jackson stopped Elizabeth when she began gathering plates and silverware. "You've done enough. Who'll take a turn washing up with me?"

Before Kayla could nudge Alex, her daughter spoke up. "I will."

Jackson smiled at her. "Thanks, DeeDee."

The rest of them played a card game while the dishes were washed and dried. Kayla had to admit, grudgingly, to herself that at least Jackson's attitudes weren't so dated that he expected only women to be on dish detail. Of course, he might have been doing it just for show.

"How about a hike?" Jackson suggested as he hung up the dish towel. "I saw a trail leading off from the campground when we pulled in."

"Sounds good," Hank said and Elizabeth nodded.

They started off together, but the three kids quickly ranged ahead.

Grams tucked her arm into her husband's. "Go on and catch up with them. We're fine."

Kayla and Jackson quickened their pace and she called out, reminding Alex and DeeDee to remain in sight.

The light was glorious. The golden radiance of the sun on the horizon cast an alpine glow over the landscape, and Kayla caught her breath at the sight of a large stag standing tall and alert in a meadow.

"Magnificent, isn't he?" Jackson murmured. "Worth putting up with me to be here?"

"We'll see."

"It's got to be worth it being here with your grandparents. I saw how emotional you got at dinner when Elizabeth talked about us being a family."

"Oh," Kayla said, abruptly feeling self-conscious; she didn't enjoy having her feelings on public display. "What makes you think I was emotional?"

"Hey, turnabout is fair play. You see my jaw muscles tense when I get uptight. I notice your eyes.

Did it mean that much to have Elizabeth call us a family?"

"It just reminded me how silly it was to stay away from them all these years."

"Why did you?"

"A lot of reasons, most of them meaningless in retrospect. I thought they'd be embarrassed that both their daughter and granddaughter had a baby in their teens. My mom made it sound… Well, it doesn't matter. I should have realized they weren't like that." Kayla didn't add that Alex's resemblance to Jackson would have made returning to Schuyler a challenge, *or* that her pride had been involved, at least in the beginning. When he'd accused her of sleeping around, she'd sworn she would never return.

"You didn't trust them."

"Maybe to some extent," she admitted. "After everything that had happened, I wasn't sure they'd want me around. But it was mostly because I didn't want them to be hurt by what I'd done or think I expected someone else to take responsibility. Now I realize it hurt them more by staying away."

He was silent a moment. "You should give yourself a break."

"Why should I when *you* won't? You're still angry that I didn't force you to accept that Alex was your child. Admit it, you still feel it's my fault, somehow."

Jackson glanced at the kids a couple hundred

feet away. "Maybe we should try to stop throwing accusations at each other. I handled it badly when you got pregnant, but we have to figure out a way to make this work."

"I didn't mean to throw accusations, and certainly not about the pregnancy. It was both our responsibilities. And now I understand why you suddenly dumped me and went back to Marcy. At the time it looked as if you'd scored a few times, so you didn't have any more use for me."

Perhaps it was the rosy light of the lowering sun, but Jackson's neck seemed to redden slightly.

"I'm sorry it came off that way."

She sighed. "Fine. Let's just enjoy this beautiful place for an hour without dredging up garbage from the past."

"That's a good idea. Shall I tell you everything I know about Yellowstone?"

"Thanks, but I'll wait for a park ranger."

JACKSON WAS GRATEFUL for the temporary truce as they retraced the trail. The youngsters had gotten spooked by something rustling in the shadowed forest undergrowth and had hastily closed the distance between themselves and the adults. They quickly recovered their composure, however, and chattered back and forth about movies such as *Gremlins* and *The Blair Witch Project*.

"Isn't DeeDee too young for those films?" he asked Kayla in a low voice.

"Yup. She saw them at a friend's house during a slumber party. She isn't allowed back there."

The corners of Jackson's mouth twitched at Kayla's stern expression; it was nice to know she was a mama bear when it came to her children.

"Luckily, DeeDee doesn't scare easily," Kayla added.

"She *does* seem self-assured."

Back at the campsite Jackson lit a fire and everyone gathered around it. He wasn't sure how Morgan would react when Elizabeth brought out marshmallows, chocolate bars and graham crackers—the last time he'd suggested making s'mores, Morgan had put up her nose and called it "kiddie stuff." But his daughter took one look at Alex and DeeDee eagerly poking marshmallows on barbecue forks and didn't waste a second doing it herself.

"Careful," Morgan warned as Alex tried to shake a burning marshmallow from his barbecue fork. "Remember what happened in *Wild Hogs*."

Alex laughed. "Yeah, but there's no way we could all share a sleeping bag. DeeDee kicks."

"Ha," DeeDee said. "You're the one who ends up with his head where his feet should be."

The charred marshmallow dropped into the glowing coals and Alex stuck a fresh one on his fork.

Wild Hogs. Jackson remembered the film about four aging friends taking a motorcycle road trip, though he didn't recall a marshmallow incident. It seemed as if most of the movies he'd seen, he hadn't truly watched. What had happened to his ability to simply enjoy the moment?

Right now was a good example. He kept averting his gaze from Kayla and how the firelight glinted on her hair, turning the color to molten gold. She was a beautiful woman in a beautiful setting; he should simply appreciate the sight. After all, neither of them was interested in each other.

So no problem.

Feeling the tightening in his groin, Jackson put a marshmallow on a barbecue fork and extended it over the fire. Maybe he was better off being cautious.

JACKSON'S METHODICAL PLAN for seeing Yellowstone was annihilated the following morning. The first thing the kids wanted to see was the Old Faithful Geyser, followed by a visit to the nearby souvenir shop.

An idea occurred to him, though, and he watched until he could talk to his daughter alone in the store.

"Morgan, DeeDee's birthday is in a few days," he said quietly. "Shall we pick out a gift?"

"I already got her something from me." Morgan hurried away to join Alex, who was looking at books.

Jackson released an exasperated breath. When could Morgan *possibly* have gotten a gift?

Jackson looked at a jewelry display and tried to

recall if he'd seen DeeDee wearing any necklaces or bracelets. He'd actually already gotten a present for her in Schuyler, but he couldn't use it now since Morgan would realize he'd suggested shopping together as an afterthought.

THE NEXT FEW days were hectic.

Jackson didn't know the Garrisons well, but he was impressed with their vigor. Unless a particularly strenuous hike was planned, both Hank and Elizabeth kept pace with the rest of them. The fourth day was an exception—they made an excuse to stay in camp so they could prepare a party for DeeDee while the others explored the Upper Geyser Basin.

"It doesn't look real. It's almost as if they painted the bottom," DeeDee suggested when they reached Morning Glory Pool.

Jackson chuckled. The brilliant hue *didn't* look real. "Nature does amazing things. Look at abalone shells."

"Or petrified wood," Alex said. "I love the Gingko Petrified Forest, though the petroglyphs are my favorite thing there."

Now he was talking about petroglyphs?

Jackson shook his head, amazed by Alex and DeeDee's aggressive curiosity. They studied roadside plaques, read guidebooks and acted as if every historical display was a treat. But the best part was seeing Morgan's blasé attitude being swept away by their enthusiasm.

Still, the trip wasn't turning out the way he'd envisioned. He'd thought there would be solo hikes with Alex when they could grow closer, along with teaching him to fish and the other things his dad had done with him and his brothers. He'd hoped for alone time with Morgan as well, perhaps getting her to open up about what was wrong. Instead, the kids were practically inseparable.

"Do Alex and DeeDee usually do so much with each other?" he queried softly. "I thought teenage boys treated younger sisters as nuisances. Not that I ever did with Madison or Alaina, of course. I was a very tolerant big brother."

"Yeah, right."

"Okay, so I ditched them at every opportunity."

Kayla snapped a picture. "Sometimes Alex ditches DeeDee, too, but this is an unusual situation, and both of them know family solidarity is important to me."

"It's important to me, as well," Jackson commented.

"That's nice," she said, though he wasn't sure she believed him.

Ironically, he was getting to know Kayla better than Alex. It wasn't a waste of time—they *needed* to get along—but it was tricky. Aside from when she got steamed and started arguing, she was pleasant, yet reserved. He admired her intelligence and enjoyed some of their debates, but she clearly had no faith in him, despite acknowledging he'd changed since high school.

Obviously, they *both* had a problem with trust.

Jackson's increasing attraction to Kayla was another complication. He'd nearly embarrassed himself a few times when she came back from an early-morning run, flushed with a healthy glow, her damp T-shirt clinging to her body. The main thing saving him was Morgan going running with her.

Kayla must have hypnotized his daughter— Morgan was *not* a morning person. But it reminded Jackson that he'd speculated whether the two might connect. They seemed to be communicating well enough. After running they went to the camp showers together and returned chatting and laughing.

Hell, he'd only heard his daughter laugh a handful of times in the past year. And then it was with her friends, not with him.

"Drat, my SD card is full," Kayla said ruefully when she tried to take a photo. "I hope they'll have some at the next gift shop."

He dug one from his pocket. "Here."

She cautiously lifted it from his palm, almost as if she was trying not to touch him. "Thanks. I'll replace it as soon as possible."

"No need."

"Of course there is," she told him. "If you're like

me, you keep the SD card as backup, even after copying everything onto the computer."

"I meant that I have plenty."

"I'll still replace it."

Naturally. Kayla Anderson wouldn't take anything from him. She wasn't even interested in child support, however determined he was to provide it.

Kayla put the new card into her camera and tucked the full one into a pocket on her shoulder pack. "We'd better catch up with the kids."

She walked by him and Jackson automatically checked the swing of her hips. The degree to which a woman was attracted to a man could often be gauged by her hip action, but Kayla moved with a feminine grace that told him nothing.

And it didn't matter anyway.

A brief affair would be impractical under the circumstances, and anything else was out of the question. From what she'd said, Kayla probably felt the same.

He caught up with her on the trail. "I've been meaning to ask, how long have you been divorced?"

The question seemed to surprise Kayla. "Er... six and a half years."

It was longer than he'd expected. "Do you think kids ever adjust to their mother and father splitting up?"

"Who knows? Surely it's better than living with parents who are miserable because they stayed together."

"Was your marriage that bad?"

Kayla regarded him for a long moment and he half expected a reminder that her private life was *private*.

"I thought we were happy, but Curtis is a perpetual adolescent," she said finally. "He isn't a bad person, he just loves falling in love…again and again. As far as I know it started with me, but now he's on his third marriage since we broke up, and I don't remember how many romances there were between each of them. Every time it falls apart—and each one falls apart faster than the last—he tells me he can't understand why."

Her comments were revealing. For one, why was she friendly enough with her ex to talk about his love life? Jackson could understand needing to discuss things such as custody issues…

His gut clenched. It was hard to think about another man sharing custody of Alex.

Kayla had said he still wanted to blame her for the years he'd missed with his son, but it was time to genuinely accept that it *wasn't* her fault. And she'd accomplished so much. Those accomplishments were even more extraordinary with the added challenges of having been a single, teen mother. Hell, she'd even started her own company.

There was also her work ethic to respect. Every morning she connected with her manager. Once they'd sent a tricky billing question to her and she'd stayed in camp to resolve the issue while everyone else left for a hike.

Kayla Anderson was someone he might eventually be able to regard as a friend. In the meantime, he needed to ignore the pain in his groin whenever he looked at her.

KAYLA'S FINGERS TINGLED where they'd brushed Jackson's palm. It was so annoying. She didn't even *like* him, so why did he get her blood moving more than any of the men she'd dated over the past few months?

Surely it was just an echo from her teenage hormones. She'd grown up with teachers' pity, social workers' critique and the contempt of students from better circumstances, so when Jackson had asked her out, she'd felt like Cinderella. It had been a wonderful dream until it turned into reality—no guy, morning sickness and a mother who was perched on a bar stool every night. Half the time Carolyn hadn't even remembered her daughter was pregnant.

Kayla hurried forward to take more pictures of the kids and the landscape, determined not to give in to memories *or* hormones.

It had been a good day so far. Because it was DeeDee's birthday, she'd gotten to choose the breakfast menu and what they'd do. Grams had stayed in camp to bake the cake, wanting that part to be a surprise, and Granddad had remained behind, as well.

"Yo, check that out," Morgan cried, pointing up a tree.

Kayla looked and nearly dropped her camera. It was an eagle. Carefully she took several photos before focusing on the children, wanting to catch the wonder on their faces.

"What is it?" Jackson murmured, coming up beside her.

Silently she pointed at the large bird and Jackson shifted into photography mode, as well.

There was a piercing cry from the eagle and Kayla turned the camera back to where he was imperiously exhibiting his wingspan. He took off and they heard the whoosh of his powerful wings beating the air.

"That was amazing," she breathed.

Jackson's camera clicked again and she realized he was taking a picture of her. She decided to ignore it.

"Did you see it, Mommy?" DeeDee squealed, bounding in their direction. "It was an eagle. A real eagle. I never saw one before except in a zoo. It's a birthday present from Yellowstone."

"I saw it."

"Dad, can we go to the gift shop later?" Morgan asked. "I want to see if they have any books on birds."

"Sure," Jackson said. "I'm an easy sell if you want books and not more souvenir kitsch."

"Great. Kayla, DeeDee said she wanted to go the store, too, or I wouldn't have asked." Morgan ran back to where Alex was now studying a rock formation.

"You and Morgan seem to have hit it off," Jackson said after a minute.

"It's nice to have company when I'm running."

Coolly, Kayla started toward the three kids, proud she was keeping an unruffled surface. She and Morgan *were* getting to know each other. The girl appeared hungry for something, but Kayla hadn't figured out what. To her surprise, she enjoyed the teenager's company. While Morgan was angry and confused part of the time, she was also clearly struggling with what it meant to become a woman, and that was something Kayla understood all too well.

Poor kid. Hormones could be a bitch.

CHAPTER NINE

JACKSON LENGTHENED HIS stride to reach Alex as he was walking ahead on the trail. DeeDee and Morgan had lagged behind with Kayla to study a clump of wildflowers. DeeDee had made up another word to describe them—pholothimbody, or something of the sort. Alex seemed oblivious to their absence, though he'd slowed and was looking down at his hands.

"Hold up," Jackson told him. "No going out alone, remember?" He and Kayla had made it a safety rule. Ironically, he wouldn't have complied himself as a teenager, but he would never admit that to his son or daughter.

Alex glanced back at his mother and sisters. They weren't more than a hundred feet away.

"I'm not going out alone," he muttered. "I was texting a friend."

"Okay, just… That's all right. Yellowstone is an amazing place, isn't it?" Jackson thought it was a stupidly obvious thing to say, but he didn't know what to talk about with Alex.

"Yeah."

"Say, your face is getting a little red. I've got an extra hat, or we can get one for you at the store."

"No, thanks." Alex looked back down the trail again. "I'm going to see what everyone is doing."

Damn.

Jackson also reversed direction and strode back to the rest of the group behind his son. Okay, so there were a few hitches along the road—that was no reason to sit on his ass about it.

KAYLA DIDN'T MIND waiting while the three kids pored over the books at the souvenir shop, and she said yes to the ones DeeDee and Alex wanted. As far as she was concerned, books were wholesome luxuries. But when she pulled out her credit card, the woman at the cash register smiled and explained "the gentleman" had already arranged for payment.

Swinging around, Kayla glared at Jackson. "I can pay for any books my kids want."

"So can I," he answered blandly.

Suddenly she saw Alex was nearby, so she swallowed her irritation. "That's very nice of you," she said evenly. But when her son was out of earshot, she muttered, "You may think paying for things is the *manly* thing to do, but one-upmanship doesn't help your case."

Jackson had the grace to look apologetic.

DeeDee came running over, pulling Morgan

along with her. "Can we get ice cream for Grandpa?" she asked. "He loves ice cream."

"So do you," Kayla countered.

Her daughter grinned. "Uh-huh. Grandpa says I take after him."

A shadow crossed Morgan's face so quickly Kayla wondered if it had been her imagination.

"I'm sure everyone would enjoy it," Kayla said.

They went to the little grocery store, chose three flavors and took the cartons out to the SUV.

"Would you like to drive?" Jackson asked, holding out the key to the Suburban.

It was an odd way of apologizing for trying to take control in the store. Or at least Kayla thought it was an apology, so she nodded and took the key ring.

ALEX OPENED HIS eyes wide as his mom got into the driver's seat. He hadn't expected to see her driving the SUV. Morgan seemed surprised, too, so it probably wasn't the way Jackson usually did things.

Five minutes later they were back at camp.

DeeDee jumped out of the car. "Grandpa, we got ice cream." Almost immediately she saw the picnic table and shrieked, "A cake!"

It was a chocolate cake decorated with "Happy Birthday DeeDee."

"If we're going to have ice cream with that cake," Grandma said, "we either eat it now or try fitting it into the RV freezer. But I don't think there's room."

"Can we save the cake for after dinner and have ice cream now?" DeeDee asked. "That way we spread dessert out."

"Good idea, kiddo."

They sat at the picnic table while Grandma served the ice cream. Grandpa ate his blissfully.

"It's good to see a man enjoying his vices," Jackson told him as they were finishing.

"Yep, I'm an ice cream lush."

"People always said that when you were mayor, most of the town's business got done at the Schuyler Soda Saloon."

"Naturally. After all, how can you argue with a man when he's eating his ice cream?"

Jackson laughed and Alex looked down at his bowl. The guy wasn't *that* awful, even if he bugged Mom sometimes, like when she got mad at him for paying their bill at the store. Mom was prickly about taking care of things on her own and she didn't like it when guys acted as if they needed to take care of her.

Even so, the camping trip had been fun so far, and it was great hanging out with Morgan. The problem with Jackson was that he sometimes tried to act like his father. Alex wished he'd stop. He remembered terrific times with his dad; then his folks had split up, and after that, Dad was kind of on and off—mostly off. Mom tried to pretend nothing had changed that much, but DeeDee and he knew better.

So Jackson couldn't take Dad's place. In fact, Alex wasn't sure whether he wanted a dad at all any longer.

KAYLA HELPED GRAMS light the candles on DeeDee's birthday cake and they sang while she blew them out.

"You get your wish," Morgan told her.

DeeDee gulped in a breath. "Nah, they'd never let a kid go into space. Maybe I'll be a general or something."

After they ate cake, Elizabeth took the leftovers into the RV and carried out a stack of wrapped gifts. DeeDee's eyes lit up and she claimed to love everything, from the Kindle her grandparents gave her to Morgan's gift cards for music downloads. She seemed surprised at receiving a present from Jackson and smiled shyly at him.

"Thanks, Jackson!" she said, holding up the hot pink Yellowstone sweatshirt and three equally bright T-shirts.

"You're welcome."

Once everything was put away and the dishes washed, they walked to the group area for a campfire program about Yellowstone put on by a park ranger. Jackson tried to engage Alex in conversation, but it didn't go well. Alex finally edged away to talk with Morgan. DeeDee was the one who started chattering to Jackson about the horse-breeding program he'd mentioned that afternoon.

"You like horses?" Jackson asked.

"They're fantabulous. I've read the Black Stallion books at least ten times," DeeDee told him.

Kayla hid a smile. She didn't know if all girls went through a horse-crazy phase, but she'd been the same at her daughter's age. She'd introduced both her children to the classic horse stories written by Walter Farley.

"Morgan used to read those books—that's why she named her stallion the Black," Jackson said. "Do you ride, DeeDee?"

"Not yet. But my friend Keri goes to a riding stable every week, and after school starts, I get to go with her."

"I could teach you when we get back to Montana. If it's okay with your mother," he added hastily.

"Yes, *puleeze*. Can I, Mom?" DeeDee begged.

"If there's time," Kayla told her. She'd originally planned to return to Seattle right after the camping trip, but the kids were asking if their two best friends could come to Schuyler for a visit. The Garrisons were ecstatic at the idea; Kayla was less sure and had said she'd decide later.

Jackson turned to Alex. "What about you? I've got several horses that are great for new riders."

Alex shrugged. "I'll think about it."

"Good…uh…just let me know."

Kayla focused on the ground as the park docent started talking. She didn't know how to fix the tense push-pull between father and son, and a less-than-noble part of her still didn't *want* it fixed. The closer Alex got to Jackson, the more *she'd* have to put up with him.

As a memory, Jackson hadn't been important to her, and she didn't want that to change. So why should she try to help? After all, did he deserve to have an easy time of it?

Deserve?

Kayla wrinkled her nose. That sounded vindictive, but she didn't hate Jackson. He was just one of the people who'd let her down over the years. Still, it almost seemed as if he should have to earn a place in Alex's life, because if he wasn't willing to work through this difficult, painful stage, he might eventually fail Alex when it mattered even more.

The internal debate raged the rest of the evening and kept her awake most of the night. As the sky began lightening, she wearily sat up. Alex and DeeDee would be asleep for another couple of hours, and even her grandparents wouldn't emerge from the RV for a while.

She looked through the open tent flap to where Morgan lay buried in her sleeping bag. Everyone had stayed up late looking at the stars through DeeDee's new telescope, so she'd likely want to sleep in.

Quickly Kayla got dressed. There was a rough path circling the camping area—it would serve for a mild workout and still leave her energy if Morgan wanted to go running later.

After passing quietly between other campsites, Kayla reached the path and set off, trying to be quiet since it passed close to sleeping campers. She'd circled the area twice when she came upon Jackson, looking grumpy and perturbed.

She slowed and stopped. "What are you doing out so early?"

"I was concerned," he snarled. "No one should take off alone here, but especially not a woman. What if you'd encountered a bear? We made rules for the kids and should all follow them."

She raised her eyebrows. "I didn't take off, as you put it. I stuck to the campground."

"I was afraid you'd gone on one of the other trails."

"Hell, Jackson, you don't even trust a woman to take care of herself."

"It's not that… *Dammit*," he cursed. "Don't I get credit for being worried about my son's mother? The last thing Alex needs is to lose you."

"That's why I'm careful. I have *two* children who need me—I don't do reckless things. And for your information, a man isn't any safer around a bear than a woman."

She was still breathing quickly and temper added to the whoosh of her lungs. They glared at each other until Jackson suddenly reached out and pulled her close, his mouth landing on hers a second later.

The endorphin high from the run was nothing compared to the adrenaline zipping through her veins. His lips moved slow at first, then pressed harder. It was much better than she remembered it from high school, but after a couple of minutes she gathered her senses and resolutely pulled away.

"Thanks, but no thanks," she said. "I'm not interested in wandering down memory lane."

"You responded."

She surveyed the way his loose sweatpants were tented around his arousal. "So did you, but I'm the one who ended it. Now excuse me, I want to finish my run."

Kayla took off, aware that he was watching her. She didn't have to question what it meant—he was frustrated at an elemental, masculine level. But Jackson had nothing to do with what she wanted. She needed to concentrate on today, and on the future.

So would that future contain sex?

Kayla almost stumbled, annoyed that her thoughts had circled back to Jackson McGregor. But it was mostly what he represented. The brief kiss had left her shaking with need, reminding her of how long it had been since she'd shared that sort of intimacy.

She didn't intend to live as a reclusive divorcée, so it had seemed reasonable to accept a few dates when friends began pushing her. The rational half of her brain said that falling in love was a good thing. The scared half told her, *Don't risk it, don't take a chance.* It wasn't just what had happened with Curtis—her mother had never recovered when she'd lost the love of her life.

After another two laps around the campground, Kayla slowly walked back toward their campsite. Only a few people were stirring, but one grizzled fellow nodded at her. "Hello, there."

"Hi."

His eyes were content and pleased with life. A golden retriever puppy dashed over, gamboling at her feet. Kayla leaned over to rub its neck. The pup quivered with pure pleasure.

"Get on back, boy," said the old guy mildly. "Don't bother the lady. 'Sides, you're supposed to be on a leash."

"That's all right, he's fine."

Kayla gave the eager puppy a last pat and continued walking, her head still arguing with itself. Whether or not she took a risk on falling in love again, she could be happy either way. A woman didn't *have* to have a man in order to be complete... Any other idea was sexist propaganda.

And there were great things to enjoy, such as puppies and geysers and children. She didn't need Jackson McGregor, though she suspected he'd learned a *lot* about satisfying a woman since they were in high school.

Briefly she wondered if Marcy had felt secure in their marriage, but decided it probably wouldn't have been one of her concerns. There were stories that suggested Marcy had stretched her wedding vows out of shape in more ways than one, which was likely another reason why Jackson didn't think highly of the opposite sex.

Kayla stretched. Things would be far less complicated if she'd waited for Morgan to take a run. Jackson wouldn't have followed her and they wouldn't have kissed.

But a kiss wasn't that big of a deal unless she turned it into one.

JACKSON RETURNED TO camp and started a pot of coffee on his Coleman stove. With seven people to feed, including two voracious teens, the stove was getting a workout, along with the one in the RV.

As the coffee perked, he sat and stared at a beetle making its way through the dirt. Running was redundant exercise for a rancher, but he envied Kayla's discipline to the sport. At the moment he desperately needed an outlet to relax, except his way required a horse, solitude and miles of rolling land. Even swimming laps didn't replace being out on the range with Thunder.

At least *one* McGregor was getting to know Alex; Morgan and her brother seemed to be on great relations.

"Need to talk?" Kayla's voice interrupted his thoughts. "You look as if you've got a lot on your mind."

Her face was a neutral mask, and Jackson figured she'd decided to act as if nothing had happened. He'd be wise to do the same…and forget how enticing she'd felt against him.

"Just wishing I could connect with Alex," he said softly, not wanting to be overheard.

She hesitated. "Remember, it hasn't been that long since he learned about you. It would be a big adjustment for anyone, much less a teenager."

"But I'm his father."

"That doesn't guarantee you'll have anything in common with your children, *or* that you'll be able to relate to them."

As if he didn't know that already—Morgan was the perfect example. Yet they'd been close once; after the divorce, he'd even wondered if Marcy had felt left out part of the time.

"Has Alex ever gone through a phase where he was angry and wouldn't communicate?"

Kayla made a face. "His phases are subtle, and whenever Curtis throws himself full tilt into a new romance, both the kids go through grouchy periods. I try to tell Curtis that he needs to be more balanced, but it doesn't seem to help."

"Do you and your ex talk often?"

"Often enough. He shows up whenever things go south in his life. I usually go to dinner with him, listen to his woes and send him off. He has a short attention span and it doesn't take long before he forgets his latest failure and moves on to something new."

"You have an unusual relationship for a divorced couple, almost as if you still love him."

She stiffened. "I stopped loving Curtis that way a long time ago. It isn't that I hate him, but he's like a puppy, always looking for a new best friend."

Jackson wanted to look into Kayla's eyes to gauge her emotions, but she jumped up and poured two cups of coffee.

"Wow, an old stove-top percolator," she observed, handing one to him. "Who'd have thought they still made them?"

"I'm not sure they do. This one used to belong to my mom and dad."

Her brow creased as she sat down. "That reminds me, your parents are another issue we haven't discussed very much."

"There isn't much to discuss. Mostly they're trying to be patient until I've gotten to know Alex better."

Kayla tapped a finger on her cup. "What have they said about all this?"

"That they should have taught me more about birth control in high school, but they're thrilled to have a second grandchild."

"Just Morgan and Alex? I thought you had other siblings."

"There are five of us altogether, including the two cousins that my parents raised."

"Whoa. Five grown children and only two grandkids?"

Jackson cleared his throat. "The others blame me, saying they got scared off after seeing me become a parent so young. None of them have even gotten married."

A wry smile played around Kayla's mouth. "There may be more to that excuse, no matter what they say."

"Maybe they just haven't met the right people yet," he suggested.

"I can't believe you're throwing out the true-love card."

Jackson ignored the red herring. "Do you think Alex will agree to meet my folks?"

"You want me to be honest?"

"Yes," he told her, his muscles clenching.

"I think you're the only person he has trouble with." She stopped and seemed to be going through a mental argument. "Just…just stop *trying* so hard. Relax and let things happen naturally."

Jackson sighed. Like it or lump it, she was right. He'd been pushing Alex, even when he didn't think that was what he'd been doing.

Kayla sipped her coffee and gagged. "Yikes. I didn't know anyone could make coffee so strong. Is this how cowboys make it?"

"It's camp coffee."

"Well, it's too much for me." She pushed her cup aside and stood. "I need a shower. See you later."

Watching her walk to her tent was a queer sort of torture, but Jackson kept his gaze fixed on her anyway. He breathed easier when she'd collected fresh clothes and left for the facilities, though he was grateful he was still wearing sweatpants rather than his more close-fitting Levi's.

Maybe he should take a shower, too...a cold one.

MORGAN BURROWED DEEPER into her sleeping bag. Just for today, she wouldn't get up and run. After they'd looked at the stars with DeeDee, she and Alex had texted each other for hours. Now her phone was dead, but that was okay. Elizabeth would let her charge it in the RV.

Sheesh, she didn't know why her dad didn't want to camp with an RV or trailer or something. It made everything easier.

She hadn't been sure she'd get along with a geek like Alex. He didn't ride horses, had never set foot on a ranch and couldn't rope a cow if his life depended on it. But it was neat that he wasn't embarrassed about not being able to do that stuff, even when she called him a nerd. In a way, he fit his life better than she fit hers.

"Are you awake, Morgan?" DeeDee whispered.

"No," she mumbled.

"Maybe you could text me sometimes, and not just Alex."

"Sure, now let me sleep."

"Okay, but just so you know, Grandma is up and she's making chocolate-chip pancakes for breakfast."

Mmm. Morgan practically drooled. The last time she and Dad had gone camping, he'd made oatmeal every morning that tasted worse than glue.

"DeeDee?" she said.

"Yeah."

"Wake me up when the pancakes are ready, okay?"

"Uh-huh."

Morgan bunched her pillow up and shoved it harder under her cheek. DeeDee was a pest at times, but it was almost as if she was becoming Morgan's little sister, too. That was cool.

And after all, it wasn't Alex's fault that her father had finally gotten the son he wanted. He probably would have been happier if she'd been a boy; he'd even given her a boy's name. Not that she disliked being called Morgan, but it reminded her that she was a disappointment in almost every way.

CHAPTER TEN

KAYLA FELT AN odd regret as they broke camp—in a way, she was sorry they were leaving.

The ten days they'd spent in the national park had been a mixed bag of fun and stress, particularly after Jackson's kiss. Drat him anyway. He'd reminded her body of needs that went *beyond* food and sleep. Since then she had remained determinedly casual toward him, hoping no one would realize something had happened.

Yet other aspects of the trip had been wonderful.

Yellowstone was spectacular, and sharing it with her kids and grandparents had made it even more special. Meals and activities had held a warmth that had been hard to find in the frantic pace of life in the city.

Once they'd packed everything and tidied the campsite, Kayla automatically climbed into the Suburban, knowing Alex, DeeDee and Morgan wanted to ride in the RV again. At least the trip home wouldn't take as long since they wouldn't be sightseeing along the way. Well, probably. A ghost of a smile lifted her mouth… Her grandparents knew every historical marker, local museum and viewpoint in Montana and Wyoming, and wanted to share all of them with their great-grandchildren.

Jackson got into the Chevy and gripped the steering wheel so tight the skin went white over his knuckles. "It isn't enough to have a daughter who avoids my company," he muttered. "Now I have a son who feels the same way."

Your ex-girlfriend isn't crazy about riding with you, either, Kayla restrained herself from saying.

With a scowl on his face, Jackson started the SUV and followed the Garrisons out of the campground.

"Hey, they're kids," Kayla said finally. "They've got a table and games in the RV, along with a built-in Blu-ray player and television. Nobody could compete with that."

"I suppose, but we went on this trip and nothing got better with either one of them," he grumbled.

Kayla frowned. "Are you giving up?"

"*Hell, no.* I'd never give up on my kids."

"Okay, then. Don't talk as if Yellowstone was a failure. Alex has had ten days to get more familiar with you. As for Morgan, the way she looks at you sometimes, when you're not watching... It's as if she wants something, and is sad or scared, though I don't know what—"

"I've never hit her," he broke in, sounding horrified. "I wouldn't dream of hurting my daughter."

"Not that," Kayla quickly assured. "It's more as if she's uncertain. I've wondered if... I mean, she's gone from being an only child to suddenly having a sibling her own age. That's quite an adjustment."

"If her behavior started with finding out about Alex, then that might be the reason. But this has been going on for over a year. Has she said anything that might explain why she's acting out?"

Kayla could tell how much Jackson hated asking. It was clear he desperately loved his daughter, and equally clear he didn't have a clue what was going on with her.

It had been a surprise when Morgan had asked if they could go running together, but Kayla hadn't minded. The teen turned out to be eager and cheerful so long as they were alone together. When she was near her father, however, she seemed both angry and sad. In fact, Kayla had gotten the impression that Morgan felt as if she was a nuisance.

"It's obvious you love Morgan," Kayla said cautiously, "but I get the strangest sense that she feels unwanted. Has she ever—"

"Are you insane?" Jackson burst out indignantly. "My daughter knows how much I love her. You just said it was obvious."

"It's obvious to me, not necessarily to her, and I don't think this has anything to do with her mother. Anyway, there's a difference between knowing someone loves you and thinking you aren't wanted, or are at least inconvenient."

"That's ridiculous."

Kayla mentally counted to ten to keep from losing her temper. "You asked my opinion and I gave it to you."

"Well, I don't agree, so let's drop it."

"Fine."

But Kayla had a sinking feeling she wasn't wrong. She'd spent a fair amount of time with Morgan over the past week and a half. It was impractical to talk much while running, but they'd chatted when they'd gone to the showers, done dishes together or happened to be hiking next to each other.

Once in a while the teenager would say something that sounded eerily familiar, echoing shades of Kayla's own childhood. Carolyn had often called her daughter a burden. Sometimes it had been the booze talking—in that respect, Morgan's situation wasn't the same—but the feelings seemed similar.

Just because Kayla was certain Jackson loved his daughter didn't mean *Morgan* felt it.

Kayla turned her head and watched the passing scenery. She'd abandoned her original idea of leaving for Seattle after the camping trip. DeeDee and Alex still hoped their two best friends could come to Schuyler for a few days, and she was going to call Sandy's and Keri's parents to discuss it. While Kayla had doubts about being around Jackson for extended periods, perhaps the time would be useful for thinking about making some changes in their lives.

After the divorce, she'd kept the home she had chosen with Curtis, thinking it would be easier for the children to adjust. But if there was one thing seeing Jackson again had accomplished, it was making her recognize they might be stuck in a rut. Buying a new house could help them push forward with their lives.

"What are you thinking about so seriously?" Jackson asked.

"Hmm?"

"You appear to be weighing the fate of the world."

She glanced at him; he seemed to have forgotten his ire. "Hardly. I was thinking about real estate. We're still in the same house where we lived with Curtis. I'm considering looking for a new one that won't have so many complicated memories."

"How would Alex and DeeDee feel about that?"

Kayla made a face. "Opposed, I'm sure. DeeDee has always lived there and Alex barely remembers any other home. But it could teach them that change isn't always bad."

"Is it hard to keep up a house without a husband?"

"Not in my case. Curtis didn't do yard work or repairs, and I was usually the one who called in a professional service."

"Oh."

"Did you think it was a case of the poor little divorcée trying to roof the house in the rain by herself?"

Jackson snorted. "I wish you wouldn't say such ridiculous things. I've known several women who had trouble managing after they were left alone. And with kids, it's even harder. I'm not saying it wouldn't be tough on a guy, as well."

Kayla decided to give him a break. "Okay, some single moms have trouble getting by, but that isn't synonymous with the condition. I just get tired of the assumptions."

"ME, TOO." JACKSON SHUDDERED. "People seem to think a divorced guy lets the housework go down the tubes and his kids eat nothing but sugary cereal and pizza." More than one woman had decided he needed help being a father...along with helping to spend his trust fund. "I headed off the marriage headhunters by hiring a housekeeper."

"Marriage headhunters?"

"That's how they came off to me. It took a while for them to accept that I'm not sticking my head in the noose again."

"That's sad."

"Sad because I'm not willing to get married again?" He snorted. "As I recall, you feel the same way."

Kayla took a swig from her water bottle. "I have my reasons, but that doesn't mean I've generally lost faith in marriage or relationships."

Hmm. Though she'd mentioned being reluctant to fall in love, she really hadn't explained why. "What reasons?" he asked.

"I don't seem to be good at picking the right guy,

and I'm not…" She let out a heavy breath. "Never mind. Anyway, you hired a housekeeper, and my company is quite profitable, so I can pay for any work needed on my house."

Jackson's gut churned. Clearly Kayla *didn't* have money problems—her car was pricey, she wore quality clothing, and while the kids weren't spoiled, they obviously enjoyed the advantages of a comfortable lifestyle. Hell, maybe he wanted to believe she was struggling because it would give him something to contribute to Alex's life. He didn't seem to be needed for anything, financial or otherwise.

"Even though you're doing well, I still want to do some things for Alex."

"And as I've told you more than once, *we don't need money.*"

He chose his words carefully. "This isn't a question of need. An honorable man takes care of his children."

"It's…" She bit her lip.

"What?"

"Okay, I concede your desire to act honorably. Some men don't have the same compulsion."

"Thank you."

Although he was focused on the road, Jackson was well aware of Kayla's movements and facial expressions. Now she squared her shoulders. "The thing is, I don't want Alex to be spoiled. The sense of entitlement so many people have is appalling. I want my kids be grateful for the good things and work for goals that matter."

"I want the same for Morgan."

"Then, don't expect money to be spent on things Alex doesn't need, or that I'll increase his allowance or hand him his own car keys when he turns sixteen. If you *have* to send money, it can go into his education account, though I still want him to have a job during college. I don't want to sound like a broken record about it, but we value what we earn."

Jackson opened his mouth, only to close it. Surely Kayla hadn't meant to prod him in a sore spot. He owned a fine ranch because Great-Uncle Mitch had given him the land, which he'd since expanded using income from his trust fund. But for the first five years he'd worked as a regular ranch hand, living on a ranch hand's salary. While Jackson hadn't minded, Marcy had hated it, along with the tiny house that had come with the job.

And for some reason, he wished Kayla knew so she wouldn't see him as someone who'd gotten everything just handed to him.

"So?" Kayla prompted in a challenging tone.

"I agree," he said. "But I want to do more than send money. I also want to…uh…" He stopped, knowing he'd almost said something that would get him into hot water. *Again.* Before Kayla's return, he hadn't realized how many of his ideas might be chauvinistic. Of course, his sisters joked about it, but he was sure there hadn't been any serious heat to the accusations…fairly sure.

"Let me guess, you want to teach him how to drive a truck and get girls. Right?" she asked with sugary sweetness.

"I didn't say that."

"Good, because even though I could teach Alex to drive myself, he's registered for driving school this fall. And while you undoubtedly know how to 'get girls,' it isn't a skill I'm anxious for him to learn."

"Yes, but a boy needs a father, and it doesn't sound as if your ex-husband is doing much on that end," Jackson said, only to wish he'd kept his mouth shut when Kayla flinched. She turned to the window again, her lips turned down unhappily.

The time passed slowly after that, the silence broken occasionally by innocuous conversations or more tense debates. In some ways, it didn't seem as if things had gotten any better with Kayla than with Morgan or Alex.

Curiously, of the three youngsters, it was DeeDee who'd been the friendliest to him, but her attitude hadn't seemed to influence her brother or Morgan in the slightest.

THAT EVENING, KAYLA called Sandy's and Keri's parents and discussed the possibility of the kids visiting Schuyler. The Kellers and the Garzas loved the idea as long as the girls could fly together.

"I'm awfully glad you're staying longer," Elizabeth said as they sat on the patio. DeeDee and Alex had fallen asleep watching baseball in the family room.

Kayla smiled. She wasn't sure that staying was the best idea, but her vaguely uneasy feelings weren't reason enough to leave.

As a child she'd longed for a life that wasn't constantly changing, with new places to live and new people to figure out. But she couldn't deny that getting away from Seattle was proving beneficial. Both DeeDee and Alex seemed to have benefited— particularly since it was buffering them from their father's preoccupation with his new family.

Her cell phone rang fifteen minutes later. It was Jackson.

"Hello."

"I talked to my parents and they'd love to see Alex tomorrow," he told her.

On the drive back from Yellowstone they'd discussed having a get-together with Jackson's mother and father.

"Alex is asleep in front of the TV at the moment, but I'll talk to him when I get a chance."

There was a long pause. "Mom and Dad will go along with any plan that seems best, so whatever he wants is fine with us."

"All right, I'll call in the morning." After pressing the off button, Kayla glanced at her grandmother. "The McGregors want to meet Alex, tomorrow if possible."

"I'd feel the same in their place. What if we all go to Riverside Park for a picnic?" Elizabeth sighed. "Oh, well, not that we have to be there."

"Alex will want you," Kayla assured her.

Later in bed, Kayla considered what the next day might be like. Back in high school she'd been certain the McGregors didn't approve of her, and a small part of her hadn't blamed them for thinking she wasn't respectable enough for Jackson. After all, how could she fit in with people who'd never lived in apartments with cardboard plugging broken windows and Social Services knocking on the door?

It was different now.

She was proud of the life she'd made, and of the children she was raising. She wouldn't even undo her marriage, because her bright, funny, word-inventing daughter had come from it. As for her ex-husband? Kayla just wished she could have been enough for him. She no longer loved Curtis, but she still cared enough to be sorry he wasn't truly happy. Worse, he was a poor role model for the children.

Thoughts of Jackson intruded. He'd grown up with loving, long-married parents and grandparents, yet he still distrusted women and marriage.

Terrific.

Alex's fatherly role models didn't seem to be improving.

AT NOON, JACKSON pulled into the lot at Riverside Park. It was a beautiful summer day, but he was already out of sorts because Morgan had gone out riding and he hadn't been able to reach her all morning.

"Looks as if everyone is here," he said.

"It's not my fault we're the last ones," Morgan muttered. "I didn't know about your big plan until I got back."

"Because you forgot to bring the satellite phone," he reminded her.

"*So* sorry," she muttered.

Morgan slid from the truck and joined the group in the covered picnic area. Jackson sat watching to see how Alex was responding to his McGregor grandparents. From a distance he seemed to be relaxed and comfortable. With one outburst of laughter, Jackson's father even playfully arm wrestled with him, and Alex laughed some more.

Jackson was glad Alex was getting along with his parents, but being a pariah to his own children was a bitter pill.

Kayla glanced toward the truck and walked in his direction. Today she was wearing black cargo pants and a loose, flowered blouse that should have hidden her figure but somehow made him more aware of the enticements underneath.

Leaning her arm on the open window on the passenger side, she raised an eyebrow. "Are you just dropping Morgan off, or are you planning on joining us?"

"Joining you. It's going well, from what I can see."

"Yeah." Her face turned pensive. "The absence of extended family for the kids has always been one of my concerns. Now suddenly there's plenty of it, especially for Alex. Maybe it'll balance other things out."

"There's still more family for him to meet," Jackson reminded, deciding not to question her cryptic remark—it likely had something to do with her ex-husband. "Aunts and uncles, cousins... The McGregors are quite a clan. And there's also the Nelson side. They're anxious to get in on the act, as well."

"It's nice you've learned to appreciate them."

Her comment was a reminder that he'd once bemoaned having too many relatives to witness his rebellious behavior and report it to his folks.

"I've grown up since then," he said mildly. "But that's an odd thing to recall about me."

"Not really. I grew up without family—I was barely even aware I had grandparents until I was fifteen. To me, you were complaining about something I would have given anything to have. How could I forget?"

Regret went through Jackson. The things he remembered about Kayla were mostly trivial—the rumors concerning her mother, her streetwise talk, her clothing that seemed racier than the other girls'. As a teenager Kayla had projected a wayward audacity that had appealed to him, but he hadn't bothered looking much under the surface.

"You never scolded me for saying those things," he finally said.

A rueful expression crossed her face. "I was a girl with her first crush. I wasn't going to risk turning you off."

"I was a teenage boy. You couldn't have turned me off with a two-by-four."

She chuckled the way he'd intended. Setting the emergency brake, he got out of the truck, trying to ignore the way his body had responded to the allure of her face, alive with humor. Maybe he should make a date with one of his occasional feminine companions to take his mind off Kayla.

"How is everything at the ranch after your absence?" she asked as they walked toward the picnic tables.

"My foreman managed everything. He could operate without me being around most of the time, but I'm a hands-on rancher. Probably drives him crazy."

Kayla wrinkled her nose. "Yeah, I almost miss

the days when I was needed more intensively at Smooth Billings. But it leaves me freer to do things such as…uh…take unexpected vacations."

He stopped a short distance from the others and looked at her. "How much longer are you staying?"

"At least another two weeks."

"Then, the kids' friends from Seattle are coming?"

"Yes, I've talked to their parents and they're making travel arrangements."

Originally Jackson had been dismayed that Alex wanted his best friend to come for a visit—after all, it would be one *more* person to grab the boy's attention. Then he'd realized it could result in a longer stay in Montana, so he'd subtly promoted the idea.

Laughter erupted from the picnic area, and Jackson tried to discern the cause. Morgan was sitting with DeeDee while they studied an iPad. Hank Garrison was talking with Jackson's father; the two had always gotten along well. Elizabeth was doing something with food, and his mother was standing with Alex.

"Now that we're all here, it's time to start cooking burgers," Parker McGregor called. "Son, do you want to jump in here?"

Jackson accepted the long-handled utensils and took over at the barbecue grill, where Elizabeth handed him a container.

"I found soy patties at the market this morning," she explained. "Don't know what they'll be like, but at least Alex will have something on his bun. Kayla suggested portobello mushrooms, but the grocer doesn't carry them."

"I knew that someday one or more of my kids or grandkids would travel the vegetarian route," Parker said with a wink at Alex. "I'll even give you a fair chance to win over this old cattleman."

Alex grinned. Jackson knew if he'd said the same thing, the teen would have just stared, or rolled his eyes and walked away. Discouraged, he grilled the burgers and heaped them on a platter. The soy patties went on another plate, which Alex examined silently.

"You're welcome to cheat," Sarah McGregor told him. "You know what they say—what happens in Schuyler stays in Schuyler."

Sarah's comment didn't seem to affect Alex. He looked briefly at Jackson before taking the vegetarian option. "No, thanks, these are fine."

He sat next to Morgan at the end of the table. Jackson stepped forward, intent on sitting opposite, when he saw a warning shake of Kayla's head. Silently he got his food and sat at an adjacent table. A moment later, she slid onto the bench across from him. Elizabeth and Hank joined them and Jackson appreciated the support.

"Everything is delicious, as usual, Elizabeth," he said. "You're a wonderful cook. I've never eaten so well on a camping trip."

"The RV kitchen helped."

"I've always been a fan of roughing it, but you may have changed my mind about that."

"I need pickles," Kayla interjected. "Anyone want anything while I'm up?"

She slid gracefully from the bench and Jackson determinedly concentrated on his plate, glad the lower half of his anatomy was hidden by the table. His attraction to Kayla was becoming a real distraction to focusing on Alex. He had to get it under control, whether it took a date with another woman or an ice-cold shower.

CHAPTER ELEVEN

MORGAN COULDN'T BELIEVE she was still getting up early to run, even though Kayla wasn't at the ranch to go with her. Not that she was getting up *that* early. By seven thirty Kayla had probably already finished and was back at the house. She was bringing Alex and DeeDee to the Crazy Horse later, though.

Alex hadn't wanted to come, but at the picnic yesterday he'd finally agreed, as long as DeeDee and his mom were there, too. That was fine with Morgan; she liked the Andersons.

With Cory at her side Morgan set off, trying to run slow at first, the way Kayla said worked best for her, before building up to a faster speed.

Her brain kept buzzing.

Alex resented doing anything with his birth dad, and she sort of got why he felt that way. After all, it was lousy to discover a huge thing about yourself wasn't actually true. And the way his creepsville stepbrother had jeered must have made finding out even worse.

At the same time, Alex thought it was odd *she* didn't get along so great with her dad. Well, she hadn't told him everything. Maybe she should, but the whole thing was stinky.

After she sped up, thoughts clouding her brain seemed to go away for a while, so she made herself go an extra mile before slowing to cool down.

"Didn't know you were a runner," Greg Taggett said as she walked past the horse barn.

"I just started," Morgan told the foreman.

"You're doing great. I go to all my son's track meets, and you set a good pace."

Morgan stopped. "Your son runs?" Owen Taggett was a senior at the high school, but she didn't pay attention to the small track-and-field team—they were usually too serious to be much fun.

"Sure does. He just got an athletic scholarship."

"Owen doesn't want to be a rancher?"

"Hasn't made up his mind yet. This way he'll have choices."

The same old sick feeling hit her stomach, so Morgan nodded and started walking again. Her dad had never gotten a choice. He was supposed to have gone to college, but he hadn't been able to because of *her*.

"Have a pleasant run?" Dad asked as she came into the kitchen. He was drinking a cup of coffee and eating a bowl of oatmeal.

She shrugged. "Cory liked it."

"Always take him when you go, okay?"

Morgan stared into the cereal bowl she was filling. Hot, chewy oatmeal, that was what she liked, none of that overcooked junk. Flora must have made it.

"Yeah," she said. "Cory always wants to go."

"True, but make sure of it anyway, and take the satellite phone. If you fell or anything, you'd be able to get help faster."

It sounded as if he was really worried about her. Okay, so maybe he was. He tried to make sure *everyone* on the ranch stayed safe and healthy; that was one of his big things, and her dad always took care of his responsibilities.

Dropping into a chair at the kitchen table, she stirred her cereal and ate a mouthful. "When is everyone coming?" she asked.

"In an hour."

"Are…um, Elizabeth and Hank coming, too?" She'd almost called them Grandma and Grandpa, same as Alex and DeeDee.

"Not today."

It was too bad. The Garrisons were pretty awesome for people that old. On the trip to Yellowstone they'd started treating her like one of their great-grandkids, too, along with DeeDee and Alex. It had been nice, even if they were just being polite.

KAYLA PULLED UP in front of Jackson's large house at nine o'clock.

"Whoa." DeeDee stared at the house. "That's not the kind of ranch you see in the movies."

"It must suit Morgan and Jackson," Kayla said.

There was no point in explaining that the McGregors came from old money and Jackson had been able to build whatever he wanted. The McGregors were true ranchers, but they didn't need to raise cattle to make a living. They had oil or something from Texas and Oklahoma.

DeeDee opened the door and jumped out.

"Come on, kiddo," Kayla urged her son. "You aren't facing a firing squad."

"I know," he muttered.

"Try treating Jackson the way you would a friend," Kayla suggested. "He's not a terrible person."

"I guess."

His continued reticence bothered Kayla, though Alex had always been hard to read.

"I know this isn't what you expected when you came to Schuyler," she said, hoping he'd open up with the right encouragement.

"Yeah."

"What *did* you expect?" she probed once more.

Alex made a face. "I don't know. It was probably stupid anyway." He unbuckled his belt and dragged himself from the car.

Kayla wasn't reassured as she followed him. If they couldn't deal with the problem, Alex might pull another stunt even more serious than running away to meet his great-grandparents.

Jackson met them on the porch, the quintessential rancher in his worn Levi's and long-sleeved work shirt—strong, muscular, *virile*. *Damn*. She hated the way her body was betraying her.

"Jackson, do you have time to teach me to ride while Morgan teaches Alex?" DeeDee asked.

"I'll teach you both."

"Naw, I'm going to show Alex," Morgan declared.

Kayla's attention was instantly hijacked from sex to the immediate situation. She didn't know whether to chortle or be sympathetic.

To his credit, Jackson gave DeeDee a warm smile. "Sure, but maybe Morgan wants to give you both a tour of the place first." Yet as the three kids went off together, Kayla watched disappointment cross his face.

"Not what you planned?" she asked.

"You urged me to relax and let things happen naturally, but what's happening is that my son gets along great with his sister and avoids me at every turn." He sighed. "Sorry. I know I shouldn't keep blasting off about it."

"You can't force a relationship," Kayla reminded him. "And if you have the idea that Alex should automatically love you, or you him, then you're wrong." She held up a hand to stop Jackson's denial. "Be honest, did you meet Alex and immediately think, 'Wow, I love this kid'?"

"I… No."

"Of course not. Look, when we got here this morning, I told Alex to treat you like one of his friends. You could give it a shot, too. Let things happen when they happen."

A long minute passed before Jackson nodded. "All right, I'll try."

Idly Kayla noted that his eyes had changed over the years. As a teenager they'd sparked with energy and daring; now they were filled with grim determination. And they were so guarded. How could Alex get to know someone who never let anyone past the surface?

"Let's go find them," Jackson said, leading her toward the outbuildings.

They found the kids in the ranch's large, airy horse barn. Alex was observing warily as Morgan saddled a powerful black stallion, while DeeDee kept dashing in to pat the animal on its neck, only to jump backward with an alarmed squeak whenever the horse moved.

"Looks as if the first lesson is already starting," Jackson murmured.

Kayla's attention was torn between her children as they learned the fundamentals of horseback riding. Not surprisingly, DeeDee was keener than her brother, who only seemed to be going along out of his friendship with Morgan. It was interesting, though—Jackson and his daughter seemed to communicate better when animals were involved.

"See if you can lift it," Jackson suggested after showing DeeDee the different parts of a saddle.

"Jipes," DeeDee yelped, almost staggering under the weight. She stuck out her bottom lip. "Poor horses."

"You'd be amazed how strong they are. But don't worry, the one you'll be using is lighter."

He put the saddle down and opened a large double stall. The mares inside had been curiously watching the proceedings and they walked out to stand quietly between Alex and DeeDee.

"These two ladies are Betty and Boop," Jackson said.

Kayla nearly choked. "Betty and Boop?"

"Yeah, I let my younger brother choose the names. Josh has a wicked sense of humor, or at least he used to."

"I wanna ride Boop," DeeDee declared. She watched Jackson slip the bit into Boop's mouth and adjust the bridle, so eager she was hopping from one foot to the other.

"DeeDee, I'm betting you're a natural-born rider," Jackson said when he'd finished saddling the horse. "Put your foot in the stirrup this way."

Morgan was showing Alex how to mount as well, and Kayla gulped when she saw her kids so high off the ground.

"Can we go out on the ranch now?" DeeDee demanded after circling the paddock several times on Boop. "I don't want to just ride in a circle."

Jackson opened his mouth, hesitated and glanced at Kayla. She nodded slowly.

"Okay," he agreed. "But don't try going off alone at any time. Kayla, shall I saddle a horse for you?"

"Yikesylvania," DeeDee exclaimed. "You know how to ride, Mom?"

"Of course she does! I taught her," Jackson said. His words evoked memories of long-ago days, when he'd patiently taught her about horses while stealing kisses whenever his parents or a ranch hand couldn't see them.

"I'd love to go," Kayla affirmed.

Several minutes later, Jackson appeared leading two saddled horses—a black-and-white Appaloosa and a golden palomino that quickly nosed Kayla's breast pocket, where she'd dropped a handful of sugar cubes.

"Hey, beautiful girl." Kayla fed her the sugar. "What is *she* called, Daisy Mae?"

"No." Jackson cleared his throat. "Madonna. It was my youngest sister's idea—Madison is a fan." He patted the Appaloosa's neck. "And this is Thunder."

Though she hadn't gotten on a horse in sixteen years, Kayla avoided Jackson's helpful hand while climbing onto Madonna. His eyebrows shot upward, but she didn't care. There were too many memories involved, such as the way he used to run his fingers up her calf or put an intimate hand on her bottom while boosting her into the saddle. Funny, she hadn't thought about those times in years, and now she could hardly *stop* thinking about them.

The five of them started out slowly at first, then as Alex and DeeDee became more comfortable, they urged the horses into a faster pace.

Mmm. Kayla had forgotten how enjoyable riding could be. No motors. No roads. No traffic. Just moving through the early-August morning and becoming part of the landscape. Jackson rode beside her. If it wasn't for the kids ahead of them, she could have almost time-warped back to her teenage days when they'd ridden out on the range to find secluded places for kisses and fondling.

ALEX DECIDED THAT horses weren't too bad. In fact, he kind of liked riding, even if it jolted his butt.

DeeDee had been wild to get on a horse for the past year. He hadn't cared that much, even though Sandy had told him he was a dope; she loved it and had gotten her parents to take her riding every week.

After a while Jackson called out for them to stop.

"Are there mountain lions or wolves ahead?" DeeDee asked excitedly.

"No, I just think we should turn back."

"We haven't gone that far at all," Morgan complained.

"Yes, but remember what happened with Kenny and Lynne."

"Oh. Right."

"Huh?" Alex asked.

"Sore bums," Morgan explained. "My cousins visited from Chicago and they got it bad. Like, they couldn't sit or lie down or walk for days without groaning and moaning."

"Uh...okay."

"But after lunch we can get in the pool, and tomorrow we can go for a longer ride. You get used to it pretty quick."

Alex nodded. Morgan expected him to come out to the ranch every day, and maybe it wouldn't be too bad. Jackson might not be too bad, either, if they could just be friends.

And he'd liked meeting the McGregors. All of a sudden he had regular grandparents, the same as most of his friends. He even had more great-grandparents that he hadn't met yet. He'd emailed to tell Sandy more about it last night; she'd written back and said it was good he was too old to get dorky birthday clothes. That had made him laugh. The first time he'd met Sandy was in the first grade and she'd been spitting mad because her mom had made her wear a sweater from her grandmother with Big Bird on the front.

Anyway, the McGregors were okay. Jackson had seemed surprised when he'd called them Grandpa Parker and Grandma Sarah, but Alex didn't mind doing it. Other than his grandparents, he only had Uncle Pete on Mom's side, but Jackson's family was *humongous*. Grandpa Parker had promised to give him a chart of the McGregor family to help sort it out.

At the barn, Morgan showed him how to unsaddle Betty. She did the same with the Black, then casually lifted her stallion's front right foot.

"Don't fuss, ya big baby," she scolded as the Black snorted, though she didn't sound annoyed. "This is a hoof pick," she told Alex, showing him how to use the tool to clean around the horseshoe.

Alex nervously took one of the picks from the grooming trays on a shelf. Luckily Betty didn't seem to mind her feet being messed with, though she leaned on his back a little.

Next came a currycomb, then the body brush; he liked doing that part more even though his arms started aching.

"We take good care of our horses on the Crazy Horse," Morgan said. "If you wanna ride, you gotta know your way around a currycomb and hoof pick."

"That's right," Jackson agreed. He was helping DeeDee, who couldn't reach as high as she needed to get Boop's head and back with the body brush.

Alex saw his mom was grooming Madonna as if she knew exactly what she was doing. For some reason he was surprised to find out that Jackson had taught her to ride a horse, but he knew they'd dated and done stuff together...yeah, a *lot* of stuff. Yuck.

He tried to think about lunch instead, hoping

it wouldn't be barbecued burgers again, or anything else that smelled real good. Being a vegetarian was *hard*, but he didn't want to stop being one in front of Jackson…or in front of Dad, not after all the snotty jokes Dad had made about vegetarians with Brant.

He and Morgan finished by cleaning Betty's and the Black's bridles and the stirrup treads and went outside to hang around and wait for the others.

"Phew," he muttered. "That's a lot of work."

"You get used to it," Morgan said, climbing up to straddle the corral fence. "The Black trusts me more because I take care of him. And this way I know where he likes to be touched the most, and what he doesn't like, all sorts of stuff."

Alex could see how it would help. He'd already discovered there was a spot on Betty's neck where she loved being scratched, but he didn't think he'd ever get used to cleaning a horse's butt…the dock, as Morgan called it. She'd told him it was the place around the tail, but as far as he was concerned, a butt was a butt.

JACKSON ENJOYED SHOWING DeeDee how to take care of Boop and even took the time to explain the basics of cleaning and oiling saddles. But it was obvious Alex wasn't interested, because he left with Morgan. At least he'd seemed to enjoy the ride.

One step at a time, Jackson reminded himself.

With every scrap of the patience he could muster, he brought everyone into the kitchen.

"Flora, I think you briefly met Kayla when she came to the house a few weeks ago, and these are her children, Alex and DeeDee Anderson," he said, resisting the urge to call Alex his son. After all, Flora didn't need to be told—even if he hadn't explained the situation to her, the resemblance was unmistakable.

Kayla shook the other woman's hand. "Hello, again."

"Hi. I hope you're all hungry. I've got enough lasagna to feed an army."

DeeDee smacked her lips. "I loooove lasagna, and Morgan says yours is fabulous."

Jackson was astonished to see a pleased dimple in his housekeeper's cheek, though she brusquely told everyone to wash up and get to the table before the food got cold. Luckily her culinary expertise with lasagna included a meatless variety and Alex consumed a vast amount, along with salad and garlic bread.

Flora sat next to Kayla during the meal and he saw the two women exchange amused glances when Alex took a third serving.

"That was wonderful," Kayla said when they were done. Both DeeDee and Alex thanked Flora, as well.

"There will be cookies and homemade ice cream later in the afternoon," she told them.

"Homemade ice cream," DeeDee said reverently. "That is so...fantastalicious."

"The squirt likes to make up words," Alex explained.

"Someone has to," DeeDee argued. "Why not me?"

"How about going to my room and playing a game?" Morgan asked DeeDee and Alex. "Dad won't let us swim until an hour after we eat."

"Swimming after eating doesn't cause cramps," DeeDee said. "I heard they proved it didn't make any difference."

"But why take a chance?" Jackson argued back with a friendly smile. "Especially after a big meal. So go have fun, there's plenty of time for the pool."

The three kids clattered out, Morgan's dog faithfully following them.

"What can I do to help?" Kayla asked Flora.

"Nothing," the housekeeper said. "That's my job."

Jackson grimaced. The kitchen was Flora's domain and she fiercely protected it. He and Morgan often fixed their own breakfast but knew better than to do more than neatly pile their dishes in the sink.

The silence in the family room was awkward as Kayla sank onto one of the large couches.

"Flora seems efficient," she said finally.

"Yes. She's one of the best cooks in the area and keeps everything organized," Jackson answered.

Kayla glanced around, likely trying to think of conversational topics. "This is quite a place. DeeDee was surprised. She expected something more traditionally Western."

He shifted uncomfortably in his chair. The design had largely been Marcy's choice. Ironically, she'd walked out less than a year after it was built.

"What's wrong?" Kayla asked.

"Nothing. The house works, though personally I would have chosen something that blends into the landscape better."

"Oh, I see." It was clear she'd understood the implication about Marcy. Kayla had always been sharp.

"My brother Trent built it," he added. "Trent is a contractor now."

"Trent is one of the cousins your folks raised."

"Yeah, but Trent and Alaina are just as much my brother and sister as Josh and Madison." That was something his parents had simply assumed was true when their orphaned nephew and niece had joined the household.

Kayla kicked her shoes off and tucked her legs beneath her. "I remember Trent. He's older than you—sort of dark and brooding?"

"Yeah, he's a loner, but we don't let him bury his head too deep."

"Alex is trying to sort out all the relatives, but he's having a hard time."

"My parents were thrilled to meet him yesterday."

"I'm glad. They always seemed…nice." Something in her tone made Jackson frown.

"Nice? You don't seem that sure of it."

Kayla glanced around as if to be certain they were alone, then shrugged. "I always liked them, but I'm not sure they felt the same about me."

"Don't be ridiculous…" His voice trailed off and she smiled wryly.

"Yeah," she said. "Admit it, they didn't approve of me as your girlfriend."

"Please understand, Mom and Dad were disappointed that I'd broken up with Marcy. Her father's ranch was next to theirs, and it must have seemed the perfect match to them."

"Yep. Marcy was the girl next door, not the one whose mother drank her way through every bar."

Puzzled, Jackson stared at Kayla. Her mother was obviously an alcoholic who'd made her childhood difficult, yet she didn't sound bitter.

"You never talked about your mom, or about your life before Schuyler."

Kayla cocked her head. "It wasn't something I enjoyed discussing. We lived on welfare in the worst sections of town. It usually wasn't that safe. Mom drank and slept around to forget the past, and sometimes resented having a kid hanging like a millstone around her neck—those are her words, by the way, not mine."

"Then, why did she bring you back to Schuyler and take you with her when she left?" Jackson still remembered the day he'd learned Kayla was gone. He'd broken up with her because of Marcy being pregnant, which had sucked, but then Kayla had made him really mad by claiming *she* was pregnant.

"Mom can't stay anywhere for long," Kayla told him. "She has a host of personal demons, starting with my dad dying so young and leaving her alone. She still loves him, but hates him, too, for the way it turned out."

"That still doesn't explain why she didn't leave you in Schuyler. Surely it would have been better for you both."

"My grandparents asked Mom to let me stay, but I didn't want her to be alone. Besides, I *couldn't* stay."

It wasn't logical, but an intense dislike for Carolyn Garrison went through Jackson. Whatever excuses Kayla might make, her mother was a nightmare, too weak and selfish to think of anyone but herself.

Hypocrite, an inner voice taunted.

Kayla might have remained in Schuyler if she hadn't been pregnant; she might have even stayed if he hadn't accused her of sleeping around. But he had, and then she'd learned he was marrying Marcy without knowing the whole story—the news about Marcy's impending motherhood hadn't come out until after the wedding.

God, no wonder Kayla disliked him. And it was

true that his parents hadn't been happy he was dating her. So even if they'd known about Alex and supported her financially, she might have resented taking the money. On the other hand, she might have felt it was owed to her.

"I'm sorry," he murmured.

"I did okay."

"You did better than okay," he told her.

They fell silent again, but it was more comfortable this time. After exactly sixty minutes, DeeDee came running downstairs. "Can we swim now?" she pleaded. "There's a neat pool house where we can change."

"Sure," Kayla told her. "I'll go with you."

Jackson went to his bedroom to put on his swim trunks, then headed outside.

Kayla stood next to the pool in her bathing suit, chatting with Morgan. She looked like a model in one of those vacation-paradise magazine ads—long legs, hair fiery in the sun and a body that made him want to howl.

He was in deep trouble.

CHAPTER TWELVE

KAYLA FOUND IT hard to concentrate as she helped Morgan apply sunblock to her back. The barely concealed heat in Jackson's gaze made her want to wrap a towel around herself. There was nothing provocative about her swimsuit, but it exposed more of her skin than he'd seen since they were teenagers.

"Thanks, Kayla," Morgan said, almost shyly as she turned around. The teenager looked at Kayla's black Lycra one-piece. "I wish I had that kind of suit."

"I'm sure you can find something similar. But yours is awfully cute."

"Do you really think so?"

"Absolutely."

The teen wore a swimsuit that reminded Kayla of the 1960s pop song "Itsy Bitsy Teenie Weenie Yellow Polka Dot Bikini," though Morgan's blue suit had white polka dots instead of yellow, and it wasn't itsy-bitsy. It looked sweet…though Kayla could well imagine Jackson's reaction the first time he'd seen his little girl in a bikini.

"I went running this morning," Morgan told her eagerly. "At least four miles."

"Running is terrific exercise."

"Yeah. Um, I wanted to say I'm sorry about your… That is, Alex told me about how his dad keeps getting married… Uh, I mean, his *other* dad, the one who adopted…" Morgan stopped, obviously unsure how to word everything.

"Don't worry about it," Kayla advised. "Families are so complicated now, we need new names to describe relationships."

"Yeah. It's weird."

"Of course it is. But we can handle weird, can't we?"

With a grin, Morgan said, "I guess so."

"Hey, Morgan," Alex yelled. "Aren't you coming in?"

"What do you think, bozo?" She cannonballed into the deep end near Alex and DeeDee and a three-sided water fight quickly started.

Steps extended across the shallow end of the long pool, and Kayla slid into the water to sit down. It was refreshing in the sultry afternoon air and she leaned against the edge, watching the kids play. Jackson dived in and swam laps with a ferocious speed. After a long time he finally stopped.

"Do you do laps every day?" Kayla asked.

He swept his hair off his forehead, breathing hard. "No, though I probably should. Are you going to do any?"

"Not right now. I had a long run this morning, so I can relax and mellow out."

Nodding, Jackson lounged a few feet away, his bronzed shoulders bare and glistening in the sunlight, his legs spread under the surface, braced again the pool bottom. Even in the cool water, Kayla had to acknowledge the heat in her abdomen. Determinedly she turned her attention to her son and daughter as they shouted and played Marco Polo with Morgan.

A few minutes later they came splashing toward them. "Let's play water volleyball," Morgan suggested.

Glad for an excuse to be active after all, Kayla nodded and pushed away from the step. After a moment, Jackson joined them.

THAT NIGHT THERE was a mild ache in Kayla's muscles, but otherwise she had few aftereffects from the horseback ride. DeeDee and Alex felt the same and the next day they took a longer ride, all of them together. On the third day, the kids were both growing confident on their mounts and eager to get more adventuresome.

"Dad, I'm going to take Alex and DeeDee up to Halloran's Meadow, okay?" Morgan said after lunch on the fourth afternoon.

It was obviously a play for time without adult supervision and Jackson considered a moment before nodding. "It's all right with me, but Kayla has to decide for Alex and DeeDee."

"Can we, Kayla, please?" Morgan begged. DeeDee and Alex gazed at her hopefully.

"Just a ride?" Kayla asked, stalling while she tried to sort out proper caution from overprotective instincts.

"There's a waterfall at the end of the meadow," Morgan admitted. "But the pool is only a foot deep. The fun part is running through the waterfall."

"The meadow is up in the hills, but with the heat spell we've been having, the pool won't be full," Jackson explained. "I've always thought it was safe, but you have to do what makes you comfortable."

Gathering her scattered nerves, Kayla nodded. "It's okay, I guess, if you all stay together."

"Awesome!" DeeDee exclaimed.

"Take Cory with you," Jackson instructed his daughter, "and one of the satellite phones."

"Ah, Dad, I'm not going to be alone. We'll all be together."

"That doesn't matter. There's a fully charged unit on my desk," Jackson told his daughter.

Heaving a sigh that only a teenager could inject so much disgust into, Morgan went to the ranch office and brought out the phone, showing it to her father. "Happy?"

"Yes. Keep it turned on."

Kayla followed the kids to the barn and watched them saddle their horses. Alex could already handle

Betty without difficulty, and DeeDee only needed help lifting the saddle over Boop's back, using a stool for everything she wasn't tall enough to handle from the ground. Jackson mostly checked that they'd gotten the girth tight enough.

"Are you really okay with them going off on their own?" he asked as the three rode out, the McGregors' German shepherd scampering ahead of them. "I can always catch up on Thunder and tell them I've changed my mind. I'll even take the heat for both of us... After a year of Morgan being in a mood, I'm almost used to it."

"As much as I'd like to wrap them in cotton wool, let's skip the teenage angst."

Jackson rested his arms on the top rail of the fence and gazed out at the tree-studded landscape. "My parents say that when you raise kids on a ranch, you have to get used to giving them more responsibility and freedom."

"So what are Morgan's responsibilities?"

"Well, Mom has hinted that I screwed up there— as in not enough responsibility *or* freedom." He shoved his cowboy hat back on his forehead. "Morgan has a few chores, but after her mother walked out, I indulged her. Maybe I always did. Marcy was never interested in being a mother, and I wanted to compensate."

"I feel the same way when Curtis dives into one of his obsessions. It's obvious when his romances are on the wane because he spends more time with the kids. I want them to have as good a relationship as possible, so I try to keep the seesaw from being too obvious."

"Meaning you indulge them, too."

"A little." Kayla gazed around at the Crazy Horse's tidy outbuildings and corrals. "As I recall, you once had a long list of daily chores. You said that your parents hoped it would keep you on the straight and narrow, but that they'd underestimated you."

Jackson turned toward her with an enigmatic expression. "And I remember you used to help me *do* those chores."

She laughed. "I doubt a city kid was much help. You didn't seem to mind the work, though."

"That's because I always wanted to be a rancher, despite my rebellion. I just don't know what Morgan wants." He looked back to where the three riders had disappeared in the distance. "I've been thinking, Morgan has friends, but this thing with Alex is different."

Because he's family, Kayla said silently. And DeeDee was being included because she was Alex's sister. "I suppose having more children wasn't likely given Marcy's lack of maternal instincts...?"

"Marcy refused to consider another pregnancy," he replied bluntly. "After my divorce I dated someone else who seemed interested in children, but it turned out she was just looking for a rich patsy."

"How can you be sure?"

"Because I surprised Patti one evening and found a man sneaking out a side window. I tackled him, thinking it was a thief, but it was really the guy she'd been living with for years. He was so scared he blurted out the whole plan…which included a couple of years of marriage, a baby, followed by a quick divorce with generous support payments."

"Oh. Sorry." Kayla was surprised Jackson was revealing so much about his romantic woes, but they'd gone past the point of being overly concerned about something not being the other's business.

"How about you and Curtis?" he asked. "Did you want a larger family?"

She stirred restlessly. "We tried to have another baby. There was nothing physically preventing a pregnancy, it just didn't happen. Then Curtis became enamored with a woman he'd met at work. He was up front, saying he wanted a divorce because he didn't want to be unfaithful."

"Real nice of him."

"It could have been worse. Everything worked out amicably, from custody to him insisting that I keep the house. He didn't even ask for a settlement from my business." Kayla swallowed, a lump in her throat. "But for months after we separated, I kept wondering if he'd sought out someone else because we weren't successful conceiving another child."

"If he felt inadequate, that was his problem, not yours." The adamant tone in Jackson's voice was

soothing to her ego. She'd dealt with the pain years
before, but even old scars can hurt when they're
poked.

She blinked rapidly but couldn't keep a tear from
falling. "Thanks. I suppose it was harder to handle
because I kept thinking about the baby that might
have been." She sniffed and a few more tears fell.

Dammit, she wasn't a crier, yet her eyes didn't
seem to know that.

"Silly, isn't it?" she asked. "That's why I've never
told anyone how it felt. I mean, I wasn't even pregnant, so why did I feel bad?"

Jackson put an arm around her waist and pulled
her close. "I don't think it's silly in the least."

FOR SOME REASON Jackson's own heart ached as silent tears trickled down Kayla's face. She wasn't
indulging in a storm of self-pity; she was grieving
over the past that should have been and the baby
she'd hoped would be born.

In a way they were alike.

He'd never talked much to his family about the
divorce or what had happened with Patti—in his
case more from stiff-necked pride than anything
else. As for Kayla? During her deplorable childhood she'd learned to tough things out, to survive
and make the best of her circumstances—lessons
that were cemented when she was a teenage mother
facing the world alone. It was no wonder she found
it hard to confide in anyone.

"Sorry," she said finally, stepping back and wiping her face. "I don't know where that came from."

"We all need a pressure valve, though preferably not the kind your mother used."

Kayla leaned against the corral fence and gave him a shaky smile. "Alcohol wasn't Mom's pressure valve, it was her escape. I decided a long time ago not to run away from life, though I'm sure I've made different mistakes. After all, my kids need *something* to complain about to a therapist one day."

Jackson laughed. "Come back to the house, Ma," he urged in his best imitation of a character in a vintage Western film. "Us old fogys will sit around until the young'uns get back."

"Okay, Pa, but you make sure that the rockin' chair is ready."

In an easy silence they returned to the house where Kayla sank onto a couch.

Flora came into the living room shortly afterward, glancing silently at Kayla's red eyes and tearstained cheeks. "Would you like some lemonade?" she asked.

"That would be wonderful," Kayla answered.

"Same here," Jackson added.

When the housekeeper returned, she handed a tall, frosty glass to Jackson and another to Kayla, along with a damp washcloth. Kayla used it to wipe her face and press against her eyes.

"Thanks," she said.

"Take it easy," Flora ordered sternly. "We've all had that sort of day. God knows, *I* have."

The two women shared a smile full of understanding. Flora had edges that stuck out everywhere, but while Jackson didn't know her entire history, he knew she'd had hard times herself.

"I'm going into town for groceries," Flora told Jackson briskly, as though embarrassed by her rare display of softness. "Anything special you want for dinner?"

"I could stand throwing steaks or chicken on the grill, but I don't know about Alex."

"He's covered. Stuffed manicotti," she said before stomping from the room. A minute later her car drove past the window, toward the main ranch gate.

"Flora is an interesting addition to your household," Kayla remarked.

"She's an odd character. I hoped she'd feel like part of the family, but I'm not sure that's ever happened."

Kayla shrugged. "Maybe there should be a family designation that doesn't have to be defined by comparison to anything else. We should make up a word for it."

"Better yet, we could submit the idea to DeeDee," Jackson suggested. "I'm sure she'd come up with something."

"Except it would probably be much longer than necessary. I suspect she's going to become a linguist and invent an entirely new language. She's already learned Klingon, from *Star Trek*."

"She actually *speaks* Klingon?"

"Fluently. It drives Alex crazy since he's the bigger *Trek* fan."

Jackson grinned and gulped a mouthful of lemonade. It was nice having a comfortable conversation with Kayla. He still hoped they could be friends, but he'd never felt toward a buddy the way he sometimes felt around her, so he'd have to find a way to deal with that.

MORGAN'S FAVORITE PLACE in the world was Halloran's Meadow. Whenever the weather was warm enough she went there to read or sit and think, sometimes even to yell her lungs out. When she was little she'd talked to a particular quaking aspen on the north side of the meadow. The idea had come from a book her father used to read to her, and later she'd given it up, but she still thought of it as her tree.

And the waterfall was a blast.

By midsummer the stream that fed it wasn't going very strong, but she always felt happy when she dashed through the cascade of water. The summer before she'd even tried skinny-dipping, but she'd felt silly and hadn't done it again.

"I got my swimsuit under my clothes, but do you guys need to change?" Morgan asked when they reached the meadow.

Alex shook his head. "Not me, I have my trunks on under my jeans."

"I need to," DeeDee said.

"There's an open spot inside those trees you can use." Morgan pointed to the grove of quaking aspens.

DeeDee dismounted and tethered the horse the way Morgan had taught her, then raced toward the trees. "Wait for me," she called over her shoulder.

It was weird having DeeDee around all the time, especially since Morgan's friends ditched their younger brothers and sisters every chance they got. She'd suggested trying it a few times, but Alex didn't want to. He said that he and DeeDee usually didn't do that much together in Seattle, but it was different in Montana—something to do with the family-spirit thing that was important to his mom.

It was okay. Morgan didn't really mind bringing DeeDee along, and for private stuff, she texted Alex or sent him a Facebook message. DeeDee might be a pain some of the time, but she was fun and seemed to think Morgan was awesome. Nobody had *ever* thought she was awesome before, so it was kind of cool.

Cory lolled on the grass as they waited for DeeDee, a big doggy smile on his face. Morgan had hated leaving him behind when they'd gone to Yellowstone but had finally admitted he wouldn't have liked being tied up all the time.

The next few hours were the best she could remember having at Halloran's Meadow. Oddly, she'd never brought her friends there—never even thought of it. But it was different with Alex and DeeDee. When she was with them, it was easier to forget her other problems.

And she wondered…if everything blew up with her dad, would Kayla let her live with them in Seattle?

KAYLA OPENED HER eyes and realized she'd fallen asleep on Jackson's couch. She felt better, though her eyes were still scratchy from tears.

She yawned and stretched.

Across the room, Jackson put down his newspaper and smiled. "You look like a cat, content from an afternoon nap."

"Except I rarely nap in the middle of the day, no matter how little I slept the night before. Sorry for conking out that way."

"It wasn't long, and you probably needed the rest. Are you interested in a swim now, or do you want to sleep longer? The kids won't be back for at least another couple of hours—Morgan always stays at the meadow as long as possible."

"Let's swim." Kayla shimmied upward on the couch. Being indoors alone with Jackson suddenly seemed a bad idea.

Jackson was waiting when she stepped from the pool house in her swimsuit. Diving in, she swam from one end of the pool to the other before turning over to float on the surface. She let herself drift, feeling oddly at peace.

The past few weeks had often seemed surreal. It was as if time had been suspended from the moment she'd learned Alex wasn't where he was supposed to be. Or maybe it had been the long drive through the night, the sun finally rising over Montana's vast reaches, making it seem as if she'd entered a dreamworld that held both good and bad.

Currents eddied around her as Jackson did laps, his powerful arms and legs slicing through the water. Kayla determinedly kept her eyes closed. She might have been celibate for a long while, but that didn't mean she had to ogle.

A shadow fell across her face and she opened her eyes to see Jackson standing nearby. "Something wrong?"

"Just wondering if you're wearing sunscreen. My hide is like leather—your skin isn't."

"Drat, I forgot."

Getting out, she fetched the bottle from her bag in the pool house. It was smart to use sunscreen, though she didn't burn easily. As for Jackson's remark about having a hide like leather…? Kayla shot a quick look at him in the pool. He was tanned from long hours working outside, but hardly leathered.

There were comfortable chaises around the pool and she sat on the side shaded by black cottonwood trees, carefully smoothing lotion over the tops of her feet and calves. She'd poured more on her palm when she realized Jackson's gaze was fixed on her.

Kayla swallowed.

Though it had been sixteen years, she recognized that look. She continued applying lotion to her legs, but she was paying little attention to the task.

Slowly he lifted himself from the water and walked toward her with the powerful grace of a wolf claiming its territory.

Heat and electricity burrowed deep into her abdomen.

"If you're going to say no, I'd really appreciate you doing it now," Jackson whispered, drawing her upward.

No?

Kayla's thoughts scattered further when he cupped her bottom, pulling her flush against him. She didn't want to say no—she wanted more. His fingers slipped beneath the edge of her swimsuit to the skin, stroking, massaging, driving her mad.

"We're alone," he whispered between kisses. "Come upstairs?"

Mutely she nodded, and let him tug her into the house and up to a large bedroom. Slowly he peeled the black suit from her shoulders, pushing it down to her waist, stopping as his eyes took in her breasts. His breathing quickened as he played with her sensitized nipples and sent ripples of sensation through her entire body.

A moment later they tumbled to the bed. His

weight settled over her, his bare chest against her breasts and his lips hard on her mouth. After a long, drugging kiss, he eased away to tug the bathing suit down her hips, freeing the hot, damp space between her legs.

It didn't take long before Jackson's own swim trunks lay on the floor and his hard length was pressed against her.

"You'd better have a condom," she gasped.

He nodded, then groaned and lunged across the room to grope through a drawer. It seemed to take an awfully long time, and she turned her head to see him tear open the package and roll the condom over his erection.

Then he dropped back down upon the bed to lay his mouth over her right breast, sucking, teasing, before edging between her legs. A thrust of pure pleasure shuddered through her abdomen as he entered and set up a rhythm, over and over until the climax shattered her thoughts.

JACKSON'S HEART SLOWED from its wild pulsing and he lifted himself on his arms to look at Kayla. Her auburn hair lay in damp ropes across his pillows, her intense blue eyes still reflecting the pleasure they'd shared.

He kissed her again, his hands seeking her taut body. Blood surged into his groin again. Damn, how long had it been since he'd wanted a woman this much?

Realizing the state he was in, Kayla began to chuckle, and the shiver it sent through her drove his need to even greater intensity. Easing away, he hurriedly dealt with fresh protection and returned to the bed.

This time he moved more slowly, restraining the wild need so he could watch how his movements affected Kayla, learning what pleased her most. She slid her hands down his back and hips and he shuddered, moving faster while her head fell back and her climax began. He kept going, pleasuring her and himself in a way he couldn't remember ever experiencing before.

Finally, he collapsed, gasping for air. He could feel her heart thrumming against his chest, the beat matching his own until both slowed and they became aware of the world.

In the distance, a horse neighed and Kayla suddenly pushed him away.

"Don't worry, the kids can't be back yet. It must be one of my ranch hands," he said lazily.

"It doesn't matter."

"You're angry." Jackson was unaccountably disappointed. "You could have said no when I asked, though I suppose women are often—"

"Don't say it," Kayla ordered. "I'm not being inconsistent because I'm a woman. I made a choice, but that doesn't mean I'm required to be happy about giving in to temptation with a guy who doesn't trust women and treats sex as casual recreation."

"I don't," he denied, though she had a certain amount of truth on her side. "Just earlier I was thinking how much I admire what you've done with your life, so you can't claim I don't trust you."

"Yeah, you admire a teenage mother who made good. That isn't the same as trusting me."

Jackson snorted. "Hey, you have just as many trust issues as I do."

"Possibly, but you're just deflecting. I'm going downstairs in case Flora comes home or the kids return early. I do *not* want them figuring out what happened up here."

Hell. He'd forgotten Flora might get back from shopping earlier than expected. While she usually visited family when she went into town, there were no guarantees.

Quickly Kayla squirmed back into her damp suit.

"I'll be down in the pool," she said, walking out.

For several minutes Jackson lay on the mattress, trying to control his unruly body. Damned if he couldn't have made love to her *again*. He'd hardly been a monk since his divorce, but there had been nothing this good—a generous give-and-take of pleasure. Still, that didn't mean it had been a smart idea.

With a sigh, he got up and remade the bed so it showed no signs of their vigorous activity. He wasn't concerned about Flora—she wouldn't be upstairs until she made the beds in the morning—but Morgan might see and wonder about it.

He'd only complicated matters by giving in to temptation. It would be wise to remember that he had two overriding goals—figuring out Morgan's issues, and building a good relationship with Alex. To help reach the second goal, he was supposed to be forming a cordial partnership with Alex's mother, not sneaking into bed with her.

As Kayla stepped into the pool, she was ready to tear her hair out. Didn't she ever learn? Jackson McGregor was bad news for her. He was sexy as hell, but he had even more issues *now* than as a teenager. He didn't listen to people, he didn't trust women and he didn't trust marriage. A triple threat. Not that she was interested in marrying him, but it was symbolic of the gulf between them.

And he had the nerve to criticize *her* struggle to trust? She'd grown up in a harsh world, where trusting the wrong person was dangerous…a world her mother had taken her back to when they'd left Schuyler. But she'd done what was necessary to survive and take care of her baby, and now that she was alone again she wasn't about to let down her defenses, especially with a horny rancher trying to force himself into her family.

It was a reminder of how careful she needed to be with Alex, as well. Jackson might not be quite as chauvinistic as he sometimes seemed, but his opinion of the opposite sex *wasn't* the best. It still worried her that Alex would pick up the wrong attitudes.

A wry grin tugged at Kayla's mouth.

Luckily Alex's best friend was a forthright teenage feminist who'd set him on his ear if he pulled any sexist nonsense.

"Something funny?" Jackson asked as he slid into the pool next to her.

"Not really." They sat silently for a long while, then Kayla stirred restlessly. "I don't understand how you let someone like Marcy affect you so much."

Jackson stared into the pool's depths. "The only thing Marcy and I had in common was being teenage parents, and she was a lousy mother. She was furious that I'd made an agreement with my greatuncle not to touch my trust fund for several years. Instead, he gave us a small house on the ranch and I worked as a cowhand. He paid me the same as his other employees and expected the same effort from me as from them."

"That's reasonable—he loved his ranch and wanted to be sure you could handle it."

"Marcy didn't see it that way. I swear, I paid for that agreement every day of our marriage. She was bitter, claiming we were living in squalor, and complained to everyone that I was treating her badly. I thought it would get better when I was able to build this house, but her complaints didn't stop. The last straw was when she started sleeping around."

Kayla couldn't help but feel bad for him. At least Curtis had been honest enough to end their marriage before cheating. It was the only semimature thing he'd ever done.

"Did Marcy's parents believe her complaints?" Kayla asked.

"No. I think the Liptons were seeing her clearly for the first time. They wouldn't give her money and told me to stick to my arrangement with Great-Uncle Mitch. They said it might save her. But I think they'd given up hope by the time my mother-in-law died. Then with Della gone, Edgar didn't have much to live for. He went soon after."

It was sad the Liptons had passed knowing their daughter hadn't turned out to be a very nice person.

CHAPTER THIRTEEN

ALEX PATTED BETTY on the neck as they rode away from Halloran's Meadow. Much as he hated to admit it, riding horses and spending time on a ranch was pretty cool.

"Let's go faster, slowpokes," DeeDee called, passing him.

He and Morgan made faces at each other. Oops, DeeDee had looked back and was sticking out her tongue.

Sometimes it *was* a pain to have a ten-year-old tagging along. Maybe when Keri got to Montana, the two of them could hang out together and let him and Morgan spend time with Sandy.

It was rad having a sister his own age, although once in a while he'd caught DeeDee looking at him funny, especially when he tried to talk to Morgan privately.

By the time they got back to the ranch, he was starving.

"Are we staying long?" he whispered to his mother. "I'm real hungry."

"No, Grams is expecting us at six."

They'd eaten at Jackson and Morgan's house for

a couple of nights, so she'd decided they should spend an evening with her grandparents.

Morgan winked as they left—a signal to remind him about messaging her later. In the car he checked his phone and saw a message from Sandy saying her parents had *finally* gotten it together, so she and Keri were flying to Montana in two days.

When they came into the house, Grandma handed him and DeeDee plates piled with mini-pizzas. "I knew you'd be hungry and dinner will be later than planned. Your grandfather got tied up helping an old client."

"Yummalicious," DeeDee said.

Elizabeth smiled. "Thank you. Why don't you watch the baseball game?"

In the family room, DeeDee plopped down on the couch, grabbed the remote and put on the game.

Alex shoved a bite of cheese pizza into his mouth. It tasted great, but he missed pepperoni. When he got back to Seattle he might have to start eating meat, no matter what jokes Brant and Dad made.

After a while DeeDee got quiet, and Alex didn't think it was because the Mariners were getting their butts kicked by the White Sox. It made him nervous.

"Okay, what gives?" he asked during the seventh-inning stretch. "You're acting all wacky, looking at me sideways and stuff."

"Nothing."

"As if I buy that. Your face looks the way it did the time you took my bike without asking and mashed up the front wheel. So?"

"I just… Did you feel left out when…" She stopped and chewed her bottom lip. "Did you feel left out when you found out Dad had adopted you?"

Alex shrugged. "Not exactly. He already didn't have any time for me and only cares about Brant."

"Yeah. Same here. Maybe you're lucky to have Jackson."

He stared and wondered what bug she'd gotten in her brain this time.

The Mariners almost managed to pull the game out of the trash can but finally lost in the bottom of the ninth. DeeDee still had the remote and put on a cartoon Alex didn't care about, so he went to find his mom.

"Something up?" she asked.

"Yeah…no. I mean…could we go for a walk?"

Her eyebrows rose. "Sure," she agreed, exchanging a look with Grandma. "Not a long one, though. Dinner is almost ready."

KAYLA SET OFF with Alex and waited for him to say something.

"Mom, DeeDee just asked me something strange," he said after they'd walked several blocks. "She wanted to know if I felt left out when I found out about being adopted."

"Did you?" she asked.

"No, I was mostly mad because no one told me. DeeDee says maybe I'm lucky to have Jackson, but I don't feel lucky."

"You might, someday."

"I dunno, but I thought you should know about DeeDee. Something's bugging her." Alex turned and watched a passing truck, his face more grown-up and sad than she'd ever seen it. "I miss the way we used to be, back before Dad split."

Kayla let out a painful breath, wishing there was some way to make things easier. "So do I. There's no going back, but that doesn't mean the future can't also be good."

"I guess not."

They returned to the Garrison house in silence while Kayla fretted about her daughter. DeeDee was the one who usually charged ahead, with less introspection. She cared, but she moved so fast she didn't always slow down to think things through. But what she'd said to her brother made Kayla want to kick herself. She'd worried so much about Alex and her mixed feelings about Jackson that she might have missed something with DeeDee.

After dinner, she went up to the attic bedroom and sat on the bed with her daughter. "Alex told me you asked about how he felt about your dad adopting him."

DeeDee rolled onto her stomach. "I just wondered."

"Any special reason?"

"Nah, just curious."

"Maybe it's more than that. How are you feeling about everything here in Montana? I mean, we've gone to a family picnic where Alex met his birth father's parents. We spend time at the ranch where he has a sister who isn't directly related to you. And tomorrow afternoon we're having a gathering where he'll meet aunts and uncles and other family."

DeeDee squirmed around to kick off her sneakers and scratch her toe. Kayla waited. It was unusual for her daughter to think first and talk second, but both her kids had been doing unusual things lately.

"Uh…" DeeDee said finally. "It's like…Alex has a whole new chance to have a dad who cares about him instead of *our* dad, who's a jerk a bunch of the time."

A jerk? Kayla flinched. She'd suspected DeeDee was angry with her father but had never heard her call him names. "Is that how you think of your father?"

"Sometimes." The word was mumbled. "He spends all his time with Brant, the way he did with Rosa and Willie before that. He only cares about us when he doesn't have someone new around."

After she spoke, DeeDee buried her face in her pillow.

Kayla's throat ached with suppressed emotion. She couldn't deny that Curtis was a troubled person. Lately she'd begun wondering if it was because of his years as a foster child. He'd been one of those kids who regularly got moved from place to place. At each new home he would court the new family, trying to ingratiate himself so *this* time he wouldn't be sent away. Maybe after a while it had become a game. He'd expected to leave after a certain amount of time and had started anticipating what he would need to do at the next place to make them like him. That kind of childhood wouldn't prepare anyone for staying in a long-term relationship.

"Your dad loves you, DeeDee," she assured gently. "He just gets easily distracted by problems that have nothing to do with you or Alex."

DeeDee looked unhappy for a moment, then shrugged as if she'd tucked the feeling away. "Okay."

"So what about everything here in Montana? How do you feel about that?"

"Uh…well, Morgan is awesome, but I'm just the little kid who tags along. And even though the McGregors are nice to me, it's *Alex* they want to know. Maybe Jackson's family will think I shouldn't be at the party tomorrow night."

Hell. Belatedly Kayla realized she should have expected something of the sort. Her daughter was strong and bold, but no one was invulnerable.

"I think the McGregors will be happy you're there," she said. "They're a nice family and probably want to meet the people Alex cares about."

"I guess."

"And as for Morgan and Alex, you know I never had any brothers or sisters. But I'm sure older kids *do* enjoy spending time on their own, the same way you sometimes enjoy being with Keri and not having Alex around, right?"

"Keri says her big sister is always calling her a squirt—just like Alex calls me—and tells her to get lost."

"That doesn't mean they don't care about each other," Kayla pointed out. "And I'll bet her sister would love to see Montana, but Keri gets to come because you're friends."

DeeDee brightened as she nodded in agreement. Kayla tugged the end of her daughter's thick braid. "There's always give-and-take in a family. You've been very understanding about everything going on here in Montana, but Alex cares about you, too. That's why he told me you might be upset about something."

Alex stuck his head through the door. "Yeah, you may be a squirt, but you're *my* squirt."

"Alex, you shouldn't be eavesdropping," Kayla scolded him mildly.

"I just got here, so I didn't hear that much."

"It's okay," DeeDee said.

"You can be a pain," Alex told her, "but you'll always be my 'oldest' sister."

DeeDee giggled.

Kayla smiled at her daughter. "If you don't want

to go to the family gathering tomorrow evening, we can—"

"*I* want her to come," Alex interrupted quickly. "Okay, DeeDee?"

DeeDee grinned. "Sure."

MORGAN OPENED THE Facebook message from Alex. He said that DeeDee was worried people thought she was in the way.

She knew how DeeDee felt. It was crummy to feel as if someone wished you weren't there.

Grabbing her cell phone, she texted DeeDee and asked if she and Alex wanted to go on a ride before the grown-ups got there and outnumbered the kids. She didn't want DeeDee to feel bad or left out.

DeeDee texted back: Can we go 2 HMdow?

Yes. CU.

One of the things Morgan liked about DeeDee was how much she loved Halloran's Meadow. Alex thought it was fun, but Morgan didn't think he understood how she felt when she sat and listened to the water falling and the breeze rustling through the quaking aspens.

The first time they'd gone to the meadow together, she'd gotten out of the pool and sat staring at a wildflower, feeling mellow in the sun and wondering if the door to another world could be nearby...maybe behind her, or to the left or right.

And if she stepped *through* the door, there was a chance she might find hobbits or elves or unicorns.

After a few minutes, DeeDee had dropped down next to her and whispered, "I like it this way, but I wish I could come sometime in the rain. It's the kind of place where fairies might wash their hair."

Morgan had opened her eyes wide. Could DeeDee have read her mind?

"It's great in the rain," she'd whispered back.

Then DeeDee had looked embarrassed. "Don't tell Alex I said something about fairies. He might tease."

Morgan knew how DeeDee had felt. Alex was a geek who loved *Star Trek*, but he was still a guy, and guys didn't always understand. Besides, it would feel silly talking about fairies and unicorns out loud—she sure couldn't tell any of her new buddies from the past year about the things she imagined. They'd laugh their heads off.

Another message came from Alex; he'd forgotten to tell her Sandy was coming in a couple of days. Morgan didn't know what to think about that. It had been nice having him and DeeDee to herself.

They wouldn't be in Montana for much longer, then they were going home. Morgan didn't want to think about it.

THE NEXT MORNING Morgan got back from her run and slumped into a chair in the kitchen. How could

Kayla do it alone every day? It was much more fun running with her.

Her dad came in from the ranch office. He was looking at some papers but set them aside when he saw her at the table.

"Still running, I see," he said.

"Yeah," she mumbled.

"You took Cory?"

"As if I could stop him from coming."

His jaw tightened. "Morgan, can't you talk to me like a normal person?"

"Jeez, sorry for disappointing you."

"I didn't say you disappointed me."

"That's what you meant," she muttered.

Her dad rubbed his forehead. "Morgan, do you miss your mom? Is that the reason for this attitude? Tell you what, I'll call her and ask her to come for a visit."

The last thing Morgan wanted was her mother coming to Schuyler. "No."

He closed his eyes the way he did when he was angry or didn't want her know what he was thinking. "Do you want to visit her in New York?"

"No, I don't," she almost yelled, the misery swelling up terribly all at once. "I just want someone to be glad I'm around."

Then, afraid of what she'd said, Morgan lunged up and ran outside to the barn. It usually made her feel better to spend time with the Black, but she wasn't sure anything would help now.

JACKSON WATCHED HIS daughter's fast disappearing figure in shock. She wanted someone to be glad she was there?

Hell.

Kayla might be right that Morgan felt unwanted.

In quiet moments he had replayed their discussion over and over in his head, regretting his reaction. He'd asked for Kayla's opinion only to snap like a bad-tempered sidewinder when she'd given it to him. After all, Morgan *had* to question whether her mom really wanted her.

But Kayla had thought Marcy wasn't the problem.

Moodily he stared out the window. Perhaps he should discuss it with Kayla again. After yesterday she might not be very friendly, but he'd have to take his chances.

Her Volvo arrived midmorning. Alex and DeeDee tumbled from the car and dashed into the house.

"Alex, DeeDee," Kayla called. "You knock and wait."

Jackson looked into the foyer and saw her hovering at the open door.

"Why don't we say that from now on, Alex and DeeDee have open-door privileges," he suggested, not wanting to point out that his own son shouldn't have to knock. "I think Morgan is in the barn, guys."

"Is it okay if we go for a ride?" DeeDee asked equally of Jackson and her mother.

"Kayla?" Jackson asked. He wanted a chance to talk but didn't want to sound eager for the kids to be gone.

"Sure."

"Check with Flora, DeeDee," he suggested. "She should have trail mix and other snacks. Water, too."

DeeDee ran into the kitchen, Alex following more slowly. A few minutes later they came out with a sack.

"Have a good time," Jackson told them. "Oh, wait, I'll get a satellite phone for you." He got it from the office and handed it Alex, who smiled more naturally than usual.

"Thanks, Jackson."

Once they were gone, Jackson looked at Kayla. "How about a drive? There's something I'd like to discuss."

Her lips tightened, then she shrugged. "Okay."

He drove his pickup to a favorite viewpoint and sat staring at the landscape.

"I don't want to talk about yesterday, if that's what you have in mind," Kayla said, breaking the silence.

He shook his head. "Let's just treat what happened as an anomaly."

"Anomaly? Thanks for the compliment."

"I can't seem to stop putting my foot in my mouth, can I?"

Kayla shrugged. "Maybe it *was* an anomaly. Coming to Montana has been a huge shake-up and I'm still sorting myself out. And you obviously haven't had one of your casual dates for a while."

"What do you know about my dating habits, casual or not?"

"Are you kidding?" she asked with a laugh. "Between my grandmother, who hears gossip at the local beauty parlor, and what I've heard in town myself, you've made quite a name for yourself."

Perplexed, Jackson stared at her. "I didn't know I had a reputation any longer."

"Everyone has a reputation—good, bad or indifferent. But is this really what you came out here to discuss?"

"No. Something happened and I wanted to see what you thought about it." He hesitated. "The thing is, you may be right about Morgan feeling that she's not wanted."

He expected Kayla to crow and tell him she'd told him so, but Morgan mattered more than his pride.

Kayla just shook her head. "That poor kid."

"This morning Morgan actually said she wanted someone to be glad she's around. I can't believe I didn't pick up on it sooner."

"We all miss things. Last night I discovered DeeDee is worried Alex's new relationships might leave her out. She doesn't know how she fits in here. I should have guessed she'd have mixed feelings about what's happened, but I was too focused on Alex to see it."

Jackson smiled grimly. "It may not be possible for parents to think of everything, but that isn't much comfort when your child is ready to self-destruct."

KAYLA FELT BAD for Jackson. He was so proud, it would have taken a lot to make him confide in her.

"What did Morgan say when you talked at Yellowstone?" he asked. "Any specifics would help."

"It was mostly an impression—little bits of things that reminded me of how I felt knowing my mom didn't want me around a lot of the time, except when she needed to show me to the welfare people."

"Marcy hasn't been much of a mother, but I couldn't imagine my life without Morgan."

Kayla shifted in the seat. "Have you ever talked about her mom already being pregnant when you got married?"

"She knows, but it hardly seems necessary to discuss it further."

"Jackson, if you do anything, learn from what *I* did wrong with Alex. Talk to Morgan about what happened with her mother."

Jackson scowled. "We've *had* the discussion about safe sex. I didn't enjoy it, but we covered the subject."

A grin pulled at Kayla's mouth. "I don't mean the

birds-and-the-bees lecture. Tell Morgan you love her, and that even if you made mistakes, you've never regretted her being born. That's what I've been doing with Alex."

Jackson's scowl deepened. "You think Morgan believes Marcy and me having to get married means she wasn't wanted?"

"I don't know, but she may have gotten the idea somewhere. Frankly, if Morgan feeling unwanted *isn't* about Marcy being an absentee mother, it most likely has something to do with you."

His fingers drummed the steering wheel. "I suppose even if something else is bothering Morgan, talking about it might help her open up."

Kayla nodded and they fell silent. For the first time, she paid attention to the view. They'd parked on a rise and she looked down over a green landscape with a breathtaking blue sky arching overhead, a few puffy clouds accentuating the color.

"I always liked Montana," she murmured. "When I first came, I couldn't believe how beautiful it is here."

From the corner of her eyes, she could see Jackson was watching her, not the terrain outside the vehicle.

"You remember my old truck?" he questioned, his voice rough.

"Sure." The close confines of the cab became even more uncomfortable as she thought about the nights when they'd thoroughly steamed the windows of his ancient Chevy pickup. Making the mistake of looking at him, Kayla felt warmth in her stomach that had nothing to do with nostalgia.

He reached out a hand and softly traced the line of her cheek. "You have the most beautiful skin, and your eyes are Montana blue."

Kayla didn't resist when he pulled her into a kiss. She'd dreamed about his caresses the night before, but reality was so much more satisfying. Sliding her fingers through his crisp dark hair, she pulled him even closer. At the moment she didn't care if they were in a truck or a bed. His hands were exploring under her shirt when he groaned and pulled away.

"I don't have a condom with me," Jackson grumbled.

Aching with both unsatisfied need and anger at her weakness a second day in a row, Kayla jerked her clothing into place.

As THE TRUCK bounced over the rough road toward home, Jackson was still gripped by the passion he couldn't seem to contain around Kayla. It couldn't *just* be the influence of heated memories. He had plenty of memories of sex with Marcy, but he felt nothing during the rare times they saw each other. Marcy had even tried to get something going on her last visit, saying she missed his stamina in bed. He'd declined as politely as possible, not wanting her to get angry and retaliate against Morgan.

The irony couldn't be escaped. He'd married the

girl next door, the nice girl his parents would have chosen for him, even if they hadn't appreciated the timing. Yet Marcy had proved as unreliable as a wisp of paper in the wind. Kayla, who'd grown up in some of the worst circumstances possible, had worked hard and never given up, even when she'd been let down by the man she'd loved.

His arousal still pressed painfully against the zipper on his jeans, and he groaned when one wheel dropped into a particularly deep rut in the track.

"A little snug there?" Kayla guessed with a knowing glance. "That'll teach you not to start something you weren't prepared to finish."

"At least you know I didn't bring you out here with ulterior motives."

"There are pluses and minuses to everything, but it looks as if you could do with a little less plus."

A pained laugh escaped Jackson.

Kayla had never been coy about sex, but thinking back, he realized she hadn't been experienced, either, which made his teenage accusations about her sleeping around even more offensive.

What would his life have been like if he'd married Kayla instead of Marcy all those years ago?

Jackson firmly dismissed the thought. It probably wouldn't have worked any better with Kayla—they still would have been too young, with too much responsibility. He'd liked Kayla best—her sense of humor and different ideas had fascinated him—but they hadn't been in love. Then again, she'd gone on to marry someone she did genuinely love, and that had still ended badly.

It was all just the luck of the draw.

CHAPTER FOURTEEN

BACK AT THE house Jackson found his ranch hands were busy setting up the backyard for the barbecue. The McGregors and his mom's branch of the family, the Nelsons, had so many family gatherings he'd purchased a forty-foot awning to use on the grassy area to one side of the swimming pool. It was already in place and his men were bringing out tables and chairs from storage.

"How many people are you expecting?" Kayla asked.

"The Garrisons will be here, along with the five of us, plus my mom and dad, my brothers and sisters, and assorted aunts and uncles, including Great-Uncle Mitch and two of my great-aunts. Also all four of my—"

Kayla held up her hand in a whoa gesture. "I don't think Alex will remember many of their names, much less get to know them all at one time."

"Of course not, but this is mostly a welcome gathering." He frowned. "Do you think it's too much? They're anxious to meet Alex, but I don't want to freak him out."

She didn't answer right away, her face thoughtful. "It should be fine if it's only a general welcome. Alex isn't used to having extended family, but he'll have to get accustomed to it, either now or later."

Jackson was beginning to recognize Kayla's pattern of trying to balance between protecting her children and letting them be challenged.

"How about DeeDee?" he asked.

"I told her she didn't have to attend, but she liked it when Alex said he wanted her to be here."

Jackson was pleased; he'd become fond of the sassy youngster and would have missed her.

As for his son? Kayla was right. Love didn't come automatically because of a common gene pool, but he had grown to love Alex.

KAYLA WENT INSIDE to help Flora, but instead was handed a plate of thick ham-and-cheese sandwiches.

"Everything is in hand," the housekeeper told her briskly. "Eat lunch and put your feet up. It's hours yet before dinner."

Smiling, Kayla went outside to sit in the shade by the pool. The sandwiches were delicious, made with crusty bread and a tangy gourmet mustard, but she couldn't manage more than one. Flora must think she had the appetite of a lumberjack.

A light breeze moderated the heat, but on the opposite side of the pool, Kayla saw Jackson and his men setting up an industrial-size evaporative cooler near the awning. It was similar to the type she'd once seen at a greenhouse in California and would make the gathering more enjoyable should the afternoon temperatures become intense.

The cowhands nodded to her courteously, tipping their hats like gentlemen from a Gary Cooper Western. They'd been unfailingly polite, watching their language around her and DeeDee and rushing to offer assistance if they thought there was the slightest need.

Perhaps on a ranch, near an isolated town like Schuyler, it was understandable that men were gender biased. Schuyler didn't even have an airport with commercial flights, just an airfield the ranchers used if they didn't have a landing strip of their own. It would be a two-hour drive into Billings the next day just to meet Sandy and Keri at the airport.

Jackson thanked his men as they finished by rolling in a large barbecue unit. Kayla wrinkled her nose—they loved barbecuing in Schuyler, and it was hard on her vegetarian son. If his pride hadn't been on the line, she was certain he would have already succumbed to temptation.

"Have something to drink," Jackson said, setting a huge ice chest near her chaise. Inside was a wide variety of sodas and fruit juices packed in ice.

"Thanks. And please eat the rest of those sandwiches so Flora isn't insulted." She opened a bottle of cranberry juice and gestured toward the awning. "I've seen professional events with less polish."

"The family likes coming here because the pool

is even larger than the one my parents built, so it made sense to get the right equipment to be comfortable," he explained between bites of ham and cheese. "Officially we're starting around five, but some will arrive earlier to swim or play volleyball or whatever. Great-Uncle Mitch and my two grandfathers are addicted to tossing horseshoes, so they'll head for the horseshoe pit."

"Obviously the Nelsons and McGregors like to both work and play hard."

"You haven't seen much evidence that *I* work hard the past few weeks," Jackson said with a rueful grimace. "Believe me, this is a busy season on the ranch and I'm normally charging around fourteen hours a day."

"I believe you. I don't think your men would respect you so much if you didn't work alongside them," Kayla murmured.

He almost seemed embarrassed by the compliment. "Thanks. Uh, how about a game while we're waiting?"

A tall stack of board games had been carried from the pool house and they pulled out an old classic, Scrabble. She laughed when he tried to score with ridiculous combinations, claiming DeeDee as his inspiration.

Yet inevitably she tensed as the family began arriving and Jackson introduced her as Alex's mother. She lifted her chin. There was nothing to be uncomfortable about—she was a successful professional with two great children, not the scared, pregnant teenager who'd fled Schuyler.

The kids returned from their ride shortly after three and Alex seemed to take meeting everyone in stride. DeeDee stuck close and got introduced along with him.

It was curious watching the group shift and talk and laugh. When her grandparents and Uncle Peter arrived, they joined in comfortably and Kayla relaxed. She'd memorized the family chart that Parker McGregor had provided for Alex and now tried to put faces and names together. Jackson's younger brother, Josh, looked like their father, and so did his sister, Madison. His brother-cousin, Trent, couldn't come after all, but Trent's sister, Alaina, had made it. Ordinarily Alaina worked in New York, but she said she was moving back to Montana soon.

With her digital camera Kayla quietly took portraits and entered the names so Alex would have a pictorial directory to use as a reference.

She was puzzling over a couple of photos, unsure she'd gotten them right, when a shadow fell across the table. It was Sarah McGregor.

"Is there something wrong?" Sarah asked, sitting down.

"No, I was just trying to attach the right names to the faces in my camera. Is this Jackson's greataunt Sally?"

She showed the picture to Sarah, who nodded. "Yes, that's Sally."

"Then, the other one has to be Great-Aunt Moira." To be sure, she showed that shot to Sarah as well, who agreed.

"What a nice idea. It'll make getting to know the family so much easier for Alex."

"That's what I thought."

An awkward silence followed as Sarah fiddled with the bracelet on her left wrist. "Kayla," she said finally, "I want to tell you how bad we feel about everything."

Kayla gave her a noncommittal smile, not sure what the other woman was trying to say.

"We've realized we didn't treat you well when you were dating Jackson," Sarah continued. "They say hindsight is twenty-twenty, but it's painful to see your mistakes so clearly. I just wish we could have helped. You must have had a hard time as a young, single mother."

"I managed," Kayla replied firmly.

"From what Jackson has told us, you've made a huge success of your life. But you shouldn't have had to do it alone, and that's partly our fault."

With a shrug, Kayla took a photo of Alex and DeeDee with Morgan. There weren't many other kids present, though a cousin had arrived with a couple of toddlers.

"It's in the past," she said at length. "I'm glad Alex has the opportunity to know you now."

Sarah leaned forward. "You're very generous. I want to say… Well, we know we were wrong to have any questions about you. Alex is fortunate to have you as his mother. DeeDee, too, of course. She's a delightful young lady."

The sincerity in her voice was unmistakable, and Kayla decided to accept her apology without trying to look for hidden messages that probably weren't there.

"Hey, Mom, it's my turn to grill Kayla," Madison McGregor announced, walking up to the table. She plopped into a chair and winked at Kayla.

"Don't you *dare* do anything of the kind," Sarah ordered.

"Okay, but go away. I want to dish on the family skeletons."

Sarah gave her daughter an exasperated look. "I'll go, but don't scare Kayla off. She should see us on our best behavior at least *once*."

When they were alone, Madison grinned. "I figured you needed a break. Mom can be rather intense when she has a guilty conscience."

Though Kayla was secretly grateful for Madison's intervention, she'd never admit it.

"I remember you from high school," Madison continued. "You were so much more interesting than the other girls—you didn't even dress like the clones."

"The clones?"

"Yeah, the popular girls." Madison made a gagging gesture. "You know, the Stepford students. They could be vicious if you weren't part of their circle. But I have to forgive Jackson for chasing after them—he's a guy and couldn't see past their cup size."

"To be honest, I didn't know *how* to fit in," Kayla explained. Feeling like an outsider had bothered her as a kid, but gradually she'd recognized the students she most disliked were the ones who fit in the best, so she'd decided conforming was overrated.

"I thought you were cool and I was *really* glad when you and Jackson started going out. For a while after he broke up with Marcy he had so many girlfriends, I figured he was going for a record." Then Madison added candidly, "Of course, I'm not sure he isn't headed for a record now."

"So I've heard," Kayla said, trying to make it sound as if she didn't care one way or the other.

Madison made a disgusted face. "Much as I hate to admit it, my brother can be a jackass when it comes to women. But he's a good dad," she added hastily, "so you can feel okay about him and Alex."

Unsure how to respond, Kayla just nodded. She was getting the idea that Madison and Alaina weren't at ease with Jackson, which was odd since the McGregors were such a close-knit clan. Kayla didn't know how deep Jackson's chauvinism went, but between that, his reputation for one-night stands and his distrust of women, it had to be a stumbling block for his sisters.

Kayla glanced at Jackson as he and his father debated whether the hickory wood coals were ready in the barbecue. They were laughing, despite the mock argument, and a curious sensation went through her. The adult Jackson *had* become a good person, who truly wanted to do what was best for his son, even if he didn't always know what that might be.

Damn.

She was starting to like him.

Resolutely, Kayla turned her attention back to Madison in time to see the other woman spill cola on her legs.

"Oh, dear, I'll be back." Madison got up and headed for the pool house.

Kayla was grateful for a quiet moment and focused on her children. Now that Alex had gotten over his initial anxiety about Jackson, he seemed happy about their extended stay in Montana, especially now that Sandy was coming for a visit. DeeDee appeared equally pleased, especially with the welcome she'd received that day from the McGregors and Nelsons.

Unfortunately, Kayla didn't share their feelings. She wasn't a quitter, but what she felt around Jackson was making her more uneasy by the minute.

AFTER HER RUN the next morning, Morgan sat and watched the big TV in the family room, stewing. She missed running with Kayla, who'd offered to join her sometime, but today she was taking Alex and DeeDee to pick up their friends at the airport in Billings.

Heaving a sigh, Morgan thought about calling some of her own friends, but didn't feel like it. She didn't feel like doing much of anything.

"What's up?" her dad asked, coming into the room.

"Nothing," she muttered. It was stupid to say stuff she *knew* made him mad, but she couldn't seem to stop.

"Can we turn off the TV?"

Crap. He wanted to have one of his little talks and they usually made her feel worse. Slowly she pressed the power button on the television remote. She glanced at him. Jeez, the last time he'd gotten so serious, it was when he'd explained to her about Alex.

"Morgan, honey," he said, "I've told you I made a lot of mistakes when I was in high school."

"That's what you said when you told me about Alex," she said flippantly. "So we've already had this chat."

"And you know that your mother was expecting you when the two of us got married."

She froze. "Uh, yeah."

"I've been wondering if you have any questions?"

Sure, she had plenty. Like, did he hate her because he couldn't go to college because he had to get married? She hunched her shoulders and stared at the floor.

"You wouldn't have married Mom if it hadn't been for me, would you?"

"Honestly, no. It's been hard to talk about because I didn't want to admit we weren't in love. But now I've realized there's something important you need to know."

He paused and Morgan gulped, butterflies jumping in her stomach. His face was so serious, she was afraid she knew what was coming.

"It was a mistake to have been so careless back then," he said, "but you were a gift that came out of that mistake, and I've always been grateful."

Morgan tried to ignore how her eyes were stinging. What he'd said was *so* nice, but she might as well ask the big question. "But…what if…what if I'm not your daughter?"

"*Lord*, why would you ask that?" he asked, and she was pretty sure he was surprised.

"Because I don't look like you the way Alex does."

"That doesn't mean anything. I don't look like Grandma and Grandpa, but nobody thinks I'm not their son."

"It's just that I…I heard Mom slept around. *A lot*." There. The horrible words were out of her mouth. Maybe now she'd know the truth. She had felt lower than a snake's belly ever since she'd overheard Aunt Madison talking about it with Grandma last summer.

Her dad's eyes closed for a second and she noticed his fists clenched until the skin turned white over his knuckles. Finally he looked at her again and came over to sit on the couch, pulling her close.

"Sweetheart, I wouldn't care one bit if I wasn't your birth father."

She pulled back and looked into his face. "For real?"

"Absolutely for real." He squeezed her hand. "Morgan, I hadn't realized you'd heard those things about your mother, but as far as I know, she was faithful until the year before we got divorced."

"I don't get why she acted that way."

"Well, I know she was unhappy, and it was partly my fault. You see, while Great-Uncle Mitch always expected to give me the Crazy Horse, it was supposed to be after I graduated college. He got worried I wasn't responsible enough to trust with the ranch, so we worked out a plan that included me living on a cowhand's earnings for several years."

"I bet Mom was *thrilled* about that."

"To be fair, I realize now that I should have talked it over with her first."

Morgan didn't think it would have made any difference. Her mom liked money. *A lot*. She kind of remembered when they'd lived in a small house.

After that they'd had a bigger one in town, and then they'd moved into this new place on the ranch.

"Dad, do you think Mom cheated on you in high school?"

"No. But if you're still wondering if we're related biologically, I can tell you that you look exactly like Great-Aunt Moira did at your age."

"Really?"

"Sure. You could be twins. I thought you'd seen Grandma Sarah's family album."

"Not for a while."

"Then, check it out. Just remember that it doesn't matter. You're my daughter. Did you know that the only thing I insisted on when your mother and I got divorced was getting custody? I couldn't bear the thought of her taking you away."

Suddenly Morgan threw her arms around her dad's neck and it felt the same as when she was a little girl.

JACKSON HELD HIS daughter tight, grateful for the kick in the pants that Kayla had given him. It would take time to deal with all the feelings Morgan had been struggling with, but at least they'd made a start.

"Come on," he said. "It's been ages since we've gone for a ride together. Let's go to Halloran's Meadow."

"Can we get in the waterfall?"

"If we have enough time."

"I'll go change." Bouncing up, she ran out of the room.

The ride went well and they were back before the others were expected. At two o'clock, the Volvo stopped in front of the house and Alex and DeeDee piled out with their two friends. Morgan was quickly introduced and they chattered away before running to change into their bathing suits.

"Rough drive?" Jackson asked Kayla, seeing her harried expression.

"Two hours with four kids who haven't seen each other for almost a month? You'd have thought it was years. I don't think any of them stopped talking the entire way."

"You'd better sit down and relax."

Together they walked to the backyard and found Morgan and the others were already at the pool's edge, barely containing their excitement.

"They're quick-change artists," Kayla said at his bewildered stare. "Superheroes in training."

"Apparently."

She sank onto a redwood chaise in the shade and put her feet up as a noisy game of water volleyball began between the five youngsters. "Morgan seems happier," she murmured, "or is that my imagination?"

"We talked this morning," Jackson replied in an equally low voice. "Apparently she'd learned about Marcy's bed-hopping and was afraid it meant she might not be my daughter."

"No wonder she was upset."

"Right. Marcy's cheating was the final blow to our marriage, but I don't think she played around in high school. Not that I'd give a damn if Morgan wasn't biologically mine. She's had me wrapped around her little finger since the day she was born."

"Ah, you were one of those goofy, weak-kneed new daddies. Love doesn't depend on biology," Kayla said. "When you love someone, it isn't about half sisters or brothers or about being an in-law or adopted."

She stretched and Jackson decided it was safer to focus on the pool rather than her trim figure and long legs.

"I meant to ask if you and the kids were hungry," he said.

"We ate in Billings after the plane landed," Kayla explained. "DeeDee hoped to go swimming as soon as we got back and remembered your one-hour rule."

"That rule frustrates Morgan, too. How about getting in the pool yourself?" he asked. "I can keep an eye on things while you change."

"Thanks."

As Kayla went into the pool house, Jackson thought about the past few weeks. She was pushing him to look at things in ways he'd never considered. How many mistakes had he made through the years, trying to make up for his past? And how much had he missed along the way because of it?

Maybe it was time to just concentrate on being the man he wanted to be.

Of course, the sight of Kayla walking out in her black one-piece was a reminder that the man he wanted to be remained bedeviled by hormones.

AT FIVE O'CLOCK Jackson headed into the house. Flora had gone to dinner and a movie with her sister, but she'd left fajita makings in the refrigerator. He started the gas barbecue on the patio and put two griddles over the grill. Soon the scent of seasoned meat and vegetables wafted through the air and he grinned when the kids appeared as if drawn by a magnet.

"That smells fantabulous," DeeDee breathed.

Fantabulous was one of her favorite words, being a relatively recent addition to the English language. She'd proudly showed him it wasn't in his older dictionary, but had been included in a newer one used by Morgan. Her dream was to have the same thing happen with some of her own words.

"Can we help?" Sandy Keller asked, prodding Alex with an elbow so he stepped forward, as well.

"Sure, you can get the sour cream and other toppings in the fridge," Jackson replied.

He tossed a mixture of soy chicken and veggies on the second grill, impressed with his son's taste in best friends. Sandy Keller was smart, lively and unafraid to voice her opinions. It was also clear that the two friends were on the verge of becoming something more.

"How can you resist this?" Sandy asked twenty minutes later, waving a plate piled with steak, peppers and onions under Alex's nose. "Don't be too stubborn to admit you want some."

Alex made a face. "Okay," he grumbled, "I'll have a *little*."

Jackson swallowed a laugh. Curious, he scooped some of the grilled protein substitute and vegetables onto a tortilla and ate a bite. The taste was pleasant and the texture wasn't bad.

"What do you think?" Alex asked.

"It's all right. I wouldn't mind eating it part of the time."

"Yeah, but DeeDee is right about pepperoni pizza. No pepperoni is the *worst*," Alex said vehemently.

"Don't they make a soy substitute?"

"Mom hasn't found one I like. You know, she's been pretty cool about the vegetarian thing."

"That must have helped," Jackson said, secretly thrilled. It was the closest thing to a normal conversation he'd ever shared with Alex.

KAYLA TRIED NOT to watch Morgan interacting with Alex and DeeDee and their friends, not wanting to make her uncomfortable. It must have been awful for her, worrying about whether Jackson was really her dad, and if he'd still love her if he wasn't.

Sometimes Kayla wondered how anyone survived adolescence.

The fajitas were delicious, but Jackson shrugged off her compliments, saying Flora had left everything ready for the grill. Apparently despite his decided chauvinistic tendencies, he didn't have a problem with cooking himself...as long as it was over a fire.

You're buying into the stereotypes you hate, Kayla scolded herself, though she'd only seen him with barbecue utensils in hand. Of course, since he had the money to hire a housekeeper, being able to cook wasn't a big deal.

"Can we go for a ride tomorrow?" Keri asked. "I know how."

"Sandy rides, too," Alex added. "Is that okay, Jackson?"

Jackson glanced at Kayla and she nodded. "Their parents told me it was fine."

"Okay," he said. "We have more than enough horses."

The next morning Kayla saw how carefully Jackson evaluated how comfortable the two newcomers were on the mounts he'd selected for them. He finally seemed satisfied and waved them out.

Being alone with Jackson again made her uneasy considering what they'd done the *last* time, so she walked to a chaise under a tree in the front yard and settled down with a book.

"Trying to avoid me?" Jackson asked as he dragged a chair next to her.

"Trying to avoid repeating mistakes," she told him bluntly.

"Oh, well, I wanted to ask you something. That is, Sandy isn't quite what I expected."

Kayla raised her eyebrows at him. "What did you expect?"

"I don't know. You talked about them being best friends and Sandy being forthright on feminist issues, so I figured she'd be more of a tomboy."

"You mean a kid with no chest, wearing jeans and a striped T-shirt?" Yet instead of being annoyed that Jackson had pigeonholed Sandy based on a few innocent comments, Kayla thought it was funny. A whole lot of things were getting turned upside down for him.

"Yeah, I suppose. It's just that Sandy is smart and pretty and I…uh…it looks as if she and Alex could become *more* than buddies."

"That's no secret, except maybe to them."

"Well, I know you must have discussed the facts of life with Alex, but maybe I should say something as his father."

A smile tugged at her mouth. "Or maybe not. While you're getting along better, I doubt either one of you is ready for that. But don't worry, I've discussed safe sex with Alex *and* that I hope he waits until he's older. I've also reminded him that protection isn't always a hundred percent. After all, that's how he got here."

"Oh." A mix of both relief and chagrin filled Jackson's face. "About that… Maybe I should confess something. The condoms I used when we were in high school might have been a little old."

"Excuse me?"

"I sneaked them out of my parents' bathroom. It didn't occur to me that they stopped needing condoms when I was eight and Mom had a hysterectomy. They were obviously out-of-date, even if I didn't realize it at the time. Do you know how hard it is for a teenage boy to buy condoms in a town the size of Schuyler?"

His shamefaced honesty made her grin. "All things considered, I hope you're using up-to-date protection now."

"Certainly." His eyes darkened and a tingle went through her. She knew exactly what he was thinking about.

Tossing her book aside, she jumped to her feet. "How about riding out and bringing a picnic lunch to the kids? I brought sandwiches since this is Flora's day off."

"Coward," he accused softly.

"No, prudent." She faced him squarely. "I don't want a repeat of the other day, Jackson. We're a Montana rancher and a Seattle businesswoman who once made a baby together. Other than that, we don't much have in common. Our goals and ideas are on opposite poles. So let's try to be on decent terms for Alex's sake and leave it at that."

JACKSON KNEW KAYLA was right, but his body clamored to make love to her until they were senseless.

Hell, he ought to be running the opposite direction. He'd broken his personal rules because of her—no women at the house, and no sex with a woman who might be looking for a husband. Not that Kayla was on the prowl for a spouse, but she still wasn't the kind of woman he'd socialized with since his divorce.

"Okay, I'll put together some things, and then we'll go," he said.

"Aren't we going to carry it ourselves?" Kayla asked when she saw a third animal waiting patiently under a pack.

"This will be easier, and lets us bring extra water and other supplies."

Riding quickly, they covered the ground to Halloran's Meadow, where they saw the kids playing in the water.

"Hi, Mom," DeeDee yelled. "What are you doing here?"

"We brought food," Kayla called back. "How does a picnic sound?"

"Spectaculous."

"Spectaculous? That isn't a bad one," Jackson murmured to Kayla as they dismounted and tethered their horses.

"Yeah, except someone already came up with it. She was crushed when she found out, though only for a few minutes. It's great having a born optimist in the family."

Jackson could imagine, though he suspected DeeDee's father was a challenge to her natural optimism. He had a curious urge to provide DeeDee with the fatherly support that Curtis Anderson was failing to offer, and promptly broke into a cold sweat at the thought.

"Are you okay?" Kayla asked.

"Uh, yeah. Sure. Are you going into the water?"

"No, I'll just sit in the shade and watch. I didn't bring my swimsuit."

Obviously he couldn't suggest skinny-dipping as an alternative, but Jackson would have loved to see Kayla dancing naked in the waterfall. Years ago, on the same day he'd planned to bring Kayla to Halloran's Meadow for the first time, Marcy's father had come to the house to say she was pregnant.

Everything had changed after that, but looking back, it was probably the day he most regretted missing. While the meadow had been a favorite of the McGregors for over a century, he'd never brought Marcy there, even after they were married...but he *had* wanted to share it with Kayla.

CHAPTER FIFTEEN

THAT NIGHT ALEX found Sandy lying on the backyard lawn, staring up at the sky.

"Hey," he said. "What's up?"

"Nothing. I've just never seen so many stars,
aside from when I was on vacation. They don't
look this way in Seattle. It's awesome."

"I know. I wish you could have come to Yellowstone with us. We slept outside and could look at
the sky all night."

Two streaks of light shot over them toward the
horizon.

"It's harder to see shooting stars in Seattle, too,"
Sandy murmured. "Except when you go away from
the city."

"Yeah. After his last divorce, Dad took DeeDee
and me out near Black Diamond to watch the meteor shower. Instead, we saw the northern lights."

"Yeah, I remember you calling about that. It was
so late my mother nearly had a cow."

Alex laughed. "Sorry."

"Doesn't matter. Mom gets in a twist about all
kinds of junk." Sandy turned on her side to look at
him. "You know, I like your birth dad."

"I guess he isn't that bad." Yet Alex squirmed. In the beginning he'd thought the guy was a jerk, but now he liked Jackson and it made him feel strange. It would be okay if they could just be friends, except it was more mixed-up than that.

"Do you think your mom and him are getting together?" Sandy asked.

Alex bolted upright. *"What?"*

She shrugged. "You know what I mean—they used to date, so they must have liked each other once. Maybe they've started liking each other again."

This wasn't what Alex had imagined at *all* when he'd come to Montana. To meet Mom's family, yeah. And since Grandma and Grandpa were terrific, that part of running away had worked out fine.

"I don't think Mom likes Jackson," he said. "A lot of the time she's really uptight around him."

"Maybe, but there's something about how they look at each other, or the way they look *away* from each other, if you get what I mean. It sure makes me wonder."

Alex hunched his shoulders and stared miserably at the house. His mom *couldn't* fall for Jackson, could she? That would screw up everything.

"I'm going in for a minute," he told Sandy.

He found his mother at her laptop computer in the family room, typing an email. "Hey."

She clicked Send and smiled at him. "I was just letting Roger know when to expect me back."

"He must need you real bad," Alex said.

His mom frowned. "What's up, kiddo? You wanted to stay longer, and now it sounds as if you're anxious to head home."

"No, but we're still leaving in a few days, aren't we?"

"That's the plan. Sandy's and Keri's folks are expecting us and we've got to start your back-to-school shopping. I know you aren't crazy about trying on clothes, but it has to be done."

Alex relaxed. "That's okay. So you and Jackson aren't, like, hooking up?"

It had to be his imagination, but even though his mom laughed, her face seemed sort of sad.

"No, we have different lives, in different states." Her eyes narrowed. "What brought all this up?"

"Sandy wondered. I thought she was full of hot air, but decided to ask anyhow."

"I see. Does the idea of me being interested in someone bother you? Someday, I mean."

He made a face. "I don't know."

"You know you can talk to me, about anything, right?"

"Sure."

Alex trudged outside and dropped down next to Sandy. "You're wrong," he announced, "Mom and Jackson aren't hooking up because they live in different states and we're going home soon."

"That doesn't mean she isn't interested."

"You're nuts."

"Okay," Sandy told him. "You know her best."

The problem was, Alex wasn't sure he *did* know his mom that well.

KAYLA SIGNED OUT of her email and sat thinking. She *had* to be more careful. She and Jackson might be sending subconscious signals if Sandy was already wondering if something was going on between them.

What if Morgan started wondering the same thing? It was hard to guess how she would react, but she'd already had her world kicked upside down by getting an unknown brother, and that was on top of her other problems.

Restless, Kayla went to the window and looked out, a curious melancholy gripping her.

There was no denying that Jackson had shaken her up. She hadn't realized how insular she'd become, falling into the habit of getting through the days, running when the pain got bad and trying to do the right things to protect her family. She'd convinced herself that they were doing all right, but obviously they hadn't been.

Now, though some things were better, others were more jumbled than ever. She wasn't proud of having gone to bed with Jackson, but at the same time, it had been an affirmation that she was alive.

Kayla sighed.

It might be good for Alex and DeeDee to see her happy with someone, but Jackson wasn't the right man. He no longer believed in love; in fact, she had no idea if he'd *ever* believed in it, while she had a healthy respect for its awesome power. Her problem was being unsure about taking the risk again.

A shiver went across Kayla's shoulders as she remembered Curtis asking for a divorce. Her world had fallen apart that day.

Drifting into the living room, she saw her grandparents working on a jigsaw puzzle. It was easy to spend time with them; they didn't insist on constant attention and understood the need to help Alex become acquainted with Jackson.

Grams looked up and smiled. "Get your emails done, dear?"

"Yes, but it's humbling to realize my company is doing so well without me."

Hank nodded. "Sometimes our best work makes us redundant."

"I never thought of it that way." Kayla laughed. "Come to think of it, that's probably a good job description for parents. You want your kids to become strong and independent and not need you for everything."

"And when you succeed, you wonder why you wanted it so badly," Elizabeth said. "It's obviously a cosmic joke."

"Too true."

Kayla sat down and pulled several blue puzzle

pieces toward her; the sky had always been her favorite part to do on a jigsaw.

"It's wonderful to be with you again," she said. "I'm sorry I didn't trust you or myself enough to come back before."

"Hey, stop that," Grams admonished. "We agreed, no regrets. We've got the future to think about."

"Does that mean you'll visit us in Seattle sometimes? We'll come here, too, but it'll be hard during the school year."

"You couldn't keep us away."

Underneath the table, Kayla knew, her grandparents were holding hands. She couldn't suppress another stab of melancholy...and the wish to be holding hands with Jackson, perhaps walking under the stars and stopping for a long, sweet kiss. Pure romance. Except it had never been that way with him; with Jackson, any romance was just foreplay.

Stupid.

She wasn't in love with the guy; she just had a mild case of lust. Years ago she'd recovered from a teenager's crush on Jackson, and she could certainly recuperate from this.

"Take the next left," Jackson told Kayla.

She was driving and he was directing her through the country roads from the Crazy Horse to his parents' spread. He'd expected to take his pickup, but the Volvo was already loaded with the kids' extra clothing and other things they'd wanted for a sleepover.

Morgan and the others were riding their horses over to the Rocking M, and the silence in the Volvo made Jackson distinctly uncomfortable.

"And then the next right," he said. "It leads straight to the house."

His folks had planned another barbecue at their home, though it was a smaller gathering than the one at his place. After that the kids were spending the night in the backyard to watch a partial lunar eclipse, his father being the closest thing to an astronomy expert they had in Schuyler.

Kayla parked under a huge black cottonwood tree and Jackson watched her stare, expressionless, at the home where he'd grown up.

"Something wrong?" he asked finally.

She jerked as though startled. "Not really. I was just thinking about the last time I was here. I haven't thought about it in a long time, but I always felt as if I was intruding."

"I should have realized my folks weren't treating you that well."

"Your mother has already apologized. But maybe I let it become too important back then, because I already felt I wasn't good enough."

"I never thought you weren't good enough."

Her head turned. "No, you didn't. I really liked you for that."

Jackson grinned. "Was that the only reason?"

Kayla's lips pressed together a second and he thought there was a spark of laughter in her eyes. "I can't recall," she answered lightly.

"Damn. Try to remember, or I might get an inferiority complex."

"You're *so* in danger of that," she said drily.

"You never know."

"We'll just have to risk it."

Kayla opened her door and climbed out, and he was treated to a terrific view of her tight behind. Letting out a heavy breath, he stepped from the car.

He started pulling the kids' backpacks from the trunk and trotting them into the house.

"Hi, Mom," he called, dropping the last set in the living room and urging Kayla into the kitchen.

Elizabeth Garrison had already arrived, and the two women seemed to be getting along splendidly. He'd known that Elizabeth and Sarah had worked together on community projects, but now that they shared a grandchild, they were becoming fast friends. From the window he saw his father and Hank in an animated discussion on the deck above the pool, complete with gesturing arms and the wide stance of two men on opposite sides of an issue.

"What gives with those two?" Jackson asked.

Elizabeth shook her head. "Lord, they've been arguing the merits of hand-churning ice cream versus an electric churn for the past forty minutes. Why don't you go break it up?"

"No way. They're going to do one of each as a test, right?"

"Naturally."

"Well, if I get involved, they'll recruit me to do the hand churning. That's an adventure I'll leave to the kids."

Elizabeth and Sarah both chuckled.

"It's good to have you here," his mother said to Kayla. Sarah awkwardly pulled her into a hug.

Kayla returned the embrace. Considering her remarks in the car, Jackson figured she'd let go of the past in a way that seemed both gracious and sensible. It also made him uneasy—he'd had trouble doing the same thing.

"When do you think the kids will get here?" Elizabeth asked.

"They left when we did," Kayla explained, "but I wouldn't count on them hurrying."

Sarah laughed. "Then, we won't put anything on the grill until they arrive. We're all set otherwise so just relax and enjoy yourself."

"Let's go for a walk," Jackson suggested to Kayla.

Her hesitation was so slight he didn't think anyone else would have noticed. "Sure, that sounds nice."

Elizabeth and Sarah beamed with approval, and as they walked through the backyard, Hank and Parker waved with equally wide smiles.

"Let's go down to the pond," Jackson murmured.

Kayla's thoughts still seemed to be elsewhere.

and she said nothing as they strolled down the tree-lined path.

"Something on your mind?" he asked finally.

"Yes, but I don't want you to misunderstand."

"What?"

"You saw how happy your folks and my grandparents were when we went for a walk?"

"Uh, yeah," he said, having a sudden suspicion where the conversation was leading.

"I don't want anyone to get ideas that we might become a couple."

"Anyone? That sounds like code for something."

Kayla nodded. "Sandy speculated about it last night with Alex. He wasn't thrilled. Then I started worrying about Morgan and whether *she* might get the wrong idea."

Jackson wasn't sure what he should be most concerned about—that he hadn't kept his sex life separate from the ranch, or that Alex was upset at the mere *suggestion* that his mother and birth father might get together.

"Morgan knows I'm not interested in getting married again," he said finally.

"That doesn't make any difference. Do you really want your daughter to figure out that we had sex in your bedroom while she was riding her horse?"

Kayla was right, but Jackson was struggling because he *didn't* want the sex to end. There were moments he felt obsessed with Kayla and it alarmed the hell out of him. But surely it would be easier to regain his equilibrium once she was back in Seattle.

"Of course I don't want her to find out."

"Okay, good." She nodded as though convincing herself. "From now on, we need to be extracareful to not suggest we're anything more than friendly."

They'd reached the pond and Kayla stood gazing across it with anxious eyes.

"What else is bothering you?" he asked.

She sighed. "I don't think Alex has resolved all the reasons he ran away to Schuyler. Or at least I don't think he's told me all of them."

"He seems to have recovered from the shock of learning he was adopted. Sometimes teenagers just react and then it's over."

"I know."

She still looked worried and Jackson frowned. Kayla had good parenting instincts, much better than his own. It might not help, but maybe he could talk to Alex about it himself.

KAYLA GLANCED AROUND the idyllic scene; it was just as beautiful as she remembered, though it really wasn't a pond. Eighty years ago the McGregors had built a small stone dam on a bend in the creek, creating a deep, clear pool. Even in a dry summer water flowed gently over the mossy top stones of the dam, while box elders and black cottonwood trees provided shade.

"That looks new," she said, pointing to a rope

hanging from a strong tree limb. "Now that they have a pool, does your family still cool off down here?"

"Sometimes." His eyes gleamed. "Want to give it a go?"

"Nope."

"We had fun."

"Of course we did. We were teenagers."

Yes, they'd had fun. It had been an unusually warm spring and Jackson had taught her how to swing out on the rope, letting go at just the right moment. The exhilaration had been even greater the time they'd swung together, his arms around her as they'd dropped into the water. At that moment she'd believed she would love Jackson McGregor forever and ever.

"You seem pensive," Jackson observed, "and not as if you're remembering something good."

"Memories can be complicated."

He pulled her down to sit on a rock and looked unusually serious himself. "I've been thinking, too, and I want to be sure you know how sorry I am. You were right that I wanted to blame you instead of remembering you'd gotten stuck with the hard road."

"I didn't get stuck, Jackson. I could have gotten an abortion, but I wanted to have the baby. And it wasn't because I had lingering romantic dreams about you—those vanished the day I told you I was pregnant. My biggest fear was what kind of parent I might be. I even considered giving Alex up for adoption, but in the end, I just decided to do my best."

"I'm still sorry I acted as if the injury was one-sided."

His sincerity got to her, except she didn't *want* to see him in an increasingly positive light; keeping her distance was easier when she could focus on his faults. She didn't want to explore the reasons why the thought of getting close was so frightening.

CHAPTER SIXTEEN

ALEX WAS GLAD that it wouldn't be a huge group coming that day. This way he'd have a better chance to watch Mom and Jackson to see if Sandy was right.

But they barely talked to each other.

Mom mostly sat with Grandma Elizabeth. Jackson moved stuff around where Grandma Sarah told him she wanted it, and he also kept skimming leaves off the pool. It wasn't as if they seemed angry—they just didn't pay much attention to each other. Of course, Sandy would say that also meant something, but she was full of hot air.

After a while Alex took a turn cranking the ice cream freezer, the same as he'd seen in an old movie. It was harder than he'd thought, but Grandpa Parker said that was because the ice cream was getting thick.

As he worked, the chicken and steaks came off the grill and he was glad he'd switched back to meat. Grilled steak smelled better than anything in the world.

"People in Montana sure barbecue a lot," he said,

getting up from the ice cream churn so Morgan could take over.

"I don't know about everybody, but we do," Grandpa Parker said. "Especially when we're celebrating new members of the family." He winked. "Hope you don't mind, but we think DeeDee should be an honorary granddaughter."

"I think she'd like that."

"How about it, DeeDee?" Grandpa Parker called across the patio. "Can we adopt you as another granddaughter?"

"Sure," DeeDee agreed enthusiastically.

"Great. It's been so good having Morgan, we'd like to double our blessings in the granddaughter department."

Alex looked at Morgan, whose cheeks had gone pink. He knew she'd wondered if everyone thought she was some kind of mistake, so what Grandpa Parker had said probably sounded good to her. They'd emailed back and forth a lot and she'd told him things that might have been too embarrassing to say out loud.

"Now, Parker, share and share alike," Grandpa Hank said. "We're making Morgan part of our family, as well."

"That makes us related, doesn't it?"

"We'll try to put up with you for Morgan's sake, even though you *don't* know what you're talking about when it comes to ice cream."

Alex laughed. Having a big family was working

out okay. Sometimes there was awkward stuff, but maybe the good stuff made it worthwhile.

It would be dope sleeping out at the ranch. Grandpa Parker had a humongous telescope and DeeDee had brought the one she'd gotten for her birthday. DeeDee was more into astronomy than him, but he liked it a whole lot.

After lunch the girls started a water volleyball game and he was going to join in when Jackson came over. "How about a ride, Alex? I can borrow a horse from my dad, and I'm sure Betty would like to get out again."

"Uh, sure." Alex's stomach churned and he wished he hadn't eaten steak after all, but he couldn't duck and run every time the guy wanted to spend time with him.

A short while later they rode in a direction Alex hadn't gone before. After a mile they came to an old log cabin.

"This is where the McGregors lived when they first came to Montana," Jackson explained. "We restored it a couple of years ago after one corner fell down."

"That's cool, I guess," Alex said, trying to imagine living in such a small, dark place.

"They didn't stay there long," Jackson said. "After a few years they built another home with milled lumber."

"Where's that one?"

"It's part of the house where my folks live. That's

where I grew up. I can show you the old part, and where they added on later."

Alex bobbed his head, wishing his stomach wasn't so tight.

"By the way, there's something I wanted to talk about," Jackson said as they turned back toward the house.

Alex scowled; he'd *known* there had to be more to the ride than just a family history lesson.

"It's about why you ran away and came to Montana," Jackson continued. "Your mom is worried. Is there something about it that you can't discuss with her?"

Alex shrugged and kept his mouth shut.

"I'm not asking you to tell me, but I wish you'd consider trusting her with it," Jackson urged.

"Why do you care what she thinks?" Alex asked, suspicious.

"Because she's your mother. She's trying to take care of you, and it's extrahard since she's mostly doing it alone."

"Yeah, my dad's kind of a loser," Alex muttered. Sometimes he didn't care if the whole world knew his father was a jackass.

Jackson didn't say anything right away, as if he was thinking something over. "Maybe, but he must have something good about him, or your mother wouldn't have married him in the first place."

Alex let go of a tight breath, glad Jackson had said that. Sometimes it got awfully hard to love his dad.

His eyes stung and he looked away. There weren't any buildings, just cows and hills and a few trees.

All of a sudden a rabbit shot out of the grass in front of them, making Jackson's horse sidestep and toss its head with a high whinny. "Whoa there, Rico," Jackson said, bringing the stallion under control as if it was no big deal.

Alex patted Betty's neck, glad she wasn't jumpy. Morgan said her dad liked to help horses that had been broken badly or mistreated. She called Thunder a nervous Nellie because he'd been treated rotten by some guy down in Wyoming before being rescued, though he was much better now that he was starting to trust her dad.

"Do you think Thunder remembers how bad it was before you got him?" Alex asked curiously.

"It's hard to say. Horses are much more sensitive and intelligent than lots of people think."

"Yeah." Alex rubbed his nose. It was strange to go from being a computer nerd with a bratty stepbrother to riding a horse he'd saddled himself. And not at a riding stable, either, on a real cattle ranch that belonged to his birth dad's family.

"So will you talk to your mother?" Jackson pushed after they'd ridden a little farther.

Alex fiddled with Betty's reins. "I don't know. She might get upset."

"I bet she'd rather have you talk to her, no matter what. Besides, I doubt you upset your mom as much as I used to upset your grandparents."

Alex wanted to ask Jackson what sort of things he'd done as a kid, but figured he probably wouldn't want to tell. Then he decided to ask anyhow.

"What's the wildest thing you ever did?" he asked, expecting to hear it was drag racing or playing chicken, or something stupid and daring like jumping off a mountain with a parachute.

"I don't know if it was the wildest, but I drove all night to Seattle on a dare. My folks thought I was camping with a friend."

Alex laughed. "Come on, that's the worst thing you ever did?"

Jackson looked surprised, then sad.

"Actually, no," he said slowly. "The *worst* thing was not believing your mother when she told me she was pregnant with our baby. It was harder for her, but I still paid a big price. You see, I would have gotten to know you a long time ago instead of waiting until you were fifteen. It may sound sappy, but if I could fix only one thing I've done wrong, that's the one I'd choose."

Alex looked down. He'd been so bent out of shape about everything he hadn't wanted to think about how Jackson felt. But maybe he should, because even if he didn't want another dad, Jackson might be a good guy to have as a friend.

MORGAN SAT ON the edge of her grandparents' pool, swinging her legs in the water and wondering when Alex and her dad were getting back. At least she had Sandy to talk to; DeeDee and Keri were too busy playing in the waterfall to notice anyone else. Her grandparents' pool was smaller than at home, but it had a hot tub on one side that sort of spilled over into the rest of the water, and a waterfall on the other. It wasn't like the waterfall at Halloran's Meadow, but it was pretty nifty.

"You know what?" Sandy said. "Our school back home has decided to offer Japanese. Alex and I are taking it together."

"Isn't Japanese hard?" Morgan asked.

"Yeah, but it would be neat to learn. And the United States does lots of business with Japan."

"I thought you wanted to be president someday."

"I've got to do something until then. You have to be, like, *ancient* before you can run for president, so I'm going to study international law."

"I guess knowing Japanese would help."

"Sure, and I'll have to learn other languages, too."

Morgan made a face. She had enough trouble in English class. "I'm taking French this fall."

"That's cool."

"Dad says Spanish might be more useful, but I want to visit Paris someday."

Talking about class starting was depressing. Not because Morgan hated school, but it was a reminder that Alex and DeeDee were going back to Seattle soon. Of course, things were probably going to get better at home now, and Alex had said he'd show her how to do video calls with him on the computer. Besides, he'd come back to Montana to see everyone, and he was going to ask if she could visit them in Seattle. It just wouldn't be the same as him and DeeDee being here all the time.

"What's the matter?" Sandy asked.

Morgan shrugged. "I'm going to be lonely when you guys leave."

"Yeah, I was lonely while Alex was gone. I could have *killed* him when he emailed and told me he'd blown off his dad to go to Montana."

Morgan nodded; she would have been mad, too.

She liked Sandy, though a jealous little part of her wanted to keep Alex to herself.

"Alex says you might come to visit Seattle," Sandy continued. "That's cool. I'll take you sailing on Lake Washington. Alex won't go, he gets seasick."

"Really?"

"Yeah. It's gross."

Morgan laughed. "I won't get sick. My grandparents have a boat and we go sailing on Flathead Lake."

"Awesome. We'll thumb our noses at him as we sail away."

"He won't care."

"No, but we'll do it anyway."

It sounded fun and Morgan wondered how soon she could go. It was a long way to Seattle. Dad would have to let her fly, but maybe he wouldn't mind. He might even want to go, too. After all, Alex was a boy and that probably meant a lot to him.

She'd always known her father had wanted a boy instead of a girl. It was what her mom had said—that he'd wanted them to have more kids because he'd hoped one would be a son. It bothered her a little, but not as much as thinking he hadn't wanted her at all.

KAYLA ANXIOUSLY WATCHED for Alex's return, wondering how he might be taking the one-on-one time with Jackson. So far, Alex had tried to stay in a group whenever his birth father was around.

Alex came into the backyard by way of the house. He'd changed into his bathing suit and immediately jumped into the pool.

Jackson followed, but stopped when he saw Elizabeth pulling the churn dasher from the ice cream maker.

"I can't tell any difference," he said after eating a spoonful, "unless it's one of those lesson things—we get more out of the stuff we have to work for."

"Hush," Hank warned, "there are kids here. Don't give away a parent's trade secrets."

"My apologies."

Keri, listening from the pool, giggled.

Kayla had always imagined an extended family gathering would be like this, filled with warmth and laughter. She was grateful Alex and DeeDee were experiencing it now, and that there'd probably be many more in the future.

The McGregors seemed genuine about wanting DeeDee to be part of their family, and she knew her grandparents felt the same about Morgan. It was partly why she'd warned Jackson to be careful about giving anyone the wrong impression—there was no sense in anyone thinking they'd get together. Of course, it was possible the McGregors didn't have that in mind since they had to be aware of Jackson's reputation. Madison certainly didn't have a high opinion of her brother's attitude toward women and marriage.

Nevertheless, Jackson seemed to have taken her warning seriously. Aside from casual friendliness, he didn't come over to talk with her, or do anything else that might suggest they were becoming a couple. So she was able to concentrate on other people…mostly.

Around eight, after another meal, the kids started getting ready for their sleep-out. Elizabeth and Hank said good-night and left for home.

"You've got everything you need?" Kayla asked her son and daughter and their friends.

"Everything's cool, Mom," Alex said.

"Then, have a good time."

The kids barely seemed to notice as she said goodbye to the McGregors and walked out to the Volvo, Jackson beside her.

"I should have brought my truck so you wouldn't have to take me home," he said.

"No problem," she assured, except now that they were alone again, the breathless surge of her hormones was reasserting itself with a vengeance.

In silence she started the Volvo and began retracing the various roads to Jackson's ranch.

"It's obviously more direct to come over on horseback," she said, hoping her voice sounded even, "but is there any problem crossing other ranches?"

"Not around here. We just have one rule—if you open a gate, close it after you." His voice was husky in the gathering darkness.

"Very neighborly."

"Yeah, though the only ranch that has to be crossed is the Balderdash, and now it belongs to my brother Trent."

Kayla stopped in front of his house. "Looks as if you didn't leave on any lights."

"I forgot Flora was spending the night with her sister. How about a swim?" he asked, his voice low and enticing.

Oh, *hell*. What was a woman to do? At least tonight nobody was around to get their hopes up about any future relationships…or be upset by the possibility.

"Sounds good."

She climbed out of the car and went inside with Jackson.

"I'll leave the pool lights off so they don't out-shine the stars. Go on out, I'll change upstairs."

A tall rolling fence had been pulled alongside the pool, blocking any lights from the ranch's out-buildings. It was quiet and private and devastating to any resolve she might have had left in her brain.

Quickly she went into the pool house to put on her suit, half surprised and half disappointed that Jackson hadn't suggested a *nude* starlight swim.

He wasn't there when she emerged, and she slipped into the dark water to float on her back. With no artificial light nearby, the stars shone with a fiery glory, and several meteors shot across the sky as she watched.

Kayla was barely aware that Jackson had come outside and entered the pool with silent grace. She had a dreamy sensation of being suspended in time, floating between worlds in the starlight. After a long time, reluctantly, she moved toward the long steps in the shallows.

"Surely you're not leaving," he murmured in the darkness.

"Perhaps I should."

His hand cupped her waist and she swallowed. "Hey," she chided, "you blew your chances when you didn't suggest skinny-dipping."

"That would have hurried things up too much." Jackson tugged her closer. "You wouldn't have wanted to miss all those shooting stars," he mur-mured. "Did you make a wish?"

She hadn't wished for anything, since the only things she still wanted were out of reach.

"No."

"I did." His fingers slipped under the shoulder strap of her suit. "Another reason for not starting out skinny-dipping is the sensuality of undressing in the water."

Kayla swallowed as he tugged the straps down until her breasts moved freely. With strong hands, he stretched the black one-piece so it slipped easily over her hips. She couldn't see his face, but had a feeling he was grinning as he swam down and eased the fabric from her legs.

As he rose, his hand brushed the inside of her thighs and stopped at the apex. The water didn't feel cool in the least as his fingers probed, and she gasped as they found the center of sensation. He drew her closer with one hand until he was kissing her while his other still touched, explored, entered, withdrew, teasing until pleasure exploded through her body.

"Mmm," he whispered. "See what I mean?"

"What about..." She stopped, realizing his own suit was gone and his erection was insistently prodding her belly.

"Much as I'd enjoyed proceeding without delay," he murmured, "being in the water isn't any protection."

She almost didn't care whether protection was involved, but she let him lift her onto the edge of the pool and lead her to one of the large redwood chaises. Only then did she realize the backrest was lying down flat. Perhaps it should have offended her that he'd assumed too much; on the other hand, she'd known it was going to happen from the moment she'd agreed to a starlight swim.

He stopped, and with the faint crackle of a condom wrapper, she knew he was covering himself before moving over her, his weight settling on her body with delicious satisfaction.

"ARE YOU COLD?" Jackson asked much later. They were still damp and a breeze was blowing through the yard.

"Not too bad. You're the one who's probably chilly, since you're blocking the wind.

Almost without thinking, he'd shifted to shield her. With only the faint light from the stars and rising moon to guide his eyes, he studied the planes of her face...her slender neck, collarbone, enticing breasts, one of them pressed against arm.

"Why didn't you wish on a shooting star?" he asked.

"I could wish for keeping my kids safe and happy, but that's more like my daily prayer. What was your wish, or should I ask?" she said in a dry tone.

He chuckled. "My wish was immediate, basic and very graphic. And I got it."

"You didn't need to wish. You knew what would happen when I agreed to stay for a swim."

True, he'd known she'd desired him as much as he had wanted her in return. But his wish… He frowned. *Had* his wish been granted? He had an odd sense that he'd missed something, though the sex had been spectacular.

In the house he could hear the clock chiming and reluctantly sat up.

"I hate to mention this," he said, "but if your grandparents don't see you soon, they may get suspicious."

"I KNOW." GETTING UP, Kayla hurried into the pool house and dressed swiftly. Outside she found Jackson with a towel wrapped around his waist.

"You *are* going to clean up the evidence, right?" she asked.

"I'll make sure everything is shipshape."

"Don't forget my suit. It's somewhere in the pool."

"I'll get that, too," he promised.

"Then, I'll see you tomorrow when I pick up the kids."

"Sleep well."

"The same to you."

It was all very polite and civilized, as if nothing had happened. And maybe, to him, nothing significant *had* happened. He enjoyed discreet liaisons, although they might not be as discreet as he imagined, since the people in town knew he had an active sex life.

Kayla settled behind the wheel of the Volvo and started the engine. She was disgusted by her lack of restraint, but it wasn't Jackson's fault that she was an idiot.

Perhaps if an attractive guy had come along at the right moment back in Seattle, the same sort of thing might have happened. Of course, in her normal environment she probably wouldn't have succumbed so easily. A number of her single friends claimed vacations were hell on self-control when it came to the opposite sex. That had to be the explanation. It was like the perfect storm, with every condition falling into place and tipping over the balance of her life.

So it actually had little to do with Jackson, other than an echo of the old teenage affection that had tugged at her. But now she was an adult and so was he. They'd changed. She still believed real love was out there, at least for some people, while he doubted it even existed, and certainly not for him.

In a few days she would return home. Thankfully, after that, her occasional contacts with Jackson would be insignificant.

JACKSON TRIED TO locate Kayla's swimsuit in the dark, but without luck; the black fabric faded into the shadows too well. So he turned on the pool lights, dived down to get it and hung it up. Outside he scoured the pool area for anything having to do with condoms.

Jackson glanced at the large, empty house. He ought to be exhausted, but instead he burned with energy.

He dived into the water and swam lap after lap, pushing for more speed, heart beating, living over and over again the feel of Kayla against him and the pleasure of making love to her. Curiously, it was a sensation that had both satisfied him and left him hungry for more. Finally, with muscles aching, he stepped from the pool, his lungs sucking oxygen from the warm night air, his heart rhythm gradually returning to normal.

He looked up at the sky.

The eclipse was beginning, and he felt curiously lonely that no one was there to watch it with him.

Still, he should feel good. Things were getting sorted out with Morgan and though he didn't imagine everything would be easy from now on, at least they'd made a start. And a terrific thing had happened—he and Alex had actually talked. Not a brief word here or there. Not a sentence on the way to someone else. Not with a glance over his shoulder to see how soon he could get away from his inconvenient birth father. Alex had looked him in the eye and shared a conversation.

Jackson knew he had Kayla to thank for that. She'd done her best to keep him from coming on too strong with Alex, urging him to let things happen naturally.

It had been risky asking Alex to talk to his mother; he could easily have blown up and told him to butt out. And since his son had seemed interested in hearing and seeing some of the McGregor family history, it had been doubly perilous to introduce the issue. Regardless, it had been the right thing to do as a parent.

But what bothered Jackson was that he'd talked to Alex as much for Kayla's sake as for his son's.

"Hey, boss, you out here?" called a voice from behind the fence, dragging Jackson's thoughts into the present.

"Yeah, Greg, what's up?"

"Ruby is edgy. She doesn't show sign of getting ready to drop her foal, but you might want to check her."

"I'll be there in a minute."

Jackson got dressed and headed to the barn where they kept the broodmares. Most of them had dropped their foals in May and June, but they'd bought Ruby from a rancher down south, who'd bred her late. She was younger than Jackson liked, too, for a first-time mother.

"Hey, girl."

Ruby pushed her nose into his chest and he rubbed her neck. She was a sweetheart, a purebred Appaloosa like Thunder, and he hoped one day to breed them together.

"Do you just want attention?" he asked the mare.

She stepped uneasily from foot to foot and he checked her over carefully. As Greg had said, there weren't any indications she was going into labor, but it wouldn't hurt to watch her.

"Go on, I'll stay," Jackson told the foreman.

"Could be a long night, boss."

"I'll have Ace call if anything happens."

Ace was the cowhand assigned to the night watch that week. Going from barn to barn and corral to corral all night long wasn't popular, so they rotated the duty between the hands, Jackson taking his turn along with the others.

"Go," he ordered. "She doesn't like you as much as me anyhow."

"Yeah, it's your killer charm with the ladies," Greg said, and ambled out.

Jackson got a grooming cloth and began wiping Ruby down, knowing it would calm her. He'd been grooming horses every day for as long as he could remember, and the familiar task didn't demand as much of his attention as he would have liked.

Why was he so restless?

He'd just enjoyed the best sex of his life. He should be supremely relaxed. After all, he'd gotten what he'd laughingly wished for in the pool. But he couldn't shake an uneasy feeling that he'd settled for much less than he could have had.

It was strange. He'd been determined never to get seriously involved with another woman, fiercely resolute never to let another Marcy or Patti come near him. But Kayla wasn't the least bit like the other two women, which was something he needed to think about very carefully.

CHAPTER SEVENTEEN

Late the next morning Kayla pulled up in front of Jackson's house and assumed her best game face.

"Hi," she called as he stepped out on the porch. "Are the kids here?"

"Not yet. At the moment they're eating my mother's pancakes and deciding whether to take a detour up to Halloran's Meadow. I told Mom we'd call if we wanted them to come straight back."

Jackson's eyebrow lifted in what she interpreted as a challenge, but Kayla refused to react. "We're going home in a couple of days. Let them have a little more vacation fun."

He frowned, though she didn't try to interpret what it meant.

"You look tired," she added, trying to look as bright-eyed as possible, despite having gotten little rest herself.

"I was up all night with a foaling mare," he explained. "I just came in to change my clothes and then head back out to the barn. But now that you're here, I'd like to show you something."

With a neutral smile Kayla followed him into his office. After all, she was an expert at survival.

At worst, Jackson was a passing heartache. That was all.

She hoped.

Silently she examined the papers he showed her. He'd established a trust fund for Alex.

"You don't have to tell him about it," Jackson said, "but it's there if needed."

Kayla returned the documents. "I'd rather he didn't know. Aside from anything else, his relationship with you should be separate from money."

"I guess you're right." He tossed the papers into a drawer and locked it.

Kayla didn't know what else to say, so she suggested visiting the new foal. Luckily two of the ranch hands were there when they arrived, keeping things light the way she wanted.

AS THEY RODE IN, Alex followed as Morgan veered toward the barn she'd said was for their broodmares. A truck with some writing on the side was parked next to the door.

"Hey, guys," Morgan called over her shoulder. "That's our vet. Dad's new mare might be foaling. Let's go check."

They tied their horses at the corral fence and trooped toward the large doors.

"We've gotta be quiet," Morgan said in a low voice. "Ruby is real nervous."

His heart thumping, Alex walked carefully toward the large stall where he saw his mom and

Jackson with an Appaloosa mare. She was mostly white with black spots, which was kind of opposite to Thunder, who was mostly black with white spots on his butt and face. In the corner of the stall another man was examining a baby horse.

"Shoot," Morgan whispered. "She already foaled."

Alex blinked. "It looks as if they're trying to keep the baby away from its mother."

"Well, yeah," Morgan agreed. "The foal sometimes fusses at the mom when she's still hurting from the birth, so you gotta try to help her not get upset."

"Wow," Sandy said. "I thought horses loved their babies right off."

"Some do," one of the hands told them as he walked by carrying a nursing bottle. "But Ruby is a first-time mom, and she's taking a while to get the hang of it."

"Can't the mother feed her baby?" Keri asked as the man with the bottle started giving it to the foal.

"Just being careful," Jackson said, looking up and smiling. "We're giving it colostrum, to help with protection against germs and such."

"What's coloster…whatever?" DeeDee breathed.

"It's something the baby gets when it nurses right off," Morgan explained. "But you can buy it, and we don't take chances with our foals."

Alex wished he'd been there to see the foal come, even though it might have been as gross as seeing the lamb born on his church youth group trip. The next time he visited the ranch... He stopped suddenly, startled. Whoa. He actually wanted to come back?

Go figure.

JACKSON WAS DETERMINED to keep things friendly with Kayla—no fights, and no challenges to the status quo.

He wanted more time with her, but it was a commodity in short supply; she'd soon be driving away. It was disturbing because Alex should be his first and *only* thought in connection to the Anderson family's departure.

They left the five kids in the barn and returned to the house. Flora had gone shopping, but there were sandwich makings in the fridge for lunch. He pulled everything out and bantered back and forth with Kayla as to whether French rolls or sourdough bread was better.

"I'll concede that since you can't get the best sourdough away from the West Coast, French rolls are probably best in Montana," Kayla finally said.

"We have sourdough bread in Montana."

She didn't have a chance to retort; the kids arrived and descended on the sandwiches like a pack of starving wolves.

"The new baby is *awesome*," DeeDee declared. "I wish I could have seen him getting born."

"Maybe another visit," Jackson told her.

"What are you going to name it?" Alex asked.

Jackson shrugged. "Not sure yet. Do you have something in mind?"

"There was an eclipse last night, so how about that?"

"Eclipse?" Sandy repeated. "That's a racehorse name, not a cow pony."

"Maybe he'll *be* a racehorse," Alex argued.

"Eclipse is a good name, no matter what he turns out to be," Jackson said firmly.

Jackson thought Kayla seemed to be avoiding looking at him, but he couldn't be sure. She wanted to leave early so they could spend the rest of the day with her grandparents but waited while the youngsters properly groomed the horses they'd ridden and mucked out the stables.

She finally got them into the car around four and waved absentmindedly as she drove away.

Looking at Morgan, Jackson saw her shoulders slump.

"Something up?" he asked. "You seem a little funky."

"I'm going to miss Alex, that's all."

He sighed. "Me, too. It's been great having him here."

"Yeah, but at least you've got a son now."

Turning she went back into the house and Jackson stared at the door, instantly ready to chew nails. He had to remind himself that he hadn't truly expected all of Morgan's issues to be resolved in one conversation.

Well, he wasn't letting it go the way he'd let too many *other* things slide by with her. He strode through the house and found her in the backyard, petting Cory.

"Okay, we're going to have this out right now," he announced. "Do you really think I appreciate Alex more than you because he's a boy?"

His jaw clenched when she wouldn't even look at him. "I don't know. But you wanted a boy. Mom said so. She told me that you wanted her to get fat and ugly again, and she wasn't about to do it just so you'd have the son you wanted."

Jackson was sure his blood pressure had gone sky-high. How could Marcy have been so insensitive? And how could she have lied that way? He'd never *once* suggested having another baby because he wanted a boy; it hadn't even occurred to him. He'd have been thrilled to have another girl.

Suddenly, he did a double take, remembering how Kayla had repeatedly accused him of bad attitudes toward women. He hadn't wanted to admit she was right on any level, but she was.

He shook his head; Morgan was the important thing right now.

Jackson breathed deeply, searching for the right words. It wouldn't help Morgan to know her mother had lied. Besides, maybe Marcy had genuinely believed that nonsense.

Cory's chin was on Morgan's knee and he gave Jackson a mournful look. She was his favorite person and hated it when she was unhappy.

"Morgan, honey, I think your mother misunderstood," Jackson said, sitting next to her. "I *did* hope for more kids, but I would have been just as happy with another girl. And no matter how big a family we might have had, none of them could have taken your place."

She stared at him, almost suspiciously. "You gave me a boy's name."

"It's also a girl's name. I liked the sound of it and your mother did, too. If we'd had a boy, it would have been Jake, not Morgan."

His gaze dropped to the jeans she was wearing. For years she'd ignored all of the dresses in her closet.

"Morgan, is that why you won't wear dresses or jewelry?"

"Uh, sort of."

"Hon, you can be any sort of girl you want to be. I'll love you just the same if you dress in lace or jeans. Or…you can dress in lace *and* jeans. Find your own style."

At that, she laughed a little. "Okay."

"And remember, we can talk about this anytime. Or anything else you want to discuss."

She nodded, still petting Cory, and he painfully recalled Kayla's accusations that he didn't trust women. She was right about that, too. Was it possible that his anger and sense of betrayal had unconsciously touched Morgan?

Uneasily, Jackson remembered a few occasions when she might have overheard him talking to one of his brothers, saying he'd hang before giving another woman the chance to stab him in the back again.

Truthfully, his ex-wife didn't deserve to have that much influence over him. And the women he'd socialized with since the divorce hadn't been any prizes, either, so maybe he'd set himself up to keep seeing the opposite sex as untrustworthy, unconsciously trying to justify the way he felt. It might even have been the reason he'd dated Patti, deep down recognizing what she was really like.

That could have affected Morgan.

And there had to be a reason his sisters had drawn away from him. He'd assumed it was because they'd grown up and had new interests, but what if it had something to do with him and his attitudes? Alaina and Madison had once visited often, even enduring Marcy, whom they'd increasingly disliked. Now they mostly stayed away except for family gatherings.

Maybe if he'd done a little more soul-searching and spent a little less time trying to be strong and impassive, he would have figured out the problem a long time ago.

All at once Morgan jumped up and asked if she could go in the pool.

"Sure."

"Will you swim with me?"

There was an appeal in his daughter's eyes, perhaps to know he *wanted* to spend time with her. He nodded. "That sounds great. We've been in a group so much, we haven't had a chance to just be together."

Jackson ran up the stairs two at a time and donned his swim trunks. Though the fabric had dried, he was still reminded of the previous night with Kayla. Desire jolted through him, but there was more to what he felt than just physical need. Kayla challenged him. She made him *want* to be a better man, and how many times did you meet someone who did that?

He needed to sort out how he felt about her, but now wasn't the right time. He needed to focus on his daughter.

As KAYLA DROVE back to her grandparents' house, the kids were full of excitement about everything from the eclipse to the new foal.

"We saw, like, a thousand shooting stars," DeeDee proclaimed.

"Uh-uh," Alex corrected. "Dozens."

"I counted fifty-six," Sandy said.

"Do you think Eclipse could be a racehorse someday?" Alex asked. "I bet he'd be happier on a ranch than some dumb racetrack."

Kayla's eyebrows rose. Alex obviously had a

growing fondness for ranch life. Of course, he'd only seen the fun parts—riding and play—but there was no question that he'd come to like Montana. But, as if to prove her wrong, Alex immediately began talking about the computer programming class he wanted to take and how exciting it would be.

"You'll be the only geek cowboy in school," DeeDee told her brother. "We'll call you a cow-punching computer nerd—sort of like cowcompnerd."

"You're *soooo* funny," he told her, rolling his eyes.

The teasing was good-natured, so Kayla didn't put a stop to it.

At the house, the two younger girls ran upstairs to the attic bedroom, a place that had enchanted Keri as much as it had DeeDee. Sandy and Alex looked at each other with complicated expressions, then Sandy went to Elizabeth's sewing room, which had been set aside for her to use.

Kayla sat down with her computer to check emails, but as she was opening her mailbox, Alex came in.

"Mom?"

"Yes?"

"Um…Jackson wanted me to talk to you."

Jackson had convinced him to open up? Perhaps it was the man-to-man influence he seemed to think was so important. She didn't care, as long as it happened.

"Sure. What's on your mind?"

"It's about why I came to Montana. Jackson says you've been really worried and I should tell you the real reason I ran away. The thing is… I guess I wouldn't have gone if not for the whole adoption thing, but I kind of *wanted* to, even before Brant blabbed."

"Were you angry at me?" Kayla asked, trying not to sound defensive. "It's okay if you are, we just need to figure out what to do."

"No, it's Dad. Sometimes I get so mad at him I could just burst."

Blinking back tears, Kayla nodded. "You've never talked about it."

"You want us to love him." Alex stopped and she held her breath. "But sometimes I don't, and that makes me feel rotten, as if there's something wrong with me."

"There's nothing wrong with you."

How complicated could life get for her kids? It was supposed to be better for them than it had been for her.

"But you're always saying you love Grandma… your mom, I mean," Alex said. "And even if I don't know much about it, I guess it wasn't very nice for you growing up."

Swallowing, Kayla thought back to her childhood, when she'd been scared most of the time, and angry, and sad. Alex needed her to be honest, so she began to tell him what it had been like growing up with a clinically depressed alcoholic mother.

His eyes grew wide.

"I loved her," Kayla concluded, "but I also hated her. I couldn't understand how she could care more about a drink than me. There were so many times I wanted to leave and never have to think about her again."

Understanding suddenly dawned on Kayla. She'd wanted to run away, too. *Far* away. She'd finally left because of Alex, knowing she couldn't let Carolyn hurt her grandson the way she'd hurt her daughter.

"But you didn't leave," Alex said.

"Not until after you were born," Kayla said slowly. "In the end I decided I couldn't stop loving her, but I wouldn't give her the power to bang my heart around. It was as if I had to put up a wall between us to protect myself. I don't know if that makes sense to you."

"It does, kind of."

"I suppose you'll have to do the same thing with your dad. Try to love him even though he's got problems, and protect yourself when you have to."

Alex sighed heavily. "I guess."

Kayla gave him hug and then looked into his eyes. "So what about Jackson? Can you give him a chance?"

"Jackson is all right. For a while I didn't want any dad at all, only now I'm kind of mixed-up."

"You'll figure it out. Just don't run away from home again. Okay?"

"Okay." He suddenly grinned mischievously. 'Well, if I do, I'll ask you to go with me."

"Brat."

"Grandma says I'm a lot like you, so I guess that means you're a brat, too."

After Alex had gone in to watch baseball with the other kids, Kayla went to find her grandparents. They were in the backyard enjoying the late afternoon.

"Alex just told me more about why he ran away," she told them, dropping into a chair. The heat spell had eased and it was pleasantly cool in the shade. "I think we've passed the hump, even if it'll take time to work it all out. Lord, divorce is complicated."

Hank nodded. "I never liked representing clients in a divorce—there's too much pain involved. But I hope it won't keep you from looking for someone else to love."

"You're just an old romantic," Kayla tried to ease.

"Guilty as charged." He lifted his wife's hand and kissed it while Grams glowed.

Kayla knew they were probably still hopeful that she'd get together with Jackson. But even if Jackson became interested in something long-term, he'd expect a woman to give everything in a relationship, to continually prove herself. There would never be any kind of partnership, no give-and-take, no compromises. Everything would have to be done his way.

In a crazy way, she felt sorry for him. He'd gotten badly burned by his marriage and the woman he'd dated after his divorce, but she didn't want to pay the price for someone else's misdeeds.

Elizabeth's voice broke into her thoughts. "We're going to miss you so much when you're gone. The time has flown by."

Kayla bobbed her head. She would miss them, too, but returning to a normal routine was attractive... and getting away from Jackson was even more attractive. Perhaps she could resolve her conflicted emotions once she was back in Seattle.

"Tomorrow is our last day. Maybe the kids and I should spend it here with you instead of going to the Crazy Horse," she suggested.

"Oh, no, they enjoy the ranch so much," Elizabeth insisted. "It would be selfish to keep Alex away from Jackson in any case, and we're invited to spend the day over there as well, along with his side of the family."

"Sure," Kayla agreed, still thinking about Jackson. Somehow he'd managed to get through her defenses, though he was the last person she should love. Not that she *did* love him, she assured herself. And even if she did, it didn't make any difference. They couldn't have a future together.

MORGAN OPENED THE package Kayla had just given her and stared at the silver-and-gold pendant on a real gold chain. It was a figure of a girl, holding up her hands and cupping a glowing round ball.

"Oh, my gosh, it's so pretty," she breathed. "What kind of stone is that?"

"It's called chrysocolla," Kayla explained. "You've had your summer turned upside down because of us, so I wanted to give you something as a thank-you."

Morgan didn't know what to say. The girl in the pendant had gold hair, and the way she was reaching up to the milky turquoise color of the stone was like…maybe a fairy tale.

"Is it from a story or something?" she asked.

"I'm not sure. A friend designed it and she loves old Irish and Welsh tales," said Kayla. "I have a similar one and asked her to send this to Montana for you as a gift. But don't feel bad if it doesn't appeal to you."

"I never had anything so incredible." No one had given her any jewelry since she'd stopped wearing girlie things. "Can you help me put it on?"

Kayla fastened the chain at the back of her neck and Morgan stood at the mirror, admiring the pendant resting in the open V of her shirt.

"Moooommm," a voice called from downstairs.

Kayla laughed. "I'd better go find out what DeeDee's crisis is *now*." She turned and left.

Down the hall, Morgan found her dad coming out of his bedroom. "Look what Kayla gave me," she told him excitedly, pointing to the necklace.

"It's real gold and everything, but I don't want to look silly. Do you think it's too fancy for me?"

He looked at her carefully. "Morgan, no woman will ever accuse me of knowing much about fashion, but if my opinion counts, it looks great."

She smiled, gave him a hug and trotted downstairs.

JACKSON STARED OUT the window into the backyard, where Morgan had emerged to talk with Alex. Score another one for Kayla Anderson. Whether by instinct or by chance, she'd found something that Morgan loved. There had been an excited glow in his daughter's eyes that he hadn't seen in quite a while.

Lord, he'd entirely missed the boat with Morgan, but the worst part was that she'd somehow gotten the idea she wasn't wanted.

He found Kayla in the living room, picking foxtails from DeeDee's socks.

"I couldn't help it," DeeDee was explaining. "Cory was there and I wanted to see what he was digging up."

"Next time look before tromping through a bunch of dry grass."

When Kayla was done, DeeDee raced off while her mother collected stray burrs from the hardwood floor. Her efforts yielded a nice view of her shapely behind, but Jackson kept a firm grip on his reaction.

"Good morning," he said.

Kayla straightened and he saw that her eyes were carefully guarded. "Hi."

"I saw the necklace you gave to Morgan. It's beautiful."

"I wanted to acknowledge the way her summer plans had to change because of us."

"It was very thoughtful."

Jackson didn't know how to say what he wanted to Kayla, and it wasn't about jewelry. Naturally, he was grateful for her insight into Morgan, but he needed to talk about the future and all the possibilities he was beginning to imagine.

Still, this wasn't the right moment. The conversation he wanted would have to wait for a time when the family wasn't expected.

"How did you know she'd enjoy jewelry like that?" he queried. "It isn't her usual style."

"I didn't know for sure, but I saw her admiring fantasy items several times at the Yellowstone gift shops, so I took a chance and asked an artist friend in Seattle to send it."

"Does your friend have a website? I'm lame at picking out things a girl would like, so it would be nice to have a good place to buy gifts for Morgan."

"I'll email the web address," Kayla told him.

"Thanks," he said, the reminder of her imminent departure causing his chest to tighten.

She seemed unaware of his restless energy, or

perhaps she assumed he was just horny. And he *was*, but that wasn't why he didn't want her to leave.

"Kayla, when we get a chance, there's something I'd like—"

"Yoo-hoo," a cheery voice called as his parents walked in the open door.

"Hey," he called back.

They warmly greeted Kayla and swept her off to look for Alex. She went without a backward glance, no doubt wanting to keep up the appearance there was nothing going on between them. And maybe from her perspective, nothing *was* going on.

It was his own fault. He'd been so determined to avoid meaningful relationships with women that he'd damaged most of his existing relationships in the process.

Hell, he hated knowing he'd turned into a cliché. He was just a guy with commitment issues who knew how to have a good time, and apparently everyone in Schuyler knew it.

But the worst part was realizing how much that cliché might interfere with the new things he wanted in his life.

CHAPTER EIGHTEEN

ALEX SAW GRANDMA SARAH come into the back-yard and smile at him. She kissed Morgan on the cheek and gave him and DeeDee a hug, her eyes looking watery.

His mom had warned him that some of the family might get emotional since they were leaving the next morning. It made him feel odd, so a little later when Morgan suggested they go for a last ride up to Halloran's Meadow, it sounded pretty good.

"Jackson says it's okay with him if we're back by lunch," he explained to his mom.

"All right, but don't stay too long," she warned. "People are coming over to say goodbye to you and DeeDee."

He nodded. It would be rude to flake out on the whole day, but a part of him wanted to disappear. There was an ache in his stomach whenever he thought about going back to Seattle.

Morgan had the horses ready and they all left together.

"You aren't going soft, are you?" Morgan asked when Sandy rode ahead of them with DeeDee and Keri.

"Nah, I'm not going anything, since I was already soft in the head before I got here. At least, that's what Sandy says."

Morgan giggled and then sighed. "I wish you were staying longer."

"I thought you'd be glad to have your dad to yourself again."

Her face scrunched up and she shrugged. "Sort of, but not really, if you know what I mean. It's been kind of weird."

"Gee, thanks for the Montana-size compliment."

"You know what I meant."

"Yeah, I guess so."

Alex turned Betty as they approached the northwest slope and he realized he'd done it automatically, before Morgan could remind him which direction they needed to go.

Back home DeeDee had been anxious to start horseback-riding lessons with Keri but hadn't been able to because of her soccer schedule. He'd thought wanting to learn was sort of stupid, but now he wondered if there was a way to go riding sometimes in Seattle. Not that it would be the same as riding on the ranch.

At least he'd gotten to see a foal only a few hours old. It would have been dope seeing it getting born, however gross it might have been. Morgan had teased, saying he'd have freaked out, but that wasn't true. He wasn't squeamish; he'd helped when the neighbor's dog got hit by a car and the blood hadn't bothered him. Well, the blood hadn't, he'd just hated seeing Ranger hurting that bad. For a while he'd even thought about becoming a veterinarian. Maybe he should think about it some more.

"Let's gallop and catch up with the others," Morgan suggested.

"Sure." Alex urged Betty into a faster pace and tried to forget his funny feelings about going home.

KAYLA WAS RESTLESS. As usual, Flora had turned down her help in the kitchen, and there was little else to do. Jackson's parents had left temporarily, going into town for some shopping, and her grandparents weren't coming over until later.

"How about the two of us take a ride?" Jackson asked. "No one will be getting here for an hour or so. And if they're early, they can just hang out at the pool."

"Okay."

She was glad he hadn't suggested a swim, since twice it had led to intimacies she should have resisted. Not that she could have succumbed this time; Flora was there and too much family was expected.

"Will you miss Montana?" Jackson asked as they rode away from the ranch center.

"Yes," she admitted. "Even as a kid I liked it here—everything was so clean and open and beautiful. Seattle is great and I love it, but it will be nice to visit my grandparents and see Big Sky Country once in a while."

"I can't imagine living anywhere else."

"They say some people's names are written on the land, and I always knew yours was carved on Montana."

Kayla wanted to relax and enjoy her last ride before leaving, but it was hard. She couldn't stop thinking about the conversation she'd had with Alex.

"A penny for your thoughts." Jackson's voice broke into her reverie.

She glanced at him. "Sorry. My mind was a million miles away. Well, a few hundred miles, at least. In Seattle."

"Because you're anxious to get home." His voice was tense, no doubt because she'd be taking Alex away from Schuyler.

"Not exactly," she answered. "I was thinking how life gets messed up, despite our best intentions."

JACKSON STOPPED AT one of his favorite views of the ranch, the sadness in Kayla's face weighing on him.

"What prompted all this introspection?" he asked.

"Alex talked to me last night. I understand I have you to thank for that, by the way."

"My pleasure. What did he say?"

"It turns out he's a lot angrier with Curtis than I thought. Maybe even more than I am."

"You mentioned your divorce was amicable."

"It was. I felt it would be better for Alex and DeeDee if we were friendly, so while I was desperately disappointed in my husband, I kept it hidden. Now I wonder if that made it harder for them to express *their* anger and disappointment. I want them to love their father, but he has real problems. Ultimately they have to learn that they can love him, despite his imperfections."

A question pressed inside Jackson—could *she* love someone else, despite their imperfections?

Someone like him?

"Maybe it would help Alex and DeeDee if you created boundaries for your ex," Jackson suggested carefully. "He should be responsible for his decisions, but he seems to rely on you for emotional support. Would it be better for everyone if you shut the door?"

A thoughtful expression crossed Kayla's face. "You may be right. Boundaries might create a safe zone for the kids. I don't want them to hate Curtis, in spite of his faults. I just don't want them to be hurt constantly because he can't give them the steady affection a kid needs."

Jackson wanted to say that *he* could do that. *He* could love both Alex and DeeDee each day of their lives and do everything in his power to protect them and make them happy. And he wanted to do that for Kayla, too. He just couldn't make that kind of declaration in the middle of a discussion about her ex-husband.

Kayla's potential reaction was hard to guess. She'd been hurt over and over, let down by the people she should have been able to trust.

The big question was whether she'd ever be willing to make another leap of faith, especially with a man who'd once let her down himself. True, he'd been a teenager when it had happened, and she knew he'd changed since then, but he'd hardly become a poster child for healthy relationships.

KAYLA WAS GLAD to see the kids return to the house soon after she and Jackson finished their own ride.

Around one o'clock her grandparents arrived, along with members of the McGregor family.

"I'm sorry you're going home," Madison told her as they sat in the shade of the awning.

"Vacations have to end sometime."

"Yeah, I know, and Seattle may be a better place to raise kids. I've been thinking about moving to the city myself."

"To Seattle?"

"Maybe. At least somewhere bigger than Schuyler. It's hard to think of leaving, but the guys are backward here. You'd think they dropped right out of the nineteenth century, especially when it comes to their women."

Kayla kept back a smile, recalling her clashes

with Jackson. "I suppose a few ranchers cling to older attitudes."

"And others, as well," Madison added darkly. Kayla had a feeling she was having problems with the man currently in her life.

"Some people in Schuyler seem relatively in step with the modern world," Kayla said. It was true. Even *Jackson* didn't have a problem with her as a businesswoman; his issues with females were based on entirely different ideas. It was possible he might shed some of his chauvinism if he was determinedly kicked in the right direction.

"Maybe. You know, you've been good for the family."

"That's nice," Kayla answered, surprised by the change of subject.

"You probably think I'm just being polite, but I mean it."

Not knowing what to say, Kayla simply smiled.

"Having more kids around has been great, too. I'm beginning to see why Mom keeps saying we need more children in the family. It keeps you loosened up, instead of trying to always do things the way you used to. I've been thinking that I don't need to have a guy to have a baby—I could go to one of those sperm banks."

Kayla leaned forward. "I'm sure that works well for lots of women. But I've had a baby alone and I've had one with my husband, and there's something to be said for doing it as a team."

Madison's chin rose determinedly. "Except I don't want to just wait around hoping something will happen."

"I understand, and my marriage didn't work out," Kayla conceded. "But you're not ancient, so don't give up, even if you decide to make a withdrawal at a sperm bank."

Madison grinned. "Withdrawal? I like that. Anyhow…" She glanced across the pool to where Jackson was talking to Josh. "It turns out that the guy I've been seeing is a real loser. Maybe I shouldn't have gone out with him, but he was different from the guys in my family."

"Oh?"

"Never mind." Madison turned around. "My mother has this crazy idea that you and Jackson might get together again."

Kayla tried not to show any reaction. "That isn't going to happen, if for no other reason than he has too much baggage left from being married to Marcy."

"I know. God, she was awful." Madison shuddered. "Alaina and I told Mom that, but she keeps hoping anyhow."

"And you were asked to scope out the possibilities with me, right?" Kayla guessed shrewdly.

Madison nodded, looking embarrassed. "She kept pushing, so we got together and drew straws. I thought Alaina would be best—she's better at diplomacy—only I got the short straw. I was supposed to be subtle and sneaky, but I'm not good at that."

"Just tell her there's nothing to report."

"Right."

Madison stayed and chatted until Kayla said she wanted to go in the water to cool off. She changed and came out of the pool house, aware of Jackson's intent gaze as she walked across the damp pavement. She could have kicked him—his mother had definitely noticed his interest.

The day wore on slowly, and when she wasn't trying to interact with people, Kayla stewed over the situation. There was an ache inside her that wouldn't subside.

How had she landed in such a mess? Somehow Jackson—a guy with worse trust issues than the ones she had herself—had gotten through her defenses. And that wasn't even counting his often archaic attitudes about the opposite sex. Even Cora had told her she wouldn't mind a visit with the caveman, she just didn't want to live with one.

Perhaps while trying to help Alex build a relationship with his birth father, she'd let herself see Jackson's positive side too clearly—his devotion to Morgan and sincere desire to live honestly and work hard. He knew how to laugh and… *Hell*. What was the point of enumerating his good qualities?

After supper she started moving the kids toward the car.

Jackson stopped her before she slid behind the wheel. "Kayla, do you have a few minutes to talk? I'd like to clarify a couple of matters before you leave for Seattle."

In frustration, she glanced at her watch. It was only seven. Although she had time, she'd hoped to avoid any *more* private moments with Jackson. "Okay, but I want to get the kids home to my grandparents' house, and I'd rather not drive back to the ranch. Can we meet at Ryan's in an hour?"

"Sure."

It was déjà vu as she later walked into the restaurant and saw Jackson waiting at the bar. He led the way to the private table they had occupied the first time they'd met to discuss Alex. She tried not to speculate what he had on his mind this time.

"So what's up?" she asked as they sat.

He seemed ill at ease. "This isn't the ideal spot for what I wanted to discuss, but I was wondering if you really have to return to Seattle."

Kayla blinked. "I know you don't want to see Alex leave—some of the barriers are coming down and you're getting more comfortable—but the kids need to be in a stable routine before school starts. Our life is in the city."

"It doesn't have to be," he returned quickly. "I was thinking we could try to be…together."

She stared, her anger growing. "Yeah, it's always been my dream to be with a guy who doesn't trust women and simply wants to keep his son in Montana," she said, sarcasm dripping from her voice. "And it's such a terrific idea, give up everything I've worked for so that you, as *a man*, can have what you want."

"Damn." Jackson ran his fingers through his hair. "I didn't say it right. This isn't about Alex. I was trying to say that I love you."

Kayla reined in her temper. "That's hard to believe. You've been up front until now, admitting you don't ever want to get seriously involved again. What am I supposed to do, keep my door open so you can stop by for sex once in a while? Or are we supposed to try living together while Schuyler takes bets on how long it will be before you start dating again?"

His jaw hardened. "No. I'm asking you to marry me, and I happen to believe in fidelity."

"Oh, now I'm supposed to accept you've suddenly changed your mind and think marriage is a good thing."

"Did you notice that I said I loved you?"

"They're just words, Jackson. Even if you *are* serious, it would never work—we both have too many issues with trust. You ought to be satisfied that Alex is willing to spend time with you. That's a big enough accomplishment for the summer."

He leaned forward, looking so sincere that her heart flipped over. "I do trust you, and I love you more than I ever thought possible."

Kayla closed her eyes to shut him out. It was the

kind of thing she'd once dreamed of him saying, except that she was a different person now, with children to protect. She couldn't take a chance on believing him.

"Kayla, I know you've been hurt, and God knows I was one of the people who was a part of that," Jackson pressed. "But we've both gone through fire to get where we are today. I finally know how precious being with the right person can be. We can make a future for each other if you just give me another chance."

Suddenly she swung her legs out of the booth and stood up. "This is pointless, Jackson. I'm heading back to Washington in the morning. We'll come to Schuyler occasionally, and you can visit Alex in Seattle, if that's what you want. But I'm not going to sit here and listen to nonsense."

With her head held high, Kayla walked toward the front of the restaurant. She was not, repeat, *not* going to cry. She'd survived a broken heart once. She could do it again.

DAMN, DAMN, DAMN, Jackson cursed silently.

Was there any way he could have managed a more pathetic marriage proposal?

All at once irony struck him. Though he'd once been married, this was actually his first proposal. The arrangements for his marriage to Marcy had been exactly that—arrangements. He'd accepted responsibility for having fathered a child and had married Marcy because that was the way his family did things.

"Did you want to order anything, Jackson?" asked a woman's voice, breaking into his thoughts.

He threw a twenty on the table. "Sorry, Lisette, I'm not eating after all."

Her smile grew more intimate. "I get off soon. How about making a night of it?"

"Thanks, but no."

Lord, what a difference one summer had made. There'd been a time when he wouldn't have turned down the invitation. Lisette was relatively new in town and they'd gotten together once or twice. She liked hot, fast sex and wasn't particular about where she got it.

But now all Jackson could think about was the auburn-haired beauty he'd lost once as a callow teenager and stood in danger of losing again, when it mattered most.

He strode out to his truck. There was no way in hell he was giving up, though he'd have to consider what his next move should be. He was in love with Kayla and was certain they could have a future together. The problem was getting her to see it, too.

But as he climbed behind the wheel, ice condensed in his gut and he stared at the remnants of the sunset. He loved Kayla so much that the thought of living without her was hardly bearable, but he couldn't force her to trust him, or to love him back.

CHAPTER NINETEEN

JACKSON TAPPED ON Morgan's door the next morning before the sun had risen. "Hey, sleepyhead, we've got to get going if we're going to see everyone before they leave."

The door popped open and his daughter, fully dressed, grinned at him. "I've been up for an hour."

"I'm impressed."

"So am I." Then her bottom lip trembled. "I just wish they weren't going."

"Me, too." He pulled her into a hug before they went down to eat a quick bowl of cereal.

Kayla was largely responsible for the quiet, friendly mood between him and his daughter. Maybe he would have figured it out eventually, but she was the one who'd opened his eyes to the problems, which was why he'd finally been able to start doing something about them.

When they arrived at the Garrison house, the kids were carrying their duffel bags out to stuff into the cargo area of the Volvo. With the exception of Kayla, they all looked half-asleep. No doubt she'd already gone out for a predawn run, giving her skin a healthy, sexy glow. It was only in her eyes that there were shadows.

Jackson drew her aside. "Please think about what we discussed last night," he pleaded, gazing intently into her face. "I'm not giving up on us."

"I thought we finished that conversation," she answered.

"I'll never finish with it. I'm just asking you to trust me one more time, please. Trust yourself. Trust us."

Her lips tightened before she turned and called, "Come on, guys. We need to say goodbye and get on the road."

Keri and Sandy thanked the Garrisons for hosting them, and Jackson for all the fun at his ranch. DeeDee threw her arms around his neck, sniffing a little, before hugging Morgan, too. Jackson looked at Alex and the two of them sort of bumped shoulders.

There were hugs and kisses all around with the Garrisons, neither of whom pretended to have a dry eye at the farewell. And in the middle he spotted Morgan giving her brother a hug, as well. Morgan stepped back, blinking furiously, and Elizabeth put an arm around her shoulders.

But Kayla simply smiled as if Jackson was a mere acquaintance before climbing into the Volvo.

"You'll let me know when you get home safely?" he asked, leaning in to look at her.

"I'll email."

Email? That was no substitute for hearing her voice.

Watching the SUV disappear down the dark road left Jackson with a twisting pain in his gut.

ALEX DIDN'T FEEL so great.

Running away had been a lousy idea that had somehow turned out okay. For a while he'd been afraid he'd messed up his whole family. But now he was leaving half his family in Montana—the new part of his family.

DeeDee was sitting in the middle seat and she turned to stare at Alex with unusually wide eyes. She almost never cried, but if she did, he had a feeling she'd be doing it right now.

"Mom, when's the next time we'll see… Grandma and Grandpa?" He'd almost included Jackson, and that was weird.

"No plans yet," his mom said. "But I'm sure it won't be too long, and you can phone or video call with them whenever you want."

"Uh, okay."

His phone signaled that he had a text, so he pulled it out and found one from Morgan.

Alrdy ms ur ugly face. When ru coming bak?

Don't know, he texted back.

Sucks.

Duh. Gotta go.

He turned off the phone since Mom always said it was rude to be in a group and ignore them while texting. As he put the phone away, he heard crackling and remembered the envelope Jackson had given him as they were getting into the car. Alex opened it and found a note. Outside it was still pretty dark, so he turned on a light to read it.

Alex,
I hope you'll feel comfortable keeping in contact with me. Take care of your mom and your sister.
—Jackson

On a small card Jackson had printed his home number, cell phone and email address.

Carefully, Alex put the card in his wallet. When he looked up, DeeDee was staring again.

"Jackson gave me one, too," she whispered.

"Good, then you won't have to bug me for it. Squirt."

"You're soooo funny."

"Let's put on a movie," Keri suggested.

Sandy was taking the first turn in the front seat so she couldn't watch, but Alex started *Wild Hogs* on one of the built-in DVD players in the headrest, and in a while he almost forgot the hollow feeling he'd gotten when they drove away from Schuyler. He knew he'd miss Grandma and Grandpa, and Morgan, of course. But he hadn't expected to miss Jackson the way he already did.

KAYLA FOCUSED ON the road ahead, her eyes stinging. Seeing the emotion in her grandparents' faces had nearly made her cry. She'd hated saying goodbye to them, as much as they'd hated seeing her leave.

Then there was Jackson and his damned marriage proposal.

She'd been trying to keep from thinking about it. A proposal was the last thing she'd expected, though maybe she should have realized it was a possibility. He cared about his daughter and wanted to be close to Alex; he was also big on responsibility, and money wasn't the only way he wanted to take care of his son.

It was admirable, but it didn't mean she could marry him. And it made no difference that Jackson had said he loved her. She knew better. After so many years of distrusting women, he'd suddenly decided to give love and the wedded state another go? Hardly. His proposal must have been an extremely rash impulse.

AS THEY APPROACHED SEATTLE, Kayla called Keri's and Sandy's families to let them know they were getting close. The Garzas and the Kellers had already arrived when she pulled into the driveway. They stood and talked while the kids chattered about their Montana adventures and gathered their belongings.

It was odd to step into the house that was so familiar yet now also felt foreign. Could she have changed that much in the weeks they'd been gone? Nothing was altered on the surface—it had to be the way her brain perceived it.

Their favorite Chinese restaurant stayed open late and she called in an order to be delivered, hoping it would help make everything seem normal again.

"It tastes different," DeeDee complained.

"We're just spoiled by Grams's cooking," Kayla said, though she agreed with her daughter. It *did* taste different. "And we're tired."

Before going to bed she phoned her grandparents and emailed Jackson. Then she crawled between the sheets to stare at the darkened ceiling; it was hours before she finally fell asleep. Her insomnia had never been this bad before.

In the morning Kayla followed her daily routine, going for her run before returning to fix a pot of oatmeal. The kids, still on Montana time, weren't quite as groggily comatose as usual.

DeeDee yawned. "Why couldn't we sleep late today?"

"School starts next week," Kayla reminded her.

"Uh-uh," DeeDee objected. "Not for a couple of weeks."

"You're thinking about Morgan's school," Alex told her. "She starts later than we do."

"Rats."

Kayla nodded. "So you need to start getting used to being awake earlier."

Alex and DeeDee groaned in chorus.

"Did you call Jackson?" DeeDee asked as she poured sunflower seeds into her oatmeal. "He wanted to know when we got here."

"I emailed him last night."

"And I told Morgan all about our trip," Alex added.

"Have you been Facebooking with her?" Kayla asked.

"Yeah. She, uh, sort of found me...before we met."

"That's what I figured. You already seemed to know her when we left for Yellowstone."

"Morgan and me text each other, too," DeeDee said.

DeeDee appeared glum, with Alex not far behind, and it didn't appear to be from sleepiness. Kayla reminded herself that an emotional letdown was to be expected after an extended vacation, even for someone as naturally buoyant as her daughter.

She left for the office and found everything operating smoothly. Everyone seemed glad to see her and she spent several hours meeting with employees and a doctor who dropped by, but she wasn't needed that badly, so she left after lunch. Her chagrin was balanced by her grandfather's reminder that she'd done her job well enough to have become redundant.

Admittedly, she was depressed herself, but that would surely pass, as it would for the kids.

So what if she was in love with Jackson? The issues between them hadn't changed, and he was probably devoutly grateful that she'd turned down his rash proposal.

Alex and DeeDee were in the kitchen when she got home and she gave them a determinedly upbeat smile. "There's a game at Safeco tonight. Want to go? We can eat junk food for dinner."

"Awesome," DeeDee said, and Alex nodded. They weren't as excited as she'd expected, but maybe she was reading too much into it.

She had to be sensible. If she ever got married again, it would be to someone in the city that she could count on. Her feelings for Jackson had nothing to do with true love—and if she told herself that often enough, surely she'd believe it.

JACKSON REINED IN Thunder and gazed at the cattle scattered along a low swale. It was his second day riding fences since Kayla had left, but the familiar task had done nothing to lessen the pain in his chest and gut.

He flexed his arm, his elbow throbbing where

he'd slashed it on a wire. It had been the result of inattentiveness, but at least the ragged cut hadn't required stitches.

Thunder snorted and Jackson urged him forward again.

Kayla had barely looked at him when she'd gotten into the Volvo. Her lack of response had stung, but was hardly surprising. And maybe it was too much to expect since she'd also been saying goodbye to her grandparents.

As he reached the top of a rise, his smartphone alerted him to an incoming text; it was from Alex

How is the new foal doing?

Grateful Alex had taken the time to type out the words, since he wasn't adept at deciphering texting language, Jackson carefully answered.

Great. Ruby is taking good care of him now.

A couple of hours later, another text arrived, this one from DeeDee.

Thx 4 Y 4 hrs 4 gr8 bbQs DD

The barbecue part of the message wasn't too difficult, but it took a while to figure out that the rest was probably a thank-you for the camping trip and teaching her to ride.

U R welcome. Glad U were here, he typed back.

The contact with the kids heartened him. But otherwise, the long hours in the saddle provided little of their usual solace.

He ached for Kayla.

It wasn't the sex, good as that had been. It was the longing for everything that made up a couple's life together. He kept imagining little moments, such as sitting on the porch as he held her hand. Riding together. Nights when they sent the kids to the Garrisons or his parents so they could be alone.

They'd eat dinner as a family, with DeeDee devising a ridiculous word to describe her day, Morgan blooming with both a father and mother to support her and Alex outlining a project he was doing at school. Knowing Kayla had wanted more children enlivened Jackson's imagination further. They could marvel together at a kicking foot and at the first cry of a new son or daughter. There would be all sorts of things to share—settling sibling squabbles, waking the kids up to see a foal being born, dealing with college applications, worrying over their decisions…countless moments.

Together.

He finally got it. When you truly loved someone, you loved each other through the good times and bad. And even when you argued, you knew at the end you'd make up and learn from it and love even more. Of course, Kayla hadn't said she loved him, but he doubted she would have been *that* upset by his proposal if she didn't have strong feelings for him.

After the long day, Jackson returned to the house and checked for voice mail on the landline phone, then checked his emails and double-checked his texts to be sure he hadn't missed any possible word from Kayla. Not surprisingly, there was nothing from her aside from the one email saying they'd arrived safely.

"Do you want me to take you shopping for school clothes?" he asked Morgan as they ate dinner, trying to inject a note of normality. They'd shared so many meals with a group it seemed unusually quiet, especially since Flora had gone into town to see the latest Bruce Willis flick.

Morgan shrugged. "Whatever."

A couple of months earlier, that "whatever" would have frustrated the hell out of him. Now he simply nodded.

"We can do it however way you like. If you'd prefer, we could even drive to Billings or Helena and see what they've got there."

She seemed to brighten. "Um...that might be nice."

"I'm sure we'll have a good time as long as you don't expect me to understand anything about women's fashion."

A tiny smile curved her mouth. "Okay."

"How about watching a movie?" he suggested.

They went into the family room and wrangled

good-naturedly over what film to watch, finally settling on the stylish Agatha Christie classic *Death
on the Nile*. They popped a bowl of popcorn and sat
sipping sodas, trading comments on the scenery.

"Some of the costumes are pretty, but I wouldn't
like wearing them," Morgan said at one point. "And
most of the wife's evening dresses look stupid, even
though they're supposed to be sexy."

Sexy?

Jackson tried not to get uncomfortable. "The
character is too obnoxious to be sexy."

"Yeah. It's like, who cares if she's toast?"

He grinned, thinking it was a good thing he
knew the movie since his mind really wasn't on the
plot. Instead, images of Kayla kept flitting through
his head, and he hoped that she was thinking about
him, as well. There was nothing else he could do.

Except…it *wasn't* the only thing he could do.
He could go to Seattle and show Kayla that he was
completely committed to a life together.

At TEN O'CLOCK that night Kayla almost wished she
hadn't suggested going to Safeco Field. The teams
were tied and the game was going into extra innings. Everyone around them was excited, but she
wanted to go home and crawl into bed. Or maybe
it was just the depression talking.

On the other hand, being at the ball game seemed
to have perked up Alex and DeeDee, along with

the hot dogs, garlic fries and ice cream sundaes they'd eaten.

During the second inning Alex had taken out his phone and texted something. Kayla didn't ask whom he was contacting, figuring it was probably Sandy. He checked the phone several times and didn't seem to get an answer until he looked again between the tenth and eleventh innings.

"Morgan and Jackson watched *Death on the Nile* tonight," he announced. "I didn't know they liked old movies."

"It's not that old," Kayla told him, hating the way her nerves tightened. She had to expect to hear Jackson's name from now on, especially since Alex had become such good friends with Morgan.

"It's older than me. Jeez, it's even older than *you*," Alex said. Obviously something being older than his mother was his benchmark for old.

The idea of sitting with Jackson and watching a movie, classic or new, was immensely appealing, and it was hard not to think how things could be if they were together. Like...what if he was at the game with them right now? His eyes probably would have crinkled with humor at Alex's definition of old. Maybe he would have put on that funny voice and suggested finding their canes and making their way to a rocking chair. And the French fries, loaded with fresh-chopped garlic, would have made him tease that they'd better *both* eat their share.

Stop, you're just making it harder, Kayla scolded herself.

It would be difficult enough to see Jackson when they visited her grandparents; she didn't have to compound the pain by considering everything that could have been.

The Mariners won at the stroke of midnight and they cheered before joining the throng heading for their cars. Kayla was grateful that it was too busy and chaotic to think about anything except making their way through the crowd.

THE NEXT MORNING Jackson sat at the kitchen table and waited for Morgan to get back from her run. Electricity seemed to be bursting in every cell of his body.

What were the best words to use when he talked to Kayla again? What tone of voice?

It was possible that if he hadn't married Marcy and Kayla had stayed in Schuyler, they might have eventually fallen in love for real. Who could say? But it didn't matter, because that wasn't how it had happened. Instead, they'd taken independent paths and become different people. And the man he'd become loved Kayla Anderson completely.

"Hey," Morgan said, entering the kitchen shortly after eight.

"Good morning," he replied. "I've got a suggestion. How about going to Seattle to buy your school clothes?"

Her green eyes opened wide. "Really?"

"You bet. It would be fun to do something different. Perhaps we could even visit the artist who made that necklace you like."

"Cool. Just wait until I tell Alex and DeeDee."

"How about surprising them instead?" he suggested. "It would be fun to see their faces if we show up and they didn't know we were coming."

"Dope!" Morgan exclaimed, presumably in agreement.

He would have emphasized not letting Alex or DeeDee know their plans, but he didn't want Morgan to wonder why he thought it was important. While it was tempting to employ her support in winning over Kayla, it wouldn't be fair to her or to Kayla.

"Why don't you go get packed?" he said. "We'll probably spend the night in Spokane, and get into the city tomorrow." Normally he'd prefer driving straight through, but with a later start, it made more sense to make it a two-day journey.

"You mean we'd leave today?"

"Why not?"

Morgan giggled. "Awesome."

She thundered up the back staircase and Jackson mentally reviewed his preparations. He'd packed, written out orders for his foreman, talked with Flora, asked Greg to watch Cory and emailed his parents to say he and Morgan were driving to the city for school shopping. He hadn't mentioned Seattle by name to his folks—there were no guarantees he'd be able to convince Kayla to marry him and he didn't want to raise anyone's hopes.

He particularly didn't want Elizabeth and Hank to anticipate Kayla and the children's return to Schuyler, in case it didn't happen.

Their return to Schuyler?

Jackson frowned.

That night at Ryan's, Kayla had accused him of expecting her to give up everything she'd worked for so he could have what *he* wanted. It was the same sort of mistake he'd made with Marcy, agreeing to live on a ranch hand's income for five years without asking how she felt about it. Jackson doubted anything would have saved his marriage, but maybe she wouldn't have been so bitter.

Damn. He really *was* the chauvinist Kayla and his sisters kept calling him. If he wanted to become a better man, he had to stop making assumptions. After all, he didn't want Morgan or DeeDee growing up thinking they had to give up everything for a man. He wanted them to stand up for themselves.

So he couldn't expect Kayla to simply drop everything and move to Montana. If they got married, they would have to work out a lot of details, and *both* of them would have to compromise.

He loaded his bag into the Suburban, glad it had been serviced after their return from Yellowstone. Morgan carried her duffel bag out and he put it next to his own. "You're already packed?" she asked.

"Sure. I come up with my best ideas in the middle of the night, so I took care of a few things in case you wanted to go."

"I hope I didn't forget anything."

She touched her throat very quickly, as if to be certain the pendant Kayla had given her was there, and Jackson had the urge to buy her every single piece of jewelry he could find, but only if it was what she wanted. It was time for her to be her own person.

"Don't worry, we can buy anything you forgot," he assured. "After all, we'll be doing your school shopping."

"Do you think Kayla might help me choose stuff?"

"You don't trust your dad's questionable taste?"

Morgan laughed, then sobered. "I'm just not sure what kind of clothes I want, and Kayla always looks super pretty."

"Yes, she does," Jackson agreed. "If you want to dress like her, that's fine, but it's also okay to experiment and find out what style fits you the best."

Morgan jumped into the Suburban and eyed the cooler on the floor behind the seat. "What's in there?"

"Snacks I raided from the refrigerator. I also made sandwiches while you were out running and grabbed that bowl of barbecued chicken from last night."

"Yum." She squirmed around the seat, opened the cooler and pulled out a sandwich.

"Hungry already?"

"Duh, I ran miles and miles."

She munched as he drove out to the main road. He'd considered having Morgan stay with his parents or Flora, but they *did* need to take care of her school shopping. Besides, how could he leave her behind when they'd finally started talking again? As much as he loved Kayla, he didn't want his daughter to think he loved her less. Once he would have thought it was impossible for Morgan to get such an idea, but lately he'd been humbled by his assumptions.

Reaching the highway, he turned toward Seattle, and resisted hitting the accelerator too hard.

CHAPTER TWENTY

WHEN KAYLA RETURNED to the house after her run, she peeked in at the kids. Yucca, their cat, lifted his head from where he was tucked under Alex's chin. He yawned and snuggled back down, closing his eyes. In her room, DeeDee was sprawled across her bed, oblivious to the world.

Kayla had told them to sleep as long as they wanted. It might make it more difficult for them to adjust to a school schedule, but she was hoping the treat of a late night at Safeco, not to mention the disgustingly fun junk food they'd consumed, had lifted their spirits.

After showering, Kayla resisted the temptation to crawl into bed again herself. It wouldn't do any good anyhow. Once she got there, her imagination would simply take over, picturing Jackson lying next to her.

Hell. If she had to fall in love again, why couldn't it have been with someone suitable who wouldn't break her heart? Why did it have to be an old-fashioned Montana rancher with a boatload of macho attitudes?

KAYLA SPENT THE rest of the day reviewing paperwork at the office. While she'd still been in Montana, Roger had mentioned there were several new clients who wanted to use Smooth Billings. He'd gotten the contracts together and she went over them carefully.

Because the new clients would expand their workload, Roger had also set up interviews for a new employee. The following morning they sat down with the first applicant. Unfortunately, despite his excellent résumé, something about the guy didn't seem right.

"He's a no go for me," Roger announced when they were alone.

Kayla nodded. "Same here. I think it's best to go with your gut."

"Definitely. I'll see if the next applicant has arrived. We need to get someone hired and trained before those contracts go active."

"Yeah. By the way, I owe you a bonus for doing such a great job while I was gone."

Roger grinned as he left.

Kayla studied the next application, wishing her head wasn't so mixed-up. Normally her instincts were fairly reliable…except when it came to romance.

They spent the next several hours in job interviews and finally agreed on a former nurse who'd applied. She'd taken early retirement due to problems with her feet and was eager to continue doing something to help patients.

Kayla tried to focus on the paperwork needing her signature. She'd expected to feel better now that she was back to her usual routine, but if anything, she felt worse. She couldn't even get away from thoughts of Jackson in her sleep. He was in her dreams, but in them, he kept slipping away, out of her reach, and she'd wake up with her pulse pounding.

Was it a message from her subconscious?

If so, it must mean one of two things—either her head was telling her that Jackson was a poor prospect and could never really be hers...or her heart was saying she'd let something wonderful go without finding out the possibilities.

But which one was it?

MORGAN TOSSED HER suitcase on the bed of the motel room. Her dad's room was through a connecting door.

Taking out her cell phone, she checked the latest message from Alex. She'd been fishing for clues about what he was doing that day, and now she knew he'd gone to Sandy's house.

Her dad knocked and peered through the door. "You settled in?"

"Sort of," she said. "I want to walk over to Sandy's and surprise Alex. I checked and it's only about ten blocks away."

He was quiet a minute before answering. "Why don't I drop you off instead, and you call when you need a ride?"

"Ah, Dad."

"Humor me."

It was strange that he wasn't asking to see Alex, too, but she didn't say anything about it. He was probably tired, or maybe he wanted to let her surprise him alone first.

Dad parked down the street from Sandy's house, but she knew he was watching while she walked to the door and waited for it to open.

It was Sandy, and her mouth dropped open. Morgan grinned. "Surprise. Alex is here, isn't he?"

"Yep. But wait a sec, I want my camera so I can catch his face when he sees you."

Morgan waved as her dad finally started the Suburban and drove down the street. This was going to be fun.

KAYLA GOT HOME midafternoon, her briefcase stuffed with a backlog of technical material to read. Usually the bustle of employees at the office didn't bother her, but today was an exception.

She was deep in an article about electronic file management when the doorbell rang. Yucca was on her lap and meowed a complaint as she shifted him onto the couch.

"Sorry, pal."

Kayla opened the front door and the air whooshed from her chest. What was Jackson doing in Seattle?

"Hey," he said. "Am I interrupting something?"

"I was just studying a business article." She glanced behind him. "Is Morgan with you?"

"She's surprising Alex at Sandy's house. May I come in?"

"I… Uh, sure."

If returning home after spending so much time in Montana had felt strange, having Jackson in her house felt positively bizarre.

"I'll make coffee," she said.

He glanced around as they walked to the kitchen. "This is nice. I see why you've been reluctant to sell."

"Yeah, but I've started searching online for real estate in the area. There's a property I want to see—it's got terrific outdoor space and lots of light, and is closer to Alex and DeeDee's schools."

"Oh."

He sat at the table while Kayla started the coffee-maker and got cream from the refrigerator. After so many meetings at the Coffee Shack, she knew Jackson invariably took his black, but she needed something to buffer her stomach.

"Have you eaten?" she asked. "I could order something."

"Not right now, unless you're hungry."

"I'm fine. I got pizza for my employees and ate a slice before leaving the office." The conversation was inane, but at least it was giving her a chance to pull her wits together.

It was unnerving to see Jackson comfortably ensconced in her bright kitchen. She would have expected him to look out of place in Seattle, but he didn't. Instead, he looked sexy and dependable and wonderful... Kayla threw the brakes on her runaway thoughts.

When the coffee finished brewing, she poured two cups and sat across from him.

"So what are you doing in Washington?" she asked finally.

"Shopping for Morgan's school clothes. She was thrilled at the idea."

Kayla tried not to feel disappointed, though she wondered why they'd come to Seattle for their shopping. "I need to get busy doing that with Alex and DeeDee. Their school year starts even earlier than it does in Schuyler."

"Morgan was hoping she could go with you and DeeDee—I think she wants a woman's point of view."

"I'd be happy to take her with us."

Jackson drank some of his coffee. "I appreciate it, but I have to admit the shopping was partly an excuse. I wanted to see you."

Kayla gulped suddenly, adrenaline taking effect far more quickly than the caffeine in the coffee. "Oh?"

He reached over and picked up her hand. "Kayla,

I love you. Being hundreds of miles apart, or all the time in the world, won't change that. I should have asked before, but I will now... Do you love me?"

A tremor went through her body and she slowly brought it under control. "Yes," she managed to say. "But that doesn't mean it would work between us."

She stared at Jackson's fingers grasping hers gently yet firmly. She'd convinced herself that he must be relieved she had turned him down. It had been safer that way—safer, because she'd always wanted to be in love the way her mother had once been in love...and was afraid to be at the same time.

"It's impossible to promise you perfection or a life without pain," he murmured huskily. "But I *can* promise to love you forever and hang on to our marriage with all my strength."

Kayla didn't doubt Jackson's sincerity. And since he'd had several days to think about it—not to mention more than fifteen hours of driving time for reflection—wanting to marry her couldn't be dismissed as simply an impulse that he'd later regret.

"I've been thinking that we could try to find a way to split our time between Montana and Seattle," he continued. "We both have good managers able to handle things when we aren't there."

"You're talking about living in Seattle part of the year?" she asked incredulously.

Jackson nodded. "You were right about me

thinking you should give up everything. In fact, I'm glad you turned me down the first time, because it made me face reality. I can't promise I won't slip into old habits, but I want you to pull me up short if I do. Because that's not the way I want Morgan and DeeDee to see men and women. Hell, that's not the model I want for Alex, either. Maybe he'll be the president's husband someday, and he should be proud of it."

It wasn't the sort of thing Kayla had expected to hear, but he was being straight with her. She doubted splitting time between Seattle and Schuyler would work; it might make more sense for her to run Smooth Billings long-distance with periodic trips to the city. But her mind was still bending around the fact that Jackson was willing to compromise, that he wasn't expecting her to give up everything so they could be together. If they were both willing to compromise...all sorts of things were possible.

"Can we trust each other?" Jackson asked. "Could you take that leap of faith with me?"

"I'm not good at trust," Kayla admitted, forcing her mind back to a second central issue. Perhaps Jackson *wasn't* the one with the biggest problem in that department.

His eyes darkened. "And you've gotten hurt whenever you *have* tried to trust someone. Y ex-husband. *Me*. You have no idea how much I regret being such a stupid, selfish clod."

"You were seventeen, Jackson."

"That's a rotten excuse." He paused and seemed to be searching for words. "But I've been thinking—all the way to Seattle—that even if someone we love *never* lets us down, someday we'll lose them, or they'll lose us. So we'll still get hurt eventually, but the cost is never having that person in our lives. That's too high a price. Would you cut yourself off again from Hank and Elizabeth because someday they'll be gone?"

"No." An awful pain went through Kayla at the thought of losing her grandparents. But it would be even worse if they were in Schuyler and she was staying away out of emotional cowardice.

HOPE SURGED IN JACKSON. At least Kayla was talking to him. It was what they'd have to do if they got married—talk and keep talking.

"Sweetheart, you're right about the way I've been for years. I haven't trusted women, and to defend that attitude, I've adopted some stupid, outdated notions. And the craziest part is that I never loved Marcy—we got married for Morgan's sake. I don't know if Marcy would have become a nicer person ~~if th~~ had been different, but I shouldn't have ~~~~ffect me like that. It was stupid and hurt ~~~~le I care about the most."

Kayla smiled gently. "We don't have to beat ourselves up about the past, do we?"

"No, it's the future that counts. I love you so much, Kayla, and I'm praying you'll marry me and we can raise our three children together. We could even make more babies, if you'd like."

She blinked. "You'd want more kids?"

"Hey, the more the merrier. But if you'd rather not, I'll be happy with three. Either way, DeeDee can invent one of her words for the complicated family we'll make."

Kayla laughed and it was the most beautiful sound in the world. "She'd love that."

"So how about it? Will you marry me and love me for the rest of our lives?"

KAYLA TOOK A DEEP, shuddering breath. Jackson was choosing her instead of clinging to his wounds. She could do the same if she was willing to follow him in that leap of faith.

His hand was strong, and she remembered how he'd stuck to his parenting responsibilities through a long, difficult year with Morgan. He loved his daughter and had never given up, though it couldn't have been easy, and he hadn't given up with Alex, either, however many times he'd fumbled. Beyond that, he was opening his mind, showing the direction in which he wanted to grow as a human being.

She hadn't wanted to risk the pain of anther messed-up relationship, but turning Jackson away wouldn't guarantee being safe from hurt. It would only mean loneliness. He was right—protecting yourself too fiercely carried too high a price, because it meant living without love.

"I love you and I want to marry you," she said steadily.

Jackson's smile flashed like a Montana sunrise as he leaped to his feet and pulled her into his arms.

ALEX HADN'T BEEN able to believe it when he'd looked up to see Morgan standing in front of him. Sandy had laughed, and he realized she'd taken a picture of him with his mouth hanging open.

"Delete that," he'd growled.

"Not a chance," Sandy had refused.

Sandy's mom had welcomed Morgan and insisted she eat with them.

"Let's go shock DeeDee, too," Morgan suggested after they'd demolished a bucket of fried chicken. "I want to see *her* face when we show up."

But they didn't get a chance to surprise DeeDee the way they'd hoped. She was looking out the window at Keri's house and both of them came out-

ming.

's Jackson?" DeeDee demanded. "And

"We had to leave Cory at the ranch," Morgan explained. "Dad dropped me off at Sandy's and said to let him know when I needed a ride. I just called and he's coming over here to pick me up."

"He didn't go in to see Alex?" DeeDee asked.

"No."

"That's funny."

Morgan shrugged. "Nah, I think he was just giving us space or whatever."

"I still think it's strange."

"Maybe he went to see your mom," Sandy suggested. "Alex says I'm wrong, but I think he has a thing for her."

"Really?" Morgan said. "That's *awesome*."

"Mom said there wasn't anything going on," Alex insisted.

DeeDee excitedly hopped from one foot to the other. "I'm with Sandy and Morgan. It would be dopeacious if they got together!"

A minute later Jackson's big SUV pulled into the driveway and Alex saw his mom in the front seat. Jackson waved and went around to open the passenger door. That was when Alex knew Sandy and DeeDee were right, because of the way they smiled at each other.

"You don't mind, do you, Alex?" DeeDee asked. "If Mom loves him, we gotta make it easy on her, because we should take care of our family. A Mom looks awful happy. It really *is* dopeac

Alex felt strange about it, but maybe it was a good kind of strange. "Yeah," he agreed. "And for once I like one of your new words. Just don't overuse it."

* * * * *

LARGER-PRINT BOOKS!

GET 2 FREE LARGER-PRINT NOVELS PLUS
2 FREE GIFTS!

⬧HARLEQUIN®

Romance

From the Heart, For the Heart

YES! Please send me 2 FREE LARGER-PRINT Harlequin® Romance novels and my 2 FREE gifts (gifts are worth about $10). After receiving them, if I don't wish to receive any more books, I can return the shipping statement marked "cancel." If I don't cancel, I will receive 4 brand-new novels every month and be billed just $5.09 per book in the U.S. or $5.49 per book in Canada. That's a savings of at least 15% off the cover price! It's quite a bargain! Shipping and handling is just 50¢ per book in the U.S. and 75¢ per book in Canada.* I understand that accepting the 2 free books and gifts places me under no obligation to buy anything. I can always return a shipment and cancel at any time. Even if I never buy another book, the two free books and gifts are mine to keep forever.

119/319 HDN GHWC

Name	(PLEASE PRINT)	

Address		Apt. #

City	State/Prov.	Zip/Postal Code

Signature (if under 18, a parent or guardian must sign)

Mail to the **Reader Service**:
IN U.S.A.: P.O. Box 1867, Buffalo, NY 14240-1867
IN CANADA: P.O. Box 609, Fort Erie, Ontario L2A 5X3
Want to try two free books from another line?
Call 1-800-873-8635 or visit www.ReaderService.com.

* Terms and prices subject to change without notice. Prices do not include applicable taxes. Sales tax applicable in N.Y. Canadian residents will be charged applicable taxes. Offer not valid in Quebec. This offer is limited to one order per household. Not valid for current subscribers to Harlequin Romance Larger-Print books. All orders subject to credit approval. Credit or debit balances in a customer's account(s) may be offset by any other outstanding balance owed by or to the customer. Please allow 4 to 6 weeks for delivery. Offer available while quantities last.

Your Privacy—The Reader Service is committed to protecting your privacy. Our Privacy Policy is available online at www.ReaderService.com or upon request from the Reader Service.

We make a portion of our mailing list available to reputable third parties that offer products we believe may interest you. If you prefer that we not exchange your name with third parties, or if you wish to clarify or modify your communication preferences, please visit us at www.ReaderService.com/consumerschoice or write to us at Reader Service Preference Service, P.O. Box 9062, Buffalo, NY 14240-9062. Include your complete name and address.

HP

LARGER-PRINT BOOKS!

HARLEQUIN

Presents®

GET 2 FREE LARGER-PRINT NOVELS PLUS 2 FREE GIFTS!

PASSION GUARANTEED SEDUCTION

YES! Please send me 2 FREE LARGER-PRINT Harlequin Presents® novels and my 2 FREE gifts (gifts are worth about $10). After receiving them, if I don't wish to receive any more books, I can return the shipping statement marked "cancel." If I don't cancel, I will receive 6 brand-new novels every month and be billed just $5.30 per book in the U.S. or $5.74 per book in Canada. That's a saving of at least 12% off the cover price! It's quite a bargain! Shipping and handling is just 50¢ per book in the U.S. and 75¢ per book in Canada.* I understand that accepting the 2 free books and gifts places me under no obligation to buy anything. I can always return a shipment and cancel at any time. Even if I never buy another book, the two free books and gifts are mine to keep forever.

176/376 HDN GHVY

Name		
	(PLEASE PRINT)	

Address		Apt. #

City	State/Prov.	Zip/Postal Code

Signature (if under 18, a parent or guardian must sign)

Mail to the **Reader Service:**
IN U.S.A.: P.O. Box 1867, Buffalo, NY 14240-1867
IN CANADA: P.O. Box 609, Fort Erie, Ontario L2A 5X3

**Are you a subscriber to Harlequin Presents® books and want to receive the larger-print edition?
Call 1-800-873-8635 today or visit us at www.ReaderService.com.**

* Terms and prices subject to change without notice. Prices do not include applicable taxes. Sales tax applicable in N.Y. Canadian residents will be charged applicable taxes. Offer not valid in Quebec. This offer is limited to one order per household. Not valid for current subscribers to Harlequin Presents Larger-Print books. All orders subject to credit approval. Credit or debit balances in a customer's account(s) may be offset by any other outstanding balance owed by or to the customer. Please allow 4 to 6 weeks for delivery. Offer available while quantities last.

Your Privacy—The Reader Service is committed to protecting your privacy. Our Privacy Policy is available online at www.ReaderService.com or upon request from the Reader Service.

We make a portion of our mailing list available to reputable third parties that offer products we believe may interest you. If you prefer that we not exchange your name with third parties, if you wish to clarify or modify your communication preferences, please visit us at www.ReaderService.com/consumerschoice or write to us at Reader Service, P.O. Box 9062, Buffalo, NY 14240-9062. Include your complete name and address.

HPLP15